GOD MADE US MONSTERS

By

Bill Neary

Ari Publishing

CHAPTER ONE

As though in a delightful dream, the Colonel, a wiry, muscular man, his bald head baked the color of oak, watched the *Roratunga* weigh anchor and raise a spinnaker sail inbound for the customs pier. He was impressed with the old slave ship as he sipped his gin stinger and smiled. *Good*, he thought, *another cargo of future agitators for the Sanford Plantation; another load of kindling for the immolation of Hawaii.*

His superiors back in London had noticed that the Americans were gaining an increasing presence in the canned goods market, particularly canned fruit, and the British didn't like these upstarts making inroads into their worldwide domination. In a surprisingly short time—less than two years—the Sanford Fruit Company established a massive pineapple plantation on the big island of Hawaii and spearheaded a remarkably extensive distribution system that included rows of warehouses with block ice as refrigerant, steamships for transport, and a spider web of delivery routes stretching from San Diego north to Seattle and east to the colossus cities of the Midwest and Eastern seaboard. The

Americans had already surpassed Tetley in the tea trade and Cavendish in coffee, and the Colonel viewed their attempts to corner the canned goods market in the States akin to stealing the crown jewels—and that simply would not do.

He put down his drink and reached for a pair of binoculars sitting on the bar as though one of its accoutrements. From the veranda of the British consulate, he focused on the *Roratunga*, a half-smile, half-smirk assembling on his otherwise taut face. *Lovely*, he thought, then spoke aloud to the three other men in attendance. "About two hundred coolies I should say."

One of his aides, a corpulent man with ferret eyes, asked, "Is that a problem, sir?"

"Not at all," said the Colonel, his tone upbeat. "In fact, it is quite the perfect number. Yes, quite." He smiled inwardly, knowing that the landing would launch the final phase of his plan.

He, and men like him, had long ago decided that an overt attack on the burgeoning American commerce in these islands was contra-indicated. No, the attack needed to be subtle yet devastating. And so, with a handshake, the Colonel had been chosen for this assignment. His service to the crown in Africa and the Caribbean, suppressing natives and pushing British interests, made him the perfect man for the job.

The Colonel estimated that the Sanford Plantation employed close to twelve hundred Chinese workers to pick, bag, and process pineapples at the onsite cannery. Sanford coolies also acted as stevedores at the company docks, loading pallets of canned goods onto the ever-waiting ships.

The coolies imported from up and down the China coast were an insular people. They did not mix with the whites or native Hawaiians or any of the myriad other races flocking to the islands. As such, they became self-sufficient (exclusive of their wages) within the plantation system. They established small groceries, loan agencies, clinics, and social clubs. The social clubs served to annul the steel-hard routine of sixteen-hour days and seven-day workweeks. They encouraged smoking, mahjong, debate, and the enjoyment of comfort women brought in on monthly rotation. The natives accepted organized prostitution as a necessary evil, at least as necessary as the banks and brokerage houses. Even the great pineapple baron, Dolan Sanford himself, a Utah-based man of faith, turned a blind eye as long as his coolies produced. And they were producing, beyond anyone's wildest dreams. Predictions were that Sanford would control the worldwide canned fruit market within two years. For that, he would shake hands with the devil himself. And some might say he had.

Sanford learned of a procurer of women, an up-and-coming broker of sin, a newcomer to these islands, a lean man with a British accent and a perpetual smirk. The two of them met, had an amicable discussion, and shook hands. The terms were simple—Sanford would allow one hundred women for a roughly 12:1 male-to-female ratio to "operate" on his plantation in exchange for one-third of the revenue generated. One-third would go to a Chinese middleman on the plantation, and one-third to the Colonel. The women would provide bread and board from the middleman's cut, and salary based on output would go to the Colonel.

"Delighted," he said to Sanford when they shook hands. *More so*, he thought when he realized how easily an American businessman could be had.

It was an easy thing. Letters were dispatched to contacts in Hong Kong, Macao, and Colombo. *The ladies,* he wrote, *should be slightly infected, but without the usual outward symptoms. Be as scrupulous as possible, perhaps engaging the services of a local doctor*

3

or one of his majesty's physicians, on my authority, of course. These women must be able to clear customs in Adelaide, Australia; then, after transshipment, clear customs and public health officials at the dock in Honolulu. The Americans are very thorough; they are positively ferocious about introducing no disease into these islands. There can be no—and I can't emphasize this strongly enough—NO outward indication of syphilis upon arrival Hawaii.

And now with these two hundred coolies fresh from a five-month sea voyage and ready to engage in the comforts of the flesh, his plan would come to fruition. Six months ago, the infected women were introduced to the Sanford Plantation, plenty of time for near-total saturation of the male workforce excluding married men, bugger's eunuchs, and boys. The Colonel would wait until a Chinese doctor in his employ reported to him that syphilis was epidemic on the plantation. British-owned newspapers (a large contingent of the American yellow press) would publish headlines screaming of a venereal disease- ridden workforce populating the Sanford Plantation. Photographs would show happy coolies picking pineapples with their hands, husking pineapples, smiling, and laughing as they fed pineapple slurry into "cans fresh from their disease to your table."

And then the Colonel would take a stab at the coup.

CHAPTER TWO

A great Morgan Company clipper, a five-master inbound from Canton, hauled her spring lines fore and aft. She had steam winches aboard, and the wooden pier groaned under the tension of tightening the ship to the dock. The hawkers, whores, and crimps barely noticed, but a diminutive figure gazed at the behemoth in awe, wondering if the vessel was going to tear the bollards out, or worse, rip the whole dock up to her decks. The heaving eventually stopped, with the dock intact, and the small priest sloshed through the rotting bananas and pineapples, occasionally stomping a piece of fish gut off his boot.

As he winced from the smell, he saw the sign he was looking for: HONOLULU BOARD OF HEALTH QUARANTINE PIER written in crude white letters and beshat with seagull and pelican droppings. An arrow beneath the board indicated he was to turn left at an elbow in the pier and follow it around the warehouse. He took the left at the warehouse and fell into the full glaze of the sun. Adjusting the straw hat upon his head, the brim wide out to his shoulders, he stopped, bent his head to light a small Dutch cigar, and then looked up.

A hundred feet down the pier lay a small interisland steamer, painted starch white with a red "H" on her stack, bobbing comfortably in her moorings. There was some scant activity alongside her, but nothing like the bustle and debauchery alongside the other vessels in this great harbor named by ancient Hawaiians for the limitless supply of pearls below. This gave him pause, but he continued on to the foot of the vessel's gangway, where a voiced boomed from above, "You must be Father Damien!"

"Yes. And you must be Captain Ross."

"Aye, that be me, and by clever deduction can I assume you'll be requestin' passage on this fine piss-cutter of mine?"

"Also true." Father Damien no longer winced at the colorful language of sailors, but he was a bit surprised the captain did not try to curtail it in his presence.

"Well, come thee aboard, Father," the captain said with a beckoning wave of his hand. "There be steak and whiskey for the likes of us; sunshine and happiness for the rest of the world."

The harbor master lifted pennants for all vessels to heave to. The little white ship had priority, so the clippers, the pineapple barges, the pearl boats, and the Navy either gave way or reduced to bare steerage to let her pass. Two men stood on her bridge wing in silence. Abeam of Diamond Head, the captain ordered a north-by-west course and relaxed imperceptibly. "It be about fifty-two nautical miles to Molokai, then two more hours steaming so's to stand for a proper tide for yer landing."

Damien nodded and said, "I feel that I am in good hands, Captain."

6

"Be ye meaning mine or God's?" the captain asked with a curious look.

The smaller man paused, then with a great laugh, slapped the burly seaman on the back. "Both, I think. Yes, both."

The vessel rounded the western spit of Molokai Island, bringing their destination into view. The peninsula was a large isosceles jut of land, mostly flat, yet not devoid of fauna or structure. At the base of the triangle, a sheer cliff, blue as the sky and green as the ocean, rose to impossible heights. "That be The Wall of Pali," the captain said. "Them be the tallest sea cliffs in the world. Make the Alps look like bumps on a frog's backside."

The cliffs, or "The Wall", were so staggering, so soaring, they gave the impression of being a life force unto themselves. At best an omnipotent overseer; at worst a malevolent guardian. "Is there any way over those cliffs, Captain?" Damien asked, taking in the magnificent sight.

"No, and that be the thing—they have The Wall at their backs and the abyss of the Pacific afore them."

Damien considered this and asked "Have any of them tried to escape by swimming?"

"Aye, there's them what tried," the Captain said, leaning down and resting his arms on the rail, "but farther out—farther than we will be—there's a current that rips like a greyhound all the way to the Aleutians. Seamen call it Thunder Road. None survive a swim in that maelstrom."

"So, there's no way out?"

The old seafarer gave a weary shake of his head. "None what's for them that's alive. The place be a living mausoleum."

Concern washed over the priest's face. "Is it true that the poor unfortunates who disembark this vessel are cast into the sea to swim to shore unaided?"

"Aye, that be true," the Captain said, lowering his head and voice. "The crew be afraid to row them to shore for fear of the disease."

"Is it also true that you suggested a buoy and rope system such that they could pull themselves to the beach without having to swim against the currents?"

The captain replied with a solemn, defeated look. "Aye, but the Honolulu Board of Health overruled me, owing to cost."

"Captain, is it your opinion that the Board wants leprosy cured?"

"No, Father," he said coldly. "I think they want leprosy eradicated."

"And what is the difference?"

"Attrition. This island be meant to kill leprosy. Every person in all the Hawaiian Islands diagnosed as a leper be sent here to kill the disease by dying their own selves until the very last one of 'em be buried in the ground."

Abeam of the point of the peninsula known as Kalaupapa, the vessel heaved to. A small skiff was made ready for the priest. Loaded aboard were a barrel of water, some blankets, and the priest's steamer trunk. The small man stood by the ship's rail ready to board. "Father," said the Captain, "I want you to take this." He handed the priest a large revolver, almost as large as one of the smaller man's arms.

"No thank you, Captain," the priest replied with a smile, "God will protect my soul."

"That be true, but when you land today, it's your body what's going to need protecting, and Samuel Colt does almost as good a job protecting the flesh as God does protecting the spirit."

"Captain, I cannot..."

"Father, please. You may never use it, but there be certain men on this island what don't have respect for God or much else. Until your good work starts taking hold, just wear it as a piece of jewelry, a gift from one shipmate to another. I'll even take it back in a couple of months' time. Maybe I'll even come ashore to do so."

The priest gave a conciliatory grin, reached out his left hand to receive the weapon, tossed a salute with his right, and swung himself over the rail to the bobbing skiff below.

The shore to the left was long and tumultuous, with human-sized rocks and violent ocean. To the right, the shoreline was equally distant, but smoother and less prone to violent surf. A massive cliff wall towered from the terminus of the left shore to the right. At the base, and within, were caves and crags from which a practiced eye could detect much human and animal habitation.

Slightly winded, Damien finally reached the shore. He had rowed as fast as he could to avoid any threat from the currents, knowing that his spindly arms could not have saved him should the threat become imminent. He beached the boat, then landed the water barrel, rolling it a short distance until it was safely out of the thinning waves. He then hauled the boat inland, removed two sets of blankets, walked beneath a banyan tree, and laid a blanket out. He sat down, quite at ease, and set about giving fire to his tobacco and a small pile of driftwood.

It was just a speck at the bottom of that blue-green curtain of stone. One might have thought it a piece of scree rock dislodged from the cliff by the increasing northwest wind, but no, it moved again and with specific

9

pattern. The wild boar had scented Damien and commenced a charge in his direction. Father Damien heard the thumping hooves, but unblessed by superior vision, he had to stare hard into the distance. Damien perspired at the mere presence of the beast, but whitened with alarm the moment he saw the red in his angry eyes and the hairs of his coarse coat standing straight up and out. His razor-sharp tusks curved upward in front of his face, rendering ineffective an opponent's nose strike or slash to the eyes. Damien felt for the colt, astonished he needed it at all, let alone so soon. Before he could cock back the hammer, a second shape emerged from the darkness—a giant white dog, sweeping and elegant. Damien's panic caused his shooting hand to tremble and he knew he could not draw a proper bead on his two fanged enemies. His chances of survival were slim no matter how desperate his prayers.

Hackles full up like porcupine quills, the dog snarled, then charged full gallop toward the pig. The bladed swine snorted and came in low to slash her. Only a body length apart, the dog dashed to the left and leapt over the boar as he struck wildly at her in the air. The moment she landed, she whipped around, leapt for his back, and came down full force between his shoulders and neck, crunching into his spine. She forced her weight upon him as her kind, the Borzoi, had been bred to do, never relinquishing the bite. She pinned the swine to the ground, immobilizing him, her teeth and powerful jaws eventually tearing through him, severing his back bone and throat. Un-winded, she sat down on her haunches and turned to Damien. He lowered his colt, his shaking barely subsided, and approached her. He reached an arm under her and scratched beneath her chin, the smallest gratitude he could give her for what he felt. When the great dog, huntress of the wild Russian steppes, slayer of boar, began to purr, he stopped scratching, patted her twice, then bent toward the pig. With a deft motion and a knife she did not see, he removed the pig's hindquarters and tossed them to the dog. "Thank you, girl. There will also be food for you." She took the meat, eyed him as a way of giving her own thanks, and trotted into the black.

Back beneath the banyan tree, Damien did not realize he ate the pig raw, but to him the water was cool, and the pig meat sweet. It was a calming moment after the events of the day. He was lulled into contemplation by the whoompf of the sea as it landed on the beach before flattening itself and speeding inland in an even hiss. He took a twig from the sand, using the burning sprig to light his pipe. As the heat in the bowl grew and the scent of the dried apple in the tobacco drifted upward, he caught a scent on the wind, *Humans!* At least he believed that it was humans, though he wasn't sure, the pipe's scent confused him as it filled his lungs and overpowered his mind...

The priest laid his pipe aside and stood. The band was still quite a ways off, and through the twilight and his spectacled eyes, a vision gathered shapes. They did not walk as humans do, but dragged themselves and swayed like thick grass in the wind.

They shambled a few strides toward the crackling fire. Some drew breath unevenly; some gurgled; some whispered. Damien stared and wondered to himself, *Are these the recipients of my ministrations? Are they the meek, the persecuted, the poor in spirit?*

But they were not enlightened spirits pursuing betterment for themselves and those around them. They were the destroyers of society, as corrupt in soul as their bodies were in disease. Their malignant minds proffered like the pus oozing from their joints, motivations of cancerous intent expanding and multiplying in filth and influence.

11

The leader, a man with no ears and only bloody mash where his nose once was spoke. "God made us monsters." He spat in disgust.

Damien gave the creature a compassionate look. "No, God made you different in body only. Your souls are as kind and beautiful as any man."

"Why have you come here?" The man eyed him suspiciously.

"To help you live in peace and comfort and dignity, as you deserve."

One of the men nodded the remains of his head to the pig bones, a reference to supper. "You eat well your first night on this island, haole, far better than any of us our first night."

"So, I have heard." Silence, broken only by the whoompf and hiss of the surf. "Please take the rest, so that we all will eat well this first night." With murmurs and gurgling, hissing and shuffling, the band of humans ripped the pig apart, stuffing bloody, fattened pieces into the rags that hung about their bodies.

"Thank you for your visit," Damien said graciously, in keeping with his role. "In the days to come, I will visit you."

There was no reply, no shuffling away. They just stared from empty eyes, their spirits still unsatisfied.

"Haole, we still hungry." Silence—no surf, no hissing, no crackling fire. One of them unsheathed a long curved knife. "Yes, haole, mebbe you good in pot." As they advanced, the wind backed a point flapping up the front tail of the priest's shirt and they froze. The band saw what he felt at his waist—the cold blue steel of the chambers and the polished grip of the Colt revolver. The band stopped, their leader nodding and waving his stump of a left arm in circular motion. He turned to leave. "God made us monsters, haole. You no forget."

The band shuffled and hissed behind him, disappearing into the night like decaying mist.

Father Damien spent an uneasy night repeatedly checking to make sure his revolver was nearby and that the fire burned to keep any beasts at bay. He dearly wished the dog would return. He would have gladly offered the larger share of his morning meal for the added protection. However, the next morning, Damien sat up, unscathed as always. He put his palms together, closed his eyes, and remained silent. It was a thing he did every day upon waking. He always felt refreshed afterwards. He spoke to the sky, thanking God for delivering him safely through the night, then put in his request. "God, you must help with something today."

The bulb of the sun rose and warmed his back in comfortable contrast to the cool east wind behind him. Damien combed the length of the western spit, and his eyes halted where the shoreline met the face of the curtain of stone. The winds had scrubbed the boulders alongside the east cliff face free of brine and weed, unlike its western counterpart. The priest gathered many pieces of old driftwood and placed them at angles to each other. He did this for half the day, experimenting with scores of combinations. Toward late afternoon he stood, surveyed his work, and with a satisfied nod, walked to the original campsite, where he knelt and prayed. After prayer, he gathered blank paper from his belongings and sat down to write a short letter, succinct and of proper importance, to be posted when the Board of Health vessel arrived the following week.

After a long draught from the water barrel, Damien changed from his hob-nailed boots and canvas work pants to grey linen trousers, white cotton shirt, and sandals. His breathing, though slow, was the result of contemplation rather than weariness. He walked inland toward the massive cliffs where, midway between them and the coast, lay the majority of the leper colony. The priest skirted small gullies filled with beach grass and walked around, rather than over, chest-high dunes. The sun descending into civil twilight cast broad rays horizontally across the peninsula, painting a bright light on the west faces of the inmates' dwellings.

It was not a village so much as a scattered sprawl of suburb and hovel. He walked between neat rows of whitewashed clapboards or shanties made from ships dunnage and driftwood. It was a place that never knew the hand of a city planner, landscaper, or humanitarian. He detected the musk of horses, the frying of palm oil, the filth of pigs, and something other…

Damien slowed his pace as the unidentified scent gained in his consciousness. It weaved like smoke around his brain and whispered fear and paralysis to his soul. Questions pierced the silent smoke as though beacons from a lighthouse. Why had he come here when they had not welcomed him yesterday? He checked to make sure his revolver was still secure in his waistband, then stepped forward again and inhaled deeply. When he exhaled, his thoughts were once again pure, his step quickened, driven to fulfill his mission from God. He would stop at the next dwelling.

The next building was no dwelling at all, but a large, three-sided wooden lean-to with a roof stenciled in upside down letters: MACHINE PARTS, U.S. NAVY, MADE IN TOLEDO OHIO. To the rear lay a crude outhouse with no door. Slow-moving pigs rooted about, a few unclean pots hanging on the outside, clanging in the wind. Damien reached the front of the lean-to and stopped. There was a small oil lamp hanging from an overhead beam. Its dim and sickly light did not allow him to discern the shapes within. But then light and keen eyesight were not needed. A deep rasping, like the hissing of a snake combined with the gurgle of a sucking chest wound, indicated the state of the man inside. The priest, as diminutive as he was, stood steadfast in his linen shirt and sandals. "I am Father Damien." The gurgling within subsided a notch. The man came to the light—he was of Polynesian stock, though small of frame and deformed. His countenance was friendly and respectful.

"We Hawaiians. We also Catholic. Why you come this island?"

"To ease your suffering."

"My wife, alive-dead, soon be dead-dead. You give confession; you give absolution?"

"Yes. Is there anything else?"

"Wife need water. Give for comfort while she pass. You bring?"

"Yes. Where is the water here?"

"Never water here. Water at Wall of Pali."

"At the wall? I don't understand."

"Years me carry water all same by bucket water at Pali to here. Weeks ago, maybe weeks before that, lose arms, rot at stumps. All same carry bucket with teeth. Teeth dead, jaw rotten. Think maybe live longer than wife, but no by much. Father, you please bring water?"

"Of course, my son, but where is the well?"

"No well. Water fall off cliff at wall. Turn 'round, walk into night. When hear thunder, keep walking. That waterfall, one mile, maybe two. Have bucket out back. Two shark bladders okay, also use. Used to string over mule; mule now dead."

Calmly and without hesitation, Damien tied together the shark bladders over his right shoulder and carried the bucket in his left hand. Turning his back on the dwelling, he set off into the night. He traveled only a short time before hearing the distant thunder. It was full night now and the blackest of the black of it was directly

15

ahead, the wall emitting no torchlight or reflection of stars and sea. Damien did not see well in the dark and tread lightly as the terrain grew uneven and filled with debris. The crags, hillocks, bumps, and misplaced stones would have made for an interesting hike in the daylight, but at night they made the walk demanding. Still, Father Damien rationalized, they rose only slightly above being a nuisance.

On the way in.

Astonishment greeted him upon his arrival. The waterfall was indeed vast, but only in height. In width, a large man could have wrapped his arms around it. The thunder came from the steep, six-thousand-foot drop, tons of water hurling itself off a cliff to plunge for whole minutes till crashing into a boulder-strewn field. The water pooled in various pockets, the remainder flooding into one of the numerous caves surrounding it. Though a relief to feel the cool water in this tropical heat, the priest, by inclination and training, recognized the temptation of lingering.

The small man filled the shark bladders first, then tied off the ends to prevent the water from leaking out. He next filled the five-gallon bucket, flashing back briefly to his school days where he recalled "One gallon of water equals ten pounds of weight." He threw the bladders over his shoulder bandolier style, hoisted the bucket into the crook of his elbow and began his journey back to the doomed husband and wife.

Damien had misjudged the afternoon. Thinking there were hours left before evening twilight, he discounted The Wall of Pali. Its Olympian height caused the sun to appear to rise later, and set much sooner and abruptly, than over a flat piece of land.

Unbalanced by weight and sloshing water, and the decreasing light, his steps became unsure and uneven. When he stepped too quickly to the right, the water surged, carrying him quickly forward. When he attempted to slow himself, the bucket slapped back against the bottom, impacting his knee. As such, he could not traverse a straight path, but tacked and jibed like a sailboat against the wind, or a sailor drunk against reality. The liana vines grasped at his linen trousers and tore rents upon them. Where the bucket slapped his knee, a small hole began, and soon the bucket drew blood that pooled around the creases of his torn skin.

He had lost the trail and the jungle began to close, the clutch of nighttime Molokai taking hold.

Damien was tending toward exhaustion, but knew that were he to collapse here, the many wild pigs would be drawn to the smell of his blood and then to a quick meal. And if they failed to overcome him, the great many vipers sidewinding their way through the brush certainly would.

The priest continued at an increasingly moderate pace. At one small slope, he gained momentum, but almost lost his balance. In trying to maintain himself, he ripped the heel from his left sandal, rendering it useless. Knowing it would be difficult, if not impossible, to carry on, he removed his right sandal, then his left, and laid them in the middle of the trail. He then gently strode forward on bare feet. The trail was hard-packed dirt, trod upon for millennia by the original Polynesian residents of this island, and more recently by its inmates, though the small beach rubble and countless shards of broken seashells made the priest's feet bleed. But he moved on, even as the volume of lacerations outnumbered the volume of intact skin. At times he felt as though he were skating on liquid. Eventually, one of his feet gave way, sliding on the gooey mass which enveloped the soles. He stumbled, then collapsed, dropping his burden seconds before spilling it. *I must rest and pray.*

And while on his bleeding knees, through courage and belief, the small man achieved a state surpassing human apprehension and human suffering, and while he had not yet achieved the divine, he achieved quietude and clarity. A thought came to him, the first thought. *Mother*. The thought solidified and took hold. "Mother, I am suffering."

"Yes, son, you are."

"Will it end?"

"No, but love of God and the purity of your work will cause the suffering to be diluted."

"Mother..."

The small man remained on his knees motionless for some time. The wind shifted a point and blew softly over the trail, bringing a whiff of sandalwood incense from the village, a reminder of his purpose here.

Damien had trouble rising until he recalled the "conversation" with his mother. His work would dilute his pain. He lifted the bucket and trod on.

Cresting a slight rise and seeing the oil lamp in the lean-to, Damien arrived alive. His linen trousers were all but gone, its remnants resembling a ragged loin cloth. His feet were caked in blood and dirt, and a vine had whipped his forehead, lancing a thin red line about his scalp as though an indentation from a hat. He pushed on with his last possible strength to reach the pounded dirt before the lean-to, and for the third time, stumbled. But aware of his limitations now, he did not spill a drop.

From within the lean-to, the hissing, tearing, liquid voice oozed, "Is that you, Father?"

"It is. I have returned with the water."

"Plenty quick, Father. Wife close death, I think."

The priest entered the little enclosure, the abattoir stench choking him. The leper took the lamp from the rafters and walked to his wife. She was wheezing from her mouth—not from the incapacity of her lungs, but because leprosy had caused her nose to become swollen and gigantic. It flopped over her lips to her chin. The same with her left ear, huge and gangrenous, upon her shoulder like a foul shawl. "Father, you help me please give water?" The priest spied a ladle hanging on a hook above the bucket, dipped it, and walked back to the woman. The leper lifted her nose and indicated for the priest to pour the water upon her lips. As he did, he looked closer into her eyes, but her eyes were no more, long since melted. She could not even cry, her tear ducts disintegrated. The priest did not shirk his ministrations, but bordering on madness and shock, wondered *Is this a vision of hell, or hell itself?* And in this lay his quandary—he didn't know if he was being tested to see if he could survive, or had been at last cast into the depths as sure as any sinner. He trickled some more water and brushed a un-lesioned portion of her cheek. She moaned in madness and despair and turned her head to face his, her hollow sockets penetrating him with infinite darkness. The priest froze in horror, a horror that lent itself to clarity. *Of course!* he thought. *I have been made to see hell's inhabitants. It is my station to bring them into the light of the world.* The woman turned her head and exhaled slightly. "There, there, my dear," he said. "Think only of sunshine and comfort, and from now on, there shall be only sunshine and comfort."

The priest watched the woman calmly fall off to sleep. Her husband thanked him and said with his rasping voice, "Go with God, Father."

There was no reply.

The sun reached its zenith as the wind soothed in its transition from onshore to offshore. The smell of hibiscus Molokai, one of the few hibiscus to carry a scent, permeated the air and instilled a tropical calm on all it touched. Father Damien pulled a fresh set of

19

trousers from his trunk, having earlier burned the rags of the night before, and began to dress. Though sore and slightly weary, he moved easily, almost to the point of stillness. He took time to stuff some apple blend into his pipe and pulled a cloth bag of beef jerky from his trunk. He bit off a piece and sat down in the sand to light the briar. He sat quietly listening to the whoompf and hiss of the surf. As the apple and tobacco burned its last, he tapped the pipe on the heel of one of his canvas shoes and dumped the dottle into the sand, making sure there were no remains alight. He stood, stretched, and without a thought, turned inland.

He came upon the lean-to he had visited the night before. The man, having seen him approach, stepped into the light of the day. "Hallo, Father, how you today?"

"Fine, my son. How is your wife?"

"She more better today. More easy breathing; more calm. We hold each other all night."

Damien smiled. *Even the damned take comfort in each other.* "What is your name, my son?"

"My name Nainoa. My wife name Mailee."

"Nainoa, please tell Mailee that I will be back to visit in a few days. I am going to be visiting your neighbors."

"You okay, go with God."

This time there was a reply: "You too, my son."

Father Damien eyed the different paths winding throughout the settlement. He noted the house closest to the lean-to was a large, whitewashed structure with a widow's walk atop. It was indeed a house, but it struck him as less home and more compound. There were a two-stall stable, a chicken coop, and a small hay barn. All the buildings lay enclosed within a white picket fence, a small scrappy terrier patrolling its internal perimeter as though centurion. There was a gated

20

entrance set far off from the house, and next to the gate stood a mounted ship's bell, with a two-foot length of nautical macramé dangling from its clapper. Damien brushed the dirt from his shoes, then rang the bell, its deep tone carrying through to the ground.

A tall man with a shock of bright red hair and dressed in starched khakis and a crisp, white-collared shirt stood on his porch and spoke to his visitor, "C'mon' up, then. You're just in time for morning tea." The small man passed through the gate and strolled the walkway to the porch. At the first step, the man with the near-orange hair reached out his hand. "Sean Corcoran."

"Father Damien from Belgium."

"Yes, I know. Now, how do you take your tea?"

The dwelling within could not have been in starker contrast to Nainoa's lean-to. Bookshelves lined the walls, the titles within diverse and eclectic; *Rights of Man, Typee, Periplus of Scylax,* Some titles were in Greek, some in English, some in Latin. There were batik sarongs from the East Indies, matted and framed about the walls; a surveyor's theodolite in one corner; and a gramophone in another. Next to a large fireplace, a glass case held a collection of Wayang puppets, while to the other side rested a glass case of guns. Nowhere did the priest see MACHINE PARTS, U.S. NAVY, MADE IN TOLEDO OHIO.

The taller of the two handed his guest a cup and saucer and motioned him to the outdoor porch. "How is the tea, Father?"

Damien sipped "It is grand, yes, grand. Russian Caravan, yes?"

Impressed Corcoran nodded, "Your nose for tea is not novice."

"We used to drink this tea by the bucket back home. I could not find it when I landed in the New World, though I tried, all the way from New York to Seattle. I am both pleased and surprised to enjoy it on this island." Damien nodded his head in thanks.

"I try to make do," said his host.

"But I am confused," said the little man, "as to the station of people in this settlement. Last night I attended to a couple that was barely alive, living as though one step above the apes."

With a puzzled look Sean asked, "Where was that, Father?"

"Just to the east. A ramshackle lean-to."

Corcoran tapped his index finger to his lips "Ah, yes that would be the Puha's. Terrible story that; one of many here, I'm afraid. They came originally from the Big Island. Nainoa was a game warden on a sheep station charged with keeping poachers and wild boar from marauding the flock. Had an excellent reputation among the planters and town fathers. Three years ago, just before Christmas, he arrested a poacher who had stolen a ewe and two lambs from the Amstutz ranch. The poacher, in turn, denounced Nainoa to the U.S. marshal as a leper. It was a blind and unfounded accusation, but one that is not ignored in Hawaii. His boss sent him to Honolulu for an exam, and by a strange and terrible coincidence, found only by a blood test, he did, in fact, carry the disease. The ramifications of such a prognosis are common knowledge on these islands: banishment to Molokai.

"Nainoa knew this and fled, but not before saying goodbye to his wife and secreting away some of the money he had earned as game warden. Nainoa is from ancient Polynesian stock, a child of the sun and the sea, and was able to blend into the islands as the color blue blends into the sky. Three U.S. marshals, ten Honolulu deputies, and a contingent from Naval Intelligence pursued him. I doubt the manhunt for Butch Cassidy or

John Wilkes Booth carried as much fervor. But it was not firepower or law enforcement that brought him in—it was love. Upon hearing of his disease, the people of his village cast out his wife. She had pleaded and begged, but was still shunned. She wandered the streets and jungles starving and destitute. Upon hearing of her plight, Nainoa sent word to the Board of Health that he would come in if his wife would be cared for. Assured that she was, he turned himself in."

"And what of his wife?" Damien said as he put down his tea.

Corcoran leaned in "The Board held that she, being wife and therefore intimate with a leper, was de facto infected herself."

"Was that the case?"

The tall planter shook his head "No. She was banished with her husband and did not contract the disease till several months ago—we think when she helped deliver a child to an infected family."

There was a staggering silence between them. "Excuse me, Mr. Corcoran…"

Sean."

"Sean. I am confused as to the degree of this sickness. I met a band of lepers on the beach that did not even appear human. This man, Nainoa, while clearly afflicted, does not seem far along, yet his wife, whom you say only contracted it a few months ago, seems near death."

"There are two forms, Father. The most severe is known as Lepromatous. This form is caused by a deep penetration of the bacteria Leprae to all organs outside the central nervous system. It disperses randomly about the skin and can devastate bones, eyes, arms, fingers, and feet. These appendages can become lesion, swell grotesquely, turn black, appear to rot, and more times than not, separate themselves from the poor unfortunate's body. The second form, known as Tuberculin or anesthetic leprosy, has an incubation period up to thirty-five years."

Damien took a moment to ponder, sipped his tea and said, "Are you telling me that a person may be diagnosed positive but not contract symptoms for three *decades?*"

"Aye, that is so."

"Am I to understand that a five-year old could be diagnosed, sent here, and not be symptomatic till he or she turns forty?"

"Yes."

"That is horrid."

"Yes, though anesthetic leprosy is not as physically devastating. The Leprae bacterium does not prey as ruthlessly as its foul cousin. The penetration is not as widespread or dense, and it is characterized mostly by some redness. The limbs may swell, but not in monstrous excess. Occasional blindness and rare separations occur. It is the form of leprosy that I have."

The priest, a reader of men's souls, knew that to offer apologies or sympathies to the man before him would be both meaningless and insulting. Instead he asked, "Would you mind if I smoked a cigar?"

The man, acknowledging this simple act of kindness, replied, "Not a 'tall, but sure I'd be insulted if you did not partake of one of mine, I have them imported from Hispaniola."

The two men each lit a cigar, and both, in different forms of contemplation, watched the smoke swirl and gather, and for a while there was no conversation between them. There was no need for conversation. As men of the world, they recognized what the other had seen and felt no need to discuss it. The cigars and their thoughts were all they needed. Unfortunately, the silence was interrupted by a skittering of nails and aggressive barking from a tiny terrier. The little dog looked up at the priest, fierce arrogance in his eyes, a teacup snarl emanating from his jaws. "Settle down there, lad, this man's a friend."

"That's quite a little dog you have there, Sean."

"Thank you. He's a Jack Russell terrier, here to stifle the rat population which, in the early days was quite high, and still poses a problem more here than on the big island."

"What is his name?"

"Tengu."

"A Hawaiian name?"

"No, 'tis Japanese. In medieval Japan, the Tengu were held to be monster spirits, supernatural demons who inhabited the bodies of dogs, birds of prey, and sea creatures. They inflicted unholy punishments on everyone they contacted. Bet you could have used him in your trip across America."

"To my surprise, I experienced not a whit of bad intent from Ellis Island to Seattle, though I must confess I could have used the little fellow when I landed upon this shoreline."

"Oh, and how's that?" The priest relayed his confrontation with the dark band of lepers on his first night. He also told him of the pistol the steamer captain had impressed upon him. "Ah, sure, Father, the good Captain Ross is a wise man."

"Indeed he is. I felt a powerful danger emanating from those poor unfortunates, as if they were inhabited by these Tengu. It was not until the wind blew open my coat and the light of the fire reflected the Colt did the band back down."

"It's a true thing that there is not much a man is scared of when he thinks himself already dead. You threw them a big one showing 'em your sidearm. I'm guessing that wee piece of metal saved your life."

25

"It is a terrible thing for a priest to defend himself with the threat of violence, but had I not lived by this 'sword' I certainly would have died by it."

"Oh, aye," said Sean with the first chuckle he had enjoyed in months, "and it would be a terrible thing if those 'poor unfortunates', as you refer to them, were indeed human."

The priest dragged deeply on his cigar. "To deny them humanity is an un-Christian act, Sean."

"Aye, that may be, Father, but you do not know these creatures as I do. I submit that you can't grant humanity to that which is inhuman. "

"I was chaplain to a French Foreign Legion battalion in Algiers. I know the horror of war and have received confession from the darkest souls."

"Sure, and as that may be, Father, but those legionnaires were men alive wishing to repent. Those as met you on beach are men dead with no repentance in their hearts."

"If I am to administer them as God's children, I must do so with courage. You must, also, with courage, relate to me their lives."

"Father, it's not that I'm lacking in Christian charity, it's only that I've paid penance enough…"

Absently Sean began to speak as though in remembrance. "The colony was more than a wind-kissed idyll that first day. The small inter-island steamer hove to, casting its stern toward the shore. The aft decks were fitted with cattle pens, though these pens saw chattel of a different sort: twelve inmates, two women, ten men, lepers all. For all intents and purposes, they were already dead. The Honolulu Board had decreed divorces for the married, executed wills, foreclosed upon their properties, and quarantined their families so they, too, could be examined.

"Upon order from the captain, the gates to the pens on the fantail were hoisted upright, and the ships boson cracked a whip, casting these people into the sea. The moans and cries were not of this earth. The eyes of the inmates were wider than those of steers pushed to the slaughter house. The seamen were equally afraid of the disease, and the boson whipped harder to drive them quickly away. The twelve plunged violently into the surf.

"They were people of the islands, and therefore of the sea. They could swim and stay afloat, but the sea was raging. They were close to shore, struggling against a swell that broke and crashed, most times on the twice-doomed swimmers. The spray blinded them, the ocean filling their lungs, and yet they swam the mile to the narrow patch of sand between the boulders. When they landed, they lay on the beach choking and gasping. That they were neither consumed by sharks or barracudas, nor shredded upon the lava rocks, was a miracle upon itself, a miracle of a god they were rapidly losing faith in.

"...I was the first white man, or haole, upon the island."

Damien, unsure of breaking the sad reverie but worried where it would bring his new friend asked, "The band I met that first night referred to me as haole. What does it mean?"

Sean shook his head to clear. "It is a derogatory term the natives use when referring to white men. Similar to the 'bog wog' the British used against us Irish, or the word 'chink' when used against the Chinese. You see, Father, while the Americans may have stolen land from the Indians stateside, it was land like New Jersey or Nevada. Here, these people feel they were robbed of paradise, and rightly so."

"So they are bitter to all white men?"

27

"No, bitter isn't quite the term. More like *aware* of what we are and what we're capable of. The Hawaiians are not a bitter people. They have a philosophy known as Aloha, a beautiful thing once you understand it. Embracing the sun and the sea and extended family is their way of life, an omnipotent force to be cherished."

"Paganism?"

"No. They do have gods, but Aloha is their virtue— a gift a people of integrity gives themselves. You'll see it soon enough."

The priest thought back to last night when Nainoa— destitute, festering, his wife on her deathbed— offered tea. "Now that you mention it, I think I already have," and wondered to himself if he'd be seeing it again.

CHAPTER THREE

The Wall of Pali, as though asserting its indifference to the rest of the natural world, caused the day to end earlier than anywhere else in the tropics. This was not a mystical occurrence or the wrath of some angry god, though, at times, the inmates felt it to be both. The massive wall—more a curtain of chasms and shear-faced rock—formed an outfacing parabola at the base of the settlement that ran from east to west. So high were the cliffs that only a short few hours after the meridian, the sun would fall behind it, leaving only the reflective light of a false sunset. The old saying was "Darkness comes earlier to the settlement than it does the settlers."

There are few secrets on any island, and word travels fast. A good distance in scope and morality from where Damien camped, a loud and heated discussion began.

"This new haole bring trouble," a massive leper named Tangata rasped, his throat burning. He took a ladle hanging from a string on the wall and dipped it in the barrel. He swirled around the mixture—Kava Kava root, Japanese rice wine, and potato spirits—dipped again, and drank deeply.

"All haoles bring trouble," came another voice from the darkness amid stampings and grunts of approval.

"This haole," his throat now cooled from the liquor, "this haole smart, have fire in eyes." Tangata, known as Terry, was a massive Polynesian, a Maori of the Cook Islands. Well over three hundred pounds and still powerful, though the disease ran rampant within, he had the distinctive facial markings of his people. Known as Moku, they resembled the tattoos of sailors, but were, in fact, much different. The Moku indicated a man's progression through life, including his warrior status. Unlike the tattoos of the white man, the Maori, rather than puncturing the skin with thousands of little holes and injecting ink, chiseled the flesh and poured dye into the ensuing wound. Tangata's lines began at the top of his nose. Two indigo lines in half concentric circles bridged to the left and right to form inverse bowls over his eyes. A dozen parallel bowls lay close atop these, reaching to the top of his forehead and the band of the brown derby he never removed, not even to sleep. Straight red lines ran parallel from the sides of his nose to his jaw and back to his ears, one of which had already rotted off, the other which had a turquoise pendant, the length of a human finger, clipped to it.

He once again dipped the ladle, drank deeply, and began to speak before being cut off by his brother Whenua, known as Willy. "No fuckin' haoles any good. Fuckin' French haoles slave us to money, to brandy. Fuckin' American haoles slave us this place." He was huge like his brother, but not as tall. Leprosy had little effect on him so far—his face such that it looked like stacked shreds of darkened leather. He had the same Moku of his brother Whenua, or Willy, but the effect of the disease made the tribal art appear as ancient petroglyphs carved on a stone wall. Willy looked like a breathing Tiki idol—fierce, defiant, and unmovable. He had no left hand, but wrapped in leather at the stump of his wrist was a whaleman's harpoon shaft and barb. He did not lose his hand to the disease, but rather a mutiny in the terrible Solomons.

Tangata and Whenua were children of the sun; Cook Islanders raised in the tradition of the Polynesian peoples. They were of a sect known as Navigators, and the South Sea islanders were the greatest navigators in the world. From a young age, Terry and Willy learned the ways of their forefathers, an art and a science passed down for a thousand years. A European mariner could, by adjusting his sextant and referring to a chronometer and printed texts, determine his location on earth at that moment. Terry and Willy needed only to *look* to the sky for the same result. They could follow cloud patterns that would lead them to the islands of Java or Ceylon. The white navigators would use lighthouses as their guides, but the Maori could scent musk in the wind to take them to the sealing grounds of the far north, or follow a star to the land with the giant wall that stretched to eternity.

When the white men came to the Pacific, they soon learned the value of the Navigators. These people, through their teachings and symbols carved on whalebone and driftwood, could chart every cove and reef the traders sought to enter or avoid. One summer between voyages, the boys, now young men, paddled a long boat to Papeete to partake of the annual solstice gathering. It was there that they met two white men, two French white men, who offered to hire them if they could navigate their two-masted clipper to Brisbane to load sheep. The boys knew the route and quickly accepted. The passage was swifter then the Frenchmen had anticipated. Terry and Willy slid though the channels and slips of the Great Barrier Reef, avoiding the claws of the hull-ripping coral with almost mystical ease. This allowed the two Europeans to arrive in Brisbane ahead of the other traders, giving them great advantage on price and selection. The two Frenchmen had staked everything on this voyage and had gained immensely. In the few days it took for customs clearance and the loading, the ship owners introduced the boys to high times. Why wait for the bliss of kava to greet you when you can put half a farthing, one-thirtieth of your month's wages, into the heady maelstrom of cane rum? No need to court girls or attend lavish ceremonies or speak to their fathers for the girls' favors. Just lay a few more farthing down and the women here, white women, would let you do things to them a stupefied Portuguese goat wouldn't allow. There were cigars from Sumatra and opium from Kowloon. The young men's appetites knew no bounds, and for the first time in history, two of the Maori people became slaves. Slaves to the pipe and the drink; slaves to the wage. The captains realized this and soon shipped rum and opium aboard, doling it out in carefully measured quantities that kept the boys always wanting a little more, thus keeping them onboard and in their employ. They, of course, changed, and as their voyages across the Pacific increased, so did their addiction. They obtained the sailor's cynicism of "life's no good till the next port" and took on the ways of the merchant. It was inevitable that they would enter the blackbird trade of the Solomons, the most lucrative and most loathsome of all cargos in the Pacific.

The bright sunshine, now four hours old, penetrated the highest jungle canopy on Guadalcanal. At sunrise, the island appeared in front of the sun, a smoldering green glob; the palms and banyans swaying in a vertical slither of rising heat waves. The morning mists were burning off in the jungle, slight wisps rising from alcove and cave, only the scant beach at the foot of the canopy calm. The beach surrounded a small cove, pincer-like, and in the cove rested a two-masted brig. It hung still against nature on its anchor, but amongst god and man there was motion.

Labor was required to fuel the coconut and hemp plantations of Australia and New Caledonia. The vast lands that these farms occupied did not exist in the Old World. Industrial farming methods on the rise in Europe and booming in America had not yet arrived in the south Pacific. New plantations—the largest in the world growing hemp, pineapples, and coconut—were on the rise. And as modern methods of agriculture had simply not arrived, neither had modern forms of morality. The bulk of the Irish diaspora in the Pacific was indentured in Australia, while other colonists engaged in small-plot agriculture or small enterprise. There simply was no large wage-earning force in that part of the world, most especially one willing to endure the rigors of the plantation system.

The irony and overwhelming revulsion of it was that it was their own people who sold them into slavery. The Solomon Islanders were the fiercest and most warlike people of the Pacific. Inter-island and inter-tribal warfare had been endemic for centuries. A great many people were already slaves, battle spoils from previous wars. Others were youths, or those simple of mind, and therefore "rented out," usually for five years, then returned to their home islands. The largest exporters of the trade were the islands of Vanuatu, Suva, and Guadalcanal; the largest importers, British and French whites who settled the South Seas. The "Trade" never went quietly.

So stifling was the heat not even the cicadas buzzed as the last of the cargo stepped aboard the imposing slave ship. The sun blazed down without mercy, rendering the island into hell's smoldering anvil.

The French captain, wearing a white blazer and pith helmet, his face drawn from malaria, stood in the stern making the final tally in a ledger, calculating the advance payment to the chief for the people "now engaged in transit." The chief, in contrast to the elegant Frenchman, was a scabrous sot of a man, toothless, and wearing a top hat. Around his neck he wore a large linked chain from which dangled a rusted bean can and several desiccated human fingers. Though frail and seemingly infantile in mannerism, he possessed a booming basso voice. "Heya Cap'n, you all like these ah blacka fella all same?" The cargo was still on deck as Tengata saddled a crosstree on the main mast, rifle in hand, scanning for any signs of mischief. Whenua stood on the bow with the other Frenchman, prepared to shunt the cargo into the hold. The old chief spoke to the Frenchman once more, "Heya Cap'n, mebbe thisa time you like all same girl black fella trip home yours?"

When the old man noticed that the Frenchman did not look up from his numbers, he lunged, then slammed his spindly knee into the white man's groin and locked his hands around his throat. Terry, seeing this out of the corner of his eye, dropped the safety on his rifle and shot the old chief dead center in the back of the neck. The shot, however, was too perfect. The bullet severed the old man's spine, causing his hands to lock in instant rigor. The impact from the bullet sent him and the Frenchman over the side. Terry could see his boss grasping at the dead chief's hands as he was carried deeper and deeper.

The moment the shot rang out, the cargo erupted. One of the young men smashed a rock smuggled in his loin cloth over the head of the other white man, killing him instantly. Terry spun in the mast, fired, and killed the boy. A second young man had smuggled a parang aboard and slashed wickedly at Willy's head. In a defensive sweep, Willy raised his forearm above his head so that his wrist received the full impact of the blow, severing it completely. His howl could be heard above the gunshot that ended his assailant's life.

Willy, spraying blood from his arm, dove toward the other dead Frenchman and grabbed the revolver from his belt. He fired wildly into the black mass while his brother methodically fired at the most imposing men. Some of the cargo dove over the side, some, in panic, dove into the cargo hold. When the decks were clear of the living, Terry swooped down and motioned to his brother to help him close the cargo hold before the rest of the mutineers came to their senses, regrouped, and searched for carelessly stored weapons. After they locked the hold, Terry tore off the dead Frenchman's shirt and tied a Spanish bowline on his brother's bloody wrist. After the bleeding stopped, he asked, "You okay, brudda?"

"This Guadalcanal no fucking good," came the calm reply.

"All haoles bring trouble," the Colonel heard through the walls.

Fucking sunniggers, he thought. "No bloody discipline, what?" He had learned in the army's special executive school that a mutiny must be suppressed at dawn's early light. It was only 1:00 pm and he was already agitated. He was an hour past his gin and scallops, and the socket of his left eye was oozing more than usual. Now with the advent of Willy's no doubt gin-induced insurrection, a most classic example of the white man's burden, he would have to forgo lunch,

35

drinks, and a round with his maholo boy. *Black bastards.* He padded barefoot to his teak armoire and chose a black silk eyepatch from amongst dozens of other colors in the top draw. He never allowed himself in public without it. He slipped on a cotton over shirt and khaki gurkah walking shorts, but chose to remain barefoot. Hanging on a nail over his bed was his favorite riding crop. Though he was never in the cavalry, nor did he ever ride a horse, he carried it with him everywhere, always the proper English gentlemen. He slipped the loop over his wrist and quickly swished the rider through the air, the czar considering a new saber.

The room he occupied—both quarters and office— was unknown to anyone on the peninsula. When he built the "Molokai Meeting Room and Relaxation Parlor", he had this room constructed in secret next to the men's lounge. The lepers who constructed it were close to death, and he paid them handsomely in women and awai for their silence. Now he slid his armoire outward and stepped on a floorboard, sliding a small portion of wall that led to a seldom-used storeroom. This, in turn, led to the rest of the common rooms throughout. No one ever saw him sleep, rest, or relax, and this added to his aura of menace. He strolled in crisp military fashion out of the storeroom, down a long hall passing the rooms with no doors, past the whores conducting business, paused for a brace of sherry in the galley, and entered the great room where the Maori, the Hawaiians, and the Fijians, lepers all, besotted themselves with poor hooch and thoughts of mutiny. The Colonel entered the room, and silence immediately fell. He chose his target. "Ah, Terry, my beautiful brown bugger. 'All haoles bring trouble,' what?'

The men were stunned. There was a belief amongst his people that the Colonel had a supernatural power to

36

see and hear things without the use of his senses, and this display only reinforced that.

"Terry, my love, do I not let you kneel before me and accept the rewards of loyalty? Do I not feed you and provide the pipe you enjoy at sundown? And now I hear 'All haoles bring trouble'? Am I not a haole? I say, what trouble do I bring you, Terry?" But before the massive Maori could answer, the Colonel slapped his face with the crop. The islander instinctively reached for his parang, but through years of acquired dependence on this white man, of fear not of death but deprival, he let his hand go slack.

The Colonel pushed the butt of his crop beneath the giant's Adam's apple till Terry's eyes went white. Without a word, the Colonel removed the crop from the throat of the giant, flipped it under his arm, did a crisp about face, and marched with military precision across the room and up a step to sit in a huge, throne-like chair.

"Right. Can't have you wogs speaking your mind. Be the end of the empire that, and right smartly, too." He shifted his eyepatch because some of the oozing fluid from the socket was drying, causing the patch to stick to his face.

"Now to this 'haole' of which you speak. You will not refer to him as 'haole', but as *Father* Damien. Titles are important, even for one's enemy. Helps one understand his station in life, and more so for all you wogs who occupy the lowest station stopped at. Ha ha." He motioned to a young girl on the other side of the room. She stood and silently departed, returning with a tray on which was a glass, a pitcher of warm gin, and a pile of betel nuts. She placed the tray on a stand next to him and poured a pint glass full. He downed it in one gulp. He replaced the glass on the tray leisurely and delicately selected a nut, cracked it in his teeth, and began to slowly chew. "Now then, as to the good Father…"

*

During their conversation, Sean offered to show his new friend about the settlement. Even though the sun was behind The Wall of Pali, there was still plenty of daylight left. Their conversation had tacked and jibed like a comfortable sailboat on a calm sea. They spoke of Sean's plantation on the big island and of Father Damien's family in Belgium. "I grew up within the business of construction," Damien said, pushing his glasses a touch higher upon his nose. "My family supplied material and labor for some of the great public works projects in Antwerp and Marseille. Originally, I was a student of engineering."

"Is that when you got the calling?"

"Oh, no, it came to me when I was very young; four or five years of age, as I recall. I was carrying split wood back and forth from the drying shed to the kitchen of our summer house in Wilgenhof. We had a very large front yard with close-cropped grass. On one of the empty-handed trips to the shed, I stopped to watch a large dragonfly perched on a single blade of grass. It was opening and closing its wings slowly, almost leisurely. Its wings were laced with a beautiful green and gold. For some reason, I became enraptured with color and motion. I felt lightness in my body, as though gravity had disappeared. I could no longer hear the singing birds and the fluttering leaves that were the signature of my summers. Without movement or thought, I was atop a blade of grass, fluttering my wings and looking at the little boy who was me. I became the wind caressing the trees and flowers; I became the sky and the color blue. Over eons and in an instant, I was once again the boy standing on the lawn, still and unafraid. I heard a silent voice on the gentle breeze—a natural voice, a

38

manifestation of truth and grace. A voice I could mistake for nothing else. A powerful calm came over me; the calm of true understanding and belief in my life's direction."

"Did you know then that you would be serving God as a priest overseas?"

The small priest looked up at his friend, his blue eyes piercing, his smile engaging. "Sean, I knew then that I'd be *here*."

The two men walked in comfortable silence for quite some time. After a while, they came to the beach where the priest first landed. "Here is where the white dog killed the pig, and where I encountered the first of the colonists."

"Aye, they didn't land you like the rest of us here."

The priest felt a twinge of guilt. "Yes, I know. Truth is, I cannot swim."

"Neither could the majority of those beached." Father Damien reached into his pocket, withdrew his rosary beads, and said a small prayer to himself. "Almost all landed just to the east of where you came ashore. See that giant pointed rock in the water?"

"Yes."

"That's Okala Island. It's a benchmark for the ships that bring the inmates in. The Chinese here are terrified of the place. They say Okala is the tooth of a long dead dragon that surely inhabits the seas around us and will likely return if riled."

"It does look frighteningly like a shark tooth I saw a seaman wearing about his neck."

"Oh, aye, I'll not deny that. Sometimes I even wonder about the dragons myself. But along here, in a few hundred yards, I'm going to show you something you thought you'd never see."

"And what is that, my friend?"

"The gates of Hell."

CHAPTER FOUR

Kalawao Cove could be mistaken for any other cove in Hawaii. Shaped like a rounded off "W", it had a short and gentle swell that rolled comfortably upon the beach. The beach itself was only about six-hundred-feet long and extended fifty feet back to the rock wall at its base. The loose sand and worn lava comprising it led up to dense and impenetrable jungle. There was only one way off, and that a small pig path heading to the west.

In the early days, Kalawao Cove could not be mistaken for any other in Hawaii. On any sunkissed and idyllic day, a steamer could be seen far out to sea. In these waters, it could have only one destination. The inmates knew this and would gather in the cove to await the new arrivals. They were there to welcome them, but not in the traditional aloha fashion.

The scabby and rusted old steamer owned by the Honolulu Board of Health had formerly done service as a cattle boat, transporting beef cattle from Hawaii's numerous ranches to the ever-growing U.S. Navy base in Pearl Harbor. The Navy had condemned it as unseaworthy and its holds unsanitary for the transportation of beef, but when the Board saw its purchase price, it did so with the blind eye of financial prudence.

On the stern were chutes where the cattle had been shunted aboard, then pronged overboard for the final departure. When the hulk was converted to "passenger service," as The Board euphemistically referred to it, raised catwalks had been assembled such that the crew could marshal the "passengers" without having any physical contact with them.

Taking abeam bearing on Okala Island, the vessel's master turned toward shore, then came about, having the stern face the cove. He did not want to get too close, for he didn't trust the bucket's engines. If they failed close in, they could be blown into the cove and ground on the island the crew referred to as "the cemetery of the walking."

Before any white men had been banished, all the colonists were Hawaiians and Polynesians—some peaceful, some warlike—but now, owing to the disease, its degradation of will and spirit, and the awful isolation, all had been reduced to barbarism. The inmates cast into the sea rolled into shore on the swells. Foam-flecked breakers tossed the condemned children, as well as their condemned mothers and grandmothers, into the shallows. Some flopped onto the beach, stunned and breathless; others, still awash in the surf, emerged gurgling and terrified, crawling toward their doom. Women of any age were instantly set upon, beaten, and brutally raped. Their husbands fought, but were unprepared for battle and the horror of the diseased creatures attacking them, and were killed easily. Single men were robbed of their possessions, then beaten or killed. Only the strongest and healthiest of men managed to survive. Children old enough to walk were taken into slavery, while the adults unable to walk were left on the beach as fodder for the wild boar and dogs.

Years passed and the vile routine of landings in Kalawao Cove never changed. One day, the steamer appeared through the mists on the horizon. The undead sauntered and shuffled, dragging feet and limbs, down to the cove. From a distance, those with sight could usually see the mass of inmates and hear their pitiful cries as the sailors dumped them into the sea.

As the boat backed its stern toward the cove, the welcoming party grew restless for the impending pillage and rape. What they saw confused them. On board were not the usual wailing families gripping the rails, vomiting from seasickness and fear. Today there was just one man, a white man standing on the stern of the little ship. He was trim and muscular and bald as an egg. He appeared to be disease-free.

The Colonel threw a watertight bundle wrapped in oilskin with a length of rope attached into the sea, turned to the crew, spit on the deck, and said, "Fuck all Americans, and fuck the world." And with the most-perfect outstretching of arms, he executed an elegant swan dive into the sea. The ship's crew hoped his large gold ring and red stone would attract barracuda. They had grown tired of him and his haughtiness and wanted to see him die almost as much as they did the lepers.

He was wise in the ways of colonists and wiser still in the way of colonialists. He was no stranger to violence or paganism. Duty here was a disgusting turn of events, not befitting a gentleman at all, but he would, he assured himself, turn crud to butter and butter to butter cream, even if he had to murder every last one of these black bastards, which, even if unnecessary, might do for a bit a sport.

Entering the shallows, he stood and pulled his bundle close in. He counted seven men on the beach, all

42

very dark-skinned and some nearly black from rotting scabs. *Gross, yes,* he thought, but no worse than the lepers of India or those pathetic tuberculoids in the Irish factories.

Emerging from the surf, he put his bundle down and calmly dropped to one knee to unwrap it. He occasionally looked up and smiled, and once even waved. The mass on the beach were confused; no one came to this island calmly or in peace.

They didn't know how right they were. He tucked an item into his belt and walked toward the group. They became nervous and were tending now toward aggression. He chose the largest one of the group, a powerfully built kanaka seemingly less mutilated than the rest. The smaller man walked up to him and smiled. There was silence on the beach; the lepers stared at the new arrival, unsure. "You will address me as Colonel." The big man looked slowly left, then right, and laughed.

"Haole, mebbe I bend you over rock, address you as wife, then feed you to pigs." At which point the Colonel exploded the man's chest with a single bullet from a British Webley pistol. He shot four more and let two purposely escape. Returning to his bundle, he dried himself off, repacked his gear, tossed it over his shoulder, and headed inland, humming an old regimental ballad.

He chose an area of greatest population. He found a hut that had two pigs in a pen. He shot them both and dragged them to a stand of palm trees. When the owner returned and heard of his pig's murder, he rushed the Colonel, brandishing a club. The Colonel shot him and his dog. He roasted the pig on a huge fire and took three days to eat it, never sleeping, and singing songs in Latin and English during the darkest parts of night. He approached three women and asked if they spoke English. When they all replied that they did, he shot one and ordered the others to gather wood and palms to build him a hut. As time increased, so did his mystery. He would go into the sea and spear nurse sharks as he had seen the people of Truk Island do. He never slept. He chewed betel nut and danced naked during the full moon. Eventually, and as he predicted, the people came to him, and in so doing, began their subjugation.

"When the Colonel gained control over the people, 'order', if you will, was established," Sean explained to Father Damien. "The wholesale rape and brutality at Kalawao Cove did not cease, but was transformed to retail. Gone were the beachside bludgeonings, mountings, maraudings, and robberies. Carnal satisfaction was no longer instantaneous, but restructured into an efficient industry. The goods of newly arrived colonists were not stolen from them at knife point, but 'appropriated' and assessed to trade back to them for the food they raised.

Father Damien listened to every word of Sean's as he stared down at the cove, only occasionally squinting or grinding his teeth. But his was no sympathetic participation—he was instantaneously and completely experiencing the despair of the victims, and in a brief, shining light, became one with them.

"Father? Father, are you with me?"

The smaller man was not. He was standing on a beach in a cove that could be mistaken for any other in Hawaii except...

"We should head up to the village," Sean said. "You still have much to see, and it's best we get indoors before full dark."

"That's fine, Sean. Forgive me—I was lost in thought."

"'Tis nuthin'."

They walked along a dirt path ascending from the cove. After a bit, the dense jungle gave way to low savannah grass and flat land. The priest stopped gape-mouthed and said, "What, pray tell, is that tree?"

"Ah, Father, you have grand taste in woodwork. That wee bush is known as a monkeypod tree."

"Wee, you say, indeed." There was nothing small about it. It had a solid trunk five feet around, and its branches extended outward one hundred feet to all points of the compass, forming a giant canopy.

"The Spanish navigators planted these throughout the Pacific four hundred years ago. They grow fast and provide the best shade in the islands." At the apex of the branches, the flowers formed in umbels and had clusters of buds with pink stamens.

"Magnificent" said Damien. "I once attended an orchid show in Le Havre, but I do not recall seeing anything this lovely."

"Oh, aye, they're a true joy, they are."

"Besides shade, do they have other gifts?"

"The wood is second to none for forming bowls and cups, small tables and such. On the other islands, almost all the villages have groves of these, and every scullery utensil comes from these trees."

"You say other islands, but not here?"

"No."

"And…"

"The people here have lost the will, the joy of creating."

The priest closed his eyes and tilted his head up and to left. With eyes still closed, he asked, "And what of the flowers, Sean? Can they be harvested for anything besides beauty?"

"That they can, Father. The flowers can be boiled and the extract mixed with flour for a children's sweet that tastes like licorice. The Kahuna ʻana woman claims

45

the same extract can be drunk to help purify the liver and other lower organs."

"The Kahuna 'ana woman?"

"Yes, Father, like a witch doctor of sorts."

The smaller man took off his glasses and exhaled. "I believe I am full to the brim this day with the South Sea eclectic. Perhaps I can just get a cook's tour till we arrive at the village."

The two men walked on, chatting about carpentry, animal husbandry, and island weather. The wind was blowing warm, causing a calm ripple through the savannah grass. In the gathering distance, the surf continued its approach and retreat, whoomp and hiss. In the deep cerulean blue of the sky, gulls mewed on the rise, and a wing of pelicans glided inland with a grace not quite possible for so ungainly a bird.

It was a single human cough that broke the soothing sounds. Then another, and another. "We'll be coming on the village shortly, Father. Just over the next hummock." The coughing increased as though some kind of staccato liquid symphony. There were throaty basso coughs, grating coughs like wood on sandpaper, and mucus-charged explosive coughs as though from a cannonade. So prevalent in every treble and tone were these expulsions that the priest wondered for a fleeting moment if he were hearing a new language.

They came to the top of the rise and greeted the advent of the leper village. Not so much a village as shacks and hovels on opposite sides of a dirt path. Their pace slowed as unseen and unheard inhospitality invaded their skin. There were no people out working; no horses or mules; no roadside stands, not a child to be seen—just shacks and hovels. Some bulky cumulus clouds had ground their way across the sun replacing the blue of the sky with pewter.

A dog barked and an enfeebled rooster crowed, but always interspersed by coughs. They advanced together, Sean Corcoran confident and alert and Father Damien confident and guarded. "Is this it?" he asked.

"Yes. Where we are now is what we in Boston called 'the wrong side of the tracks,' but here it has a far worse name: The Village of the Deceased, the leper colony's leper colony. This is where they come to die. On other parts of the island, some of the poor unfortunates are administered by helpers, or kokua. Those are non-lepers, usually family members The Board allows on the island as nurses or cooks, gardeners or whatever."

They passed a structure that was no more than stacked driftwood covered with palm fronds. Next to it another, some old ship's dunnage and flotsam saturated with waste oil, crude holes cut into it for windows. Other abodes were nothing more than slight stone walls forming a domestic perimeter, pigs and dogs cohabitating with the residents. They heard scurrying, scraping, whispers, hacking, labored breaths, coughs. "These people have no kokua. As the disease advances, they retreat to this place of pestilence. Notice off to the left?"

"What, those rocks?"

"No, that field."

"Yes. It looks to have been crudely tilled."

"Not so, I'm afraid. You see, Father, that's the graveyard. Trouble is, people here do not have the strength to dig a grave. The deepest one is a shallow as a puddle. The result is the pigs or the wild boar dig up the remains and consumes them, leaving the pits you see now."

"That's ghastly! And unholy."

"Yes, but worse still, sometimes a poor soul with no arms or legs and who can no longer be administered to

47

either by design or desire, is unceremoniously dumped via wheel barrow while still alive, and sorry to tell, the pigs do not recognize the distinction between life and death." The priest shook his head, open-mouthed, and took note in his mind. "How many are here?"

"A dozen. Maybe more, maybe less, but it's always populated."

There was a sound amongst the coughing, a sound just on the periphery of identification. It was slight, both treble and bass, and increasing minutely. As it approached, the treble changing ever so slightly to hiss, the bass to a muted bellow. The hiss increased to scraping and the bellows to slow-liquid inhales and exhales. Even still, the men thought it something ugly on the wind; something animal in combination with mechanical; something they forced themselves to dismiss.

It was the scent that finally identified the sound: a shriveled and hunched creature dragging a useless leg, the foot, unfeeling from the disease, bleeding wildly. One arm was gone, rotted off at the stump and oozing gray-green fluids. It had no nose and one eye socket was hollow. It uttered a sound, "Sh-sh-Sean?"

The taller of the men froze, stunned in amazement and recognition. "Anne? Anne, darling?"

She nodded and hissed a "Yeh-yeh-yes."

"Oh, lass, I didn't know you were so far along." And unafraid of the ravage and the ooze, or the sight and smell her, he brought her into his arms. She whispered something into his ear that the priest could not hear, but Sean nodded. "Father, there is a bench around the other side of that shack. Could I trouble you to take a seat for awhile while I tend to this fair lady? No one here will bother you." Damien consented, and the planter picked up his charge and carried her down the road.

Father Damien sat on the coral bench puffing a West Indian cigar. His mind was racing. He saw stroboscopic images of his life since leaving Belgium— whales on the wild Atlantic, the impossible skyline of New York, the Mississippi River with its banks so far apart that he first mistook it for the Pacific. He recalled his crossing from Seattle to Honolulu, Captain Ross, the bad lepers, the mad pig. He was so engrossed with his visions that he was startled upright when a gentle voice called out to him.

"Father... Father, will you help me bury my friend?"

"You mean the women we just..."

"Yes."

"But Sean, she was..."

"Please, Father, it's almost dark. The creatures of the night will begin to root. We must move quickly."

He led the priest through a warren of hovels to an open field. The walking was not easy. There were endless small hummocks and unseen bony roots which the two constantly tripped through. Damien's poor night vision forced him to rely on his friend for guidance. "Won't be too much longer, Father. Twenty yards or so." After a few more hummocks, he called for a stop. "Step easy there. I've already dug the hole. I've some rags about her hands and ankles. If you can just help me lower her, I'll fill it in." Clumps of dirt, one after the other, heaped in no departing sounds of soil upon wood or marble lid slid over a tomb—just another void in rancid earth to be filled. After the dirt was level with the surface and tamped down, Sean asked if Father Damien could pray for her soul.

"Was she Catholic?"

Sean nodded, his eyes closed "Yes."

"Then I shall administer the last rites." And after a brief silence that Sean felt could never be long enough, Damien said, "Amen."

Sean brushed the sand and lava dust from his hands and said, "Father, would you like to stay at my compound this night?"

"No thank you, lad. I think I'll return to my Pandanus Tree. You need time alone with your thoughts, and I'd like to pray under the stars tonight."

CHAPTER FIVE

His gait, like his thoughts and the tropic night around him, was quiet and flowing. He found his campsite with little difficulty and commenced his nightly ritual. The sand was mercifully soft upon his knees, unlike the stone benches and hardwood pews in the seminary of his none-too-distant youth. This relative physical comfort allowed his mind to reach out and pray deeply and soothingly.

In his upward gaze toward the heavens, he focused unintentionally on a single star. It was Arcturus, one the brightest in the night sky. For centuries, the Tahitian navigators in their longboats followed this star eastward. When it was, eventually, directly over their heads, it signaled that they were amongst the Hawaiian Islands. The Tahitians, and over time the Polynesians, referred to this star as Hokulue' a, or "The Star of Joy". The white men who came much later to Hawaii referred to Arcturus as "The "Keeper of Bears".

The creatures of the night had begun to root, but on this island, other dangers always lurked.

"Now as to the good Father," the Colonel said, stroking his clean-shaven chin, "we shall draft a plan, paint a canvas, or compose a symphony if you will. Do any of you whores or invalids know what a symphony is?" He held up a hand, palm outward. "No, don't bloody answer. I'd be content not to soil myself if one of you did know." He pointed to Terry and Willy. "Right, lads, pinch me a couple of the Filipinos none too far along, what."

The Maori strongmen were the Colonel's "lieutenants" in charge of all "recruitment" at Kalawao Cove. The two giants each selected a teenage boy they knew—one from Luzon, one from Mindanao. Upon their arrival, the colonel said, "Hello, my little bastards. What are your names?" The boy from Luzon, lithe and alert, replied, "Angel," and the lad from Mindanao, thick and square-shouldered, said, "Jesus."

"Dee-lightful," said the Colonel. "And are you two monkeys followers of the Roman church?" They both replied they were. The Colonel nodded to Terry and Willy, who slapped each of the boys in the face. "Not in my presence, lads. I'll not have anyone bowing to Rome five times a day." Angel lowered his head as Jesus stared defiantly. The Colonel took silent notice of this. "Well, my tailless little simians, there will be no churching here, but soon you'll be confessing your sins over to the Pandanus Tree. Spend your last night as pagans and enjoy my hospitality here, for tomorrow you go to work elsewhere." And as if the boys were not there at all, he asked Terry, "Do they enjoy women, men, or the pipe?"

"All."

"Dee-lightful! Give them all in abundance, and make sure they don't get hurt." Before the Maori and their two charges could depart, the Colonel said, "Willy, when the boys have had their jollies, have them cleaned and oiled like the good weapons they'll soon be. Terry, when your brother is done with the boys, I want you to acquire four pigs. Also, have the boy and girl virgins start chewing kava. Have the whores collect enough driftwood for a fire, a huge fire. A fire that can be seen in Honolulu. I want to have a luau—my kind of luau—and I want it ready for tomorrow night. If it's not, my beautiful brown sun-god bugger, I'll feed you two to the pigs we're going to dine on."

*

Damien paced between his post marks, writing down the lengths and directions. His was picturing in his mind where he would place the baths and where he'd place the latrine. He wanted part of the structure butted to The Wall of Pali for support, and part on pilings. It was his intent to channel a spillway from the base of the waterfall a quarter mile up, leading under the buildings and out to the sea to carry away the effluence.

This rushing water could also be hauled and stored for bathing and cleaning. While pacing close to The Wall, he kicked up some loose lava and rock scree and noticed a bit of white that somehow didn't belong. Curious, he bent and picked it up. Larger than he first thought, the object had a clump of dried seaweed on it. Untangling it, he was surprised to see it was a fishhook, or actually two fishhooks, on one shaft as long as his palm. Also of surprise was its composition: bone or ivory with a crude eye drilled at the top rather than metal. A fishhook, for sure, but he had noticed in his few days here that no one fished, an oddity on a peninsula in the middle of the Pacific. With a bit of a boyhood thrill, he kicked up some more loose earth and saw more bits of white. He placed the fishhook on a flat rock and dropped to his hands and knees to look amongst the debris. There were bits of broken bowls—also made of bone—and a remarkable oval piece as long as his thumb and carved with small eels. It, too, had a crude eye drilled in the top, and he surmised it to be a woman's earring. His excitement mounting, he turned to speculation. *Did this wash ashore? Did people live here?* His reverie was interrupted by two men approaching in the distance—two men he did not yet recognize. Remembering Captain Ross's warning that his body needed protecting, he sauntered casually to his tool box to remove the Navy pistol, if necessary. He willed himself not to reach in till circumstance or fate forced him to.

*

As the big Maori turned on his heels, the Colonel stopped him. "Ah, Terry old chap, one more thing. You know those two Russians that live in the shack by the beach?"

He nodded.

"Right, now after you've collected the pigs, etcetera, would you be a dear and invite those two to our soiree tomorrow? Tell those two Cossacks they'll be my special guests. Cocktails before sundown. Now off you go."

*

The priest still could not focus on the approaching figures, but a friendly voice reached him over the wind and surf. "Father, top of the morning to ya."

As the two came into focus, Damien could see one was only half clothed, bronzed by the sun and confident in his stride.

"Father Damien," said Sean, "allow me to introduce his own good self, Jeemo." The smaller man was perplexed, and he gave his friend a tilt of the head. "Jeemo...?"

The larger man chuckled, "Father most people in these islands have only one name. Jeemo is, well, only Jeemo."

54

"And whom I am very pleased to meet," he said, recovering quickly. The young man, sensing the kindness, reached out his hand. Father Damien shook it heartily.

"Jeemo has a very special job here on the island, Father."

"Oh, and what is that?"

"Postman."

"Indeed? But I took no note of post drops or mail office."

"You're right there. Well, partially anyway. 'Tis true, mail's not delivered to the home, but we do have a post office where folks can pick up and send out their parcels. You simply have yet to see it. Jeemo here is not a postman such as you and I know. Once a month, when the steamer arrives, he swims out to where it lays off. He totes an oil skin bag with his teeth that the crew hauls aboard. He then swims back with a bag from the post office on the big island."

"There is a post office here?"

"Aye, a full-service one with a grand American flag flying over it."

"There is so much I have not been told."

"Father, you couldn't *be* told the likes of what transpire here."

"Yes, yes, that is so." Damien was silent a moment, then lit a cigar, the wind snapping out his first two matches.

Sean went on. "Father I came out today not just to introduce this young man, but to recommend him, as well."

"Oh?"

"Well, if I'm recallin' in the not-too-distant past of yesterday afternoon, you mentioned building a latrine and bathhouse. Jeemo here is a fine carpenter; built most of my place. Can read plans, too." He nodded almost imperceptibly to the young man's feet, the left of which had no toes.

"Well, I am sure that I can use one more hand. What kind of wages does he require?"

"The Board of Health gives three dollars a month to those lads willing to build. If the Church can see fit for a dollar or two extra and some meals, I think you'll see a fine day's work done." The priest nodded, and the three shook hands on it. "I'll send the lad out tomorrow and bring a pot out this afternoon for tea."

"That would be grand, Sean, to both." The two walked away, Damien thinking it odd that the boy had not said a word.

Preparations were under way for the grand luau. Forty girls and boys stood aligned before large wooden vats made from monkeypod wood. Their task, starting from sunrise, was to chew and soften the rough and bitter root from the kava kava plant. Water bearers brought barrels of fresh water from the falls of Pali to pour into the mash. The Colonel authorized kegs of saki brought in by Japanese fisherman and traded for women to be tapped, and hundreds of wooden cups set about the casks. Rum produced by sugar cane in this part of the colony would be made available, as the Colonel said, "For white men only." In the morning, the whores were instructed to get plenty of rest, and the younger boys and girls were instructed to bathe and "Do what you're told" throughout the coming night.

Damien beamed. "It's enchanting! I've always been a devotee of the Russian teas, but this, this is most refreshing. Stately almost."

"I'm glad you like it. It's from an island called Ceylon. The Hawaiian Growers Association imports it by the ton, and we'll soon be selling it in San Francisco."

"Well, thank you for bringing it to my attention now. It is an unexpected pleasure during the middle of one's workday."

"Ah, you're welcome then. Father, I wanted to discuss with you—or more true to the point—ask about this bathhouse you intend to build."

"Oui. Ask your question."

"Well, truth is, it's not the first thing I expect a missionary to build."

The priest nodded and smiled. "My friend, I fear you proceed from a false presumption…"

The older man was stunned, his head swimming in implication. *Was this what they were trying to get across in church all these years? And why was it this priest was able to do so in a few words?* The smaller man felt something rare from his friend—a divine comprehension; an acceptance in the divine which is all around but so seldom witnessed or understood. The priest recognized this, and realizing he need not say more, put his hand on his friend's shoulder.

"Come along, Sean. We must now speak of earthly things."

They walked the distance of the crude survey markers, Damien indicating where the baths and latrine would be, and explaining his clever idea of a canal cut to carry the waste away.

"Father, with respect, and for clarity's sake, are you implying that leprosy may be cured by excessive cleanliness?"

"No, no, not by any means. I do say cleanliness in body and quarters can severely limit, almost restrict the spread of any disease, however, leprosy included."

"Ah, sure, Father, grand enough for Europe or America, but as you're seeing all around you, we all have the disease anyway. There is no one to spread it to."

"Yes, yes, of this I am aware, but there is another component. Basic sanitation reduces the ravages and byproducts." He noted the quizzical look on the man's face. "Listen, my friend, did you not tell me that many people die of pneumonia long before the 'separating sickness' takes hold?"

"Aye, I did."

"Well, pneumonia is transmitted by touching any surface, be it clothing, blankets, or outhouses, where someone infected."

"So?"

"So… pneumonia germs outside the body can be killed with strong soap and very hot water. Did you not tell me that infection is what separates the limbs; that hepatitis kills these people in droves?" The older man stayed silent. "Infection can be prevented by scrupulous cleansing of the body, as well as one's clothes and living quarters, and hepatitis by clean medical instruments and food serving procedures. It can all be controlled!"

"And to what end, Father?"

"No one deserves to have arms fall off or their own throat rot to starve them of air. No one deserves to have their bones eaten by pigs in a shallow grave no matter how condemned they see themselves. Over time, the perpetual darkness on this perpetually bright island will give way to a brighter light. What you see before you are the first rays on the horizon."

*

The lower limb of the setting sun touched the oceans with an unseen bubble and unheard hiss. The pyre that had yet to be put to flame was taller and wider than any building on the peninsula, its potential fearsome and fascinating. The coals of the pig pit were lit, and the four mighty beasts slain by skilled hunters from Nu-Gunu (or New Guinea as the white man called it), then laid stomach down and face up, vacant eyes pointing in each direction of the compass. There were races from all over the world—Chinese and Annamese, Ecuadorians and Mexicans, seamen and farmers, merchants and paupers, diseased all.

The Colonel sat with two men upon a raised dais at the head of the pig pit. He wore starched khaki shorts and a starched white shirt, the tusks of the freshly killed pigs around his neck. The man to his left was wiry, slightly bald with a sharpened hircine beard. He wore gold spectacles, had an air of intelligence, and gave off the shifty impression that daylight would not hit him at full noon. His companion to the right was burly, with a large white beard. He, too, wore glasses, which he removed when others spoke.

The three sat in silence, watching the sun set and wondering if, when the upper limb sank, it would produce the green flash often seen in these islands. To their disappointment, it did not, but the other attendees collectively breathed a sigh of relief.

No green flash meant no spirits, and with the sun down, no shadows could be cast on the ghost-eating stones scattered about the compound, but the natives realized that this did not mean that evil was not afoot, even if it had taken the form of the Colonel.

CHAPTER SIX

My dearest brother,
I open hoping you are well and that the children are behaving. Before reading on, please give my fond regards to your loving wife, Adele.

The sun has set upon this, my third day upon Molokai, and in these scant seventy-two hours, I have witnessed sights that would strain the soul of Job and touch the heart of Christ himself...

That is not to say the island is a theater of horror, for it is not. Physically speaking, the terrain and the ocean surrounding it are without equal in beauty or intensity. The whole island seems thrust from the deep as through a spontaneous and lovely thought of the Creator. There is land to grow upon, limitless food in the ocean, and an abundance of wild game.

As to the inhabitants, where to start? The Honolulu Board of Health refers to them as "Patients", the Territory of Hawaii,

"Colonists" the rest of the Pacific as
inmates, castaways, or the walking dead.
Make no mistake, my dear brother, leprosy
is a horror, a horror almost unendurable,
but I have things in mind...

Those same inhabitants were now safely enjoying the sunset and ensuing luau. The Polynesian people drank deeply of the kava, as was their custom for this event and this time of day; the Europeans indulged the rum; and the Asians waited for the fire to heat their cups of Saki.

Roasting pig permeated the area with a hedonistic and hungry scent. The entrails on the pit spit and burst, enticing the dogs and primitive peoples who let no part go to waste. The Colonel adjusted his eyepatch, tonight made of apricot-colored silk, and stood. The crowd murmured to silence. He raised his hand and with one eye smirking in consonance with his perpetual smirking grin, slowly lowered it, signaling Terry and Willy to move ahead with their torches. With great drama and perfect synchronicity, each hurled a flaming stick end over end into the pyre. Previously, and unknown to the partygoers, it had been drenched in kerosene, and when ignited, exploded in a mighty flash, every stick an inferno. The crowd stunned by the largesse and thrilled by the violence, burst into cheers, then settled down comfortably into the promised chaos and decadence.

The fire fed upon itself, consuming wood and debris in a manner that starved it of oxygen and caused it to roar back in anger. The flames licked the top of the pyre like the desperate hands of sinners attempting to escape hell. Its power unchained the primitive and unleashed the primordial.

The pig facing to the north was the smallest and therefore finished cooking first. Terry and Willy skewered it, placed it upon a wooden platter and presented it to the three men on the dais. "Very good, you two. Now go do whatever it is you savages do in the dark." The Colonel whisked a large Gurkha knife from a sheath beside his chair and deftly sliced the pig. "Gentlemen, I'll do the honors. Help yourselves, at your leisure, and then we'll get down to business."

Men and women copulated while eating pig and drinking kava. Throughout the compound came howls and grunts, moans and the panicked bleating of a goat. "So, you gentlemen say the pogroms were not directed solely against the Jews?" asked the Colonel, less interested in these carnal activities than civilized conversation.

The smaller man brushed imaginary lint from his shirt and said, "Da, this is correct. The Jews were the bureau-cratic and polit-ical reason. However, there was more to it."

"You see," the other spoke up, waving a half-chewed pig bone, "the czar had many emergent enemies, particularly in the east. It is a wild and nearly ungovernable place. The czar's enemies took advantage of this."

"So," finished the Colonel, "the czar called upon you two?"

The heavier of the two removed his glasses and nodded. "Da."

"Why you?"

"We were Catholic. We understood the Church."

"The Church was plotting against the czar?"

"By no means," came the languorous reply. "It was simply that the czar did not want anyone even appearing to challenge his authority in the east." He drank deeply of his rum.

"So he sent you to in to destroy the Church?"

"During the pogroms, it was easy to elim-inate any enemies of the state."

"Including the Church and its devotees?" They both nodded. "But you're both Catholic!"

"Yes, this is true, but we are Russians first, and czar paid very well."

"Have some more pig." said the Colonel, impressed by men who could be motivated by money to bring order to chaos.

*

Damien finished his letter, folded it, and placed it in his trunk. He was weary from the day's events and looked forward to curling up in his blanket on the sand. Even the huge bonfire burning to the north did not tempt him to leave his makeshift camp. But before he could lay down, a feeling overcame him. It was a powerful feeling, as strong as the tides and seductive as sleep, a feeling insubordinate to his good nature and faith. It grew within him, and he could feel it speaking a declaration of intent which he finally grasped and whispered aloud: "Annihilation!" But who or what would be annihilated he could only wonder with a calm detachment that frightened him.

End of Part I

PART II

The slave trade had been good to Terry and Willy.
Through their navigational prowess and knowledge of
Oceania, they were able to cover far more ground,
service more plantations, and raid more villages for
stock than European and American "Blackbirders"
combined.

But as they grew older and their love for material
goods grew, their taste for danger subsided. In between
slaving trips, the two brought their vessel to the Celebes
to obtain teakwood to replace their aging masts.

There, another white man approached them with a
proposition: acquire cheap labor for the railroads and
plantations of Hawaii. "It's like this, boys—we sail up to
the province in Gaodung where I got an office. I put a
notice out to the local warlords that I'm looking for
coolies. I give the warlords some 'fragrant grease,' they
put the word out, and thousands of peasants swarm to
the docks. I pick the best and the fittest, give them a
small advance on wages, and pow, we're off to the
islands."

"Hey, brudda," said Terry, "you mean these peoples
are paid?"

"That's right, pal. Cash in the beginning, then wages when they're working."

Terry turned to his brother. "You know what dat mean, man?"

"Yeah," came the reply. "No more mutinies. No more fucking Suva Island or Guadalcanal. No more cannibals. No more fucking haoles trying to cheat us monies." He glared at the white man. "Dat right, haole? No more cheating at monies?"

The labor agent was unperturbed. "Cash on the barrel head when we reach Canton; cash for each coolie landed when we reach Honolulu, plus the Growers Association will pick up the tab for food, water, and stores before we depart China."

"What terms?" asked Terry.

"Simple. I make the trip across the Pacific with the cargo for no charge, and you fly an American flag on the stern."

"You pay for flag?"

"Done."

Terry looked at his brother and received a slow-hinged nod. "Done."

The Colonel never recalled a mother or father, though in his dreams he felt he heard a hint of paternal whisperings. His earliest recollection in life was appearing entity-like on a floor in a plant in Britain's industrial midlands at the age of nine.

He often recalled, as though it were yesterday, the large group of children, roughly the same age as he, poised on and about and under heavy moving machines. There was no spark of animation upon the children— only a dull automatonic glaze. He felt as though only he and the machines were alive, as only the machines had souls, red hot and billowing steam, spewing danger and conveying malignant omnipotence.

He remembered being thrilled.

A second recollection, clear as the first: three men in a room with him, as malignant as the machines. Two were standing, their thickset and ugly hands callused and massive like slabs of beef. One thug wore a massive gold ring with a bright red sapphire inset. A third man sat behind a huge black desk. His skin and voice had the color, consistency, and tone of parchment paper. "Och, laddie, we see somethin' in ya." The boy remained silent, just a half grin on his face. The man behind the desk sighed, letting out foul vapors as the parchment of his face crackled. "Angus, would ye be so kind as to wipe the smirk from the wee lad's face?"

The thug to the left of the boy backhanded him across the cheek with skillful force, enough to hurt but not to injure, the mark already showing the facets of the uncut sapphire. The boy, still standing, shook his head to clear it. The man behind the desk raised his eyes in surprise, the bright white tufts of his eyebrows flaring upward like the hackles of an angry badger. Angus cocked his forearm back for another blow. Parchment held up his hand. "Not yet, boyo." He leaned in curiously. "We still need him breathin'. Don't ya know, laddie, we're thinkin' of martyrin' ye?"

The smirk resumed and the green eyes lit as though there were a fire within.

Before the tea whistle sounded, signaling their ten-minute meal was done, he was brought up the ancient wooden steps worn thin from the trudging of generations of eight-year-olds. The vibrations of the machines pounded the entire factory, throbbing its artificial heartbeat into the young boys' bones.

The mill floor was the most densely populated and most crowded place in the whole plant. Women who worked with men who worked above children who scurried between the moving parts of the four hundred odd looms did so without speaking. There was no point—they could not be heard, and were they to open their mouths, they would soon be coughing dust and soot. So when an unseen hand brought the machines to a roaring silence, there was a feeling of shock and near-panic on the mill floor.

Still, the workers did not speak. A pause most purposeful was left to hang before being shattered by a statement from the goon with the gold ring.

"Right, now, the lad 'ere," he said, pointing to the smirking boy, "'as of late been agitating for a better wage. Imagine that! Four shillings a month and two meals a day, and the boy ain't proper 'appy. Our feelings be 'urt by this. The guv'nor o' this mill be right proper sad upon 'earing this and asked yours truly to relate 'ow sad 'e is at what we now 'afta do."

And with great deliberateness and annunciation of every movement of his arm and shoulders, the man with the ring backhanded the boy below his left eye. The nauseating crack of the broken cheekbone carried across the plant. But once again the boy stood firm, as though nothing had happened. There was a collective gasp on the mill floor. The goon thought, *Eh, little bugger being cheeky? Well, the guv'nor ain't 'ere at present, so we'll see just 'ow tough the little bastard is.*

It was savagery. The ring opened up skin on the boy's face; the sapphire broke bones in his nose and behind his ears. Ribs were cracked and testicles flattened. Finally, when the boy became bored, he lay down and feigned defeat. Satisfied, The Ring bent down and whispered into the boy's ear, a tactic he thought would intimidate the spectators. "Now they'll trust you. Don't muck it up. Oh, and I 'ope it 'urts."

But it didn't. The boy did not feel pain.

After the beating, the workers trusted him, and over time and in a most surreptitious manner, he did everything in his power to prey upon and abuse their trust. When a fellow worker grieved about long hours, a decent interval would pass, and he, too, would be beaten. A complaint about watery gruel at breakfast would result in docked wages and, sin of sins, if talk were ever heard of unions, the speaker and all those listening would disappear without a trace. The mill, of course, could not reward him outright, at least not at first, because that would have been a death warrant. What they chose to do was to not deduct the two weeks wages every month for the bangers, mash, and board at the company dormitory adjacent to the mill. That was fine with him. He had long-range plans, and it was whispered in his dreams they required money.

*

Though the brothers had traveled far and wide, their eyes had never beheld the equal of the city before them. Kwangtung, unlike Sydney or Port Moresby, had not been birthed overnight to fulfill the expediency of colonial rape. It was an ancient city in an ancient land. Within its walls were thoroughfares, canals, parks, and public baths designed by architects at a time when the majority of Europe was still scuffling about in caves. Five hundred languages and a thousand different dialects were spoken by the scholars, soldiers, slaves, and transients ad infinitum. It was also the major port in China for export labor. Laborers flowed into the funnel of Kwangtung from the vast interior, be it the scorching Gobi Desert or the frozen forest of Manchuria. They streamed in by the millions to expatriate themselves to the service of the American railroads, Brazilian mines, and French canals, carrying no more than ragged bundles on their backs, the desire for a better life, and on the rare occasion, something unseen, unfelt, and deadly.

The brothers' vessel was moored alongside an American trading cantonment, a quasi-military mercantile outpost containing warehouses, dormitories, offices, and post offices catering to a specific company: the American Independence Lines of New York.

The buildings were whitewashed and immaculate, and though built by Westerners, they retained Chinese details like tiled pagoda roofs and latticed paper windows. Astern of their own vessel lay the *Golden State,* a massive clipper offloading cotton bales. Coolies, two to a bale, strained down the gangway in a never-ending stream of sweat and exertion. Astern of the *Golden State* lay the *Empire State,* a sleek, all-white steamship loading raw copper bound for Baltimore. As the copper poured into the holds, dust rose and swirled around the harbor, giving the air a reddish tint. On the wind could be scented the cooking oil, opium, and foul odor of the largest mass of humanity on earth.

After their vessel cleared customs and cigars were shared with the ship's chandler and the cargo agent, Terry and Willy unstowed the rolls of barbed wire they used without fail in the blackbird trade. The agent, puffing away, said, "Whaddya youse doin' wit dat?"

Terry said, "Put dis around rails so cargo no jump over rails. You musta seen dis Solomon Islands and other places."

"Yeah, I seen it." He flicked an ash on the deck. "But you don't need it for these Chinese. This cargo is paid, remember? They want to go. Not like the other birds you two used to ship."

Terry turned. "He right, brudda—no mutinies with them that wants to go."

"And while you're at it, I'm suggesting you fire your current crew and hire Chinese for the outbound passage."

"Why?" Terry asked with a suspicious look.

The agent leaned in and with a hushed hustler's voice, said, "Because Chinese are amongst the best seamen in the world, almost as good as American sailors." The two brothers stiffened, and Terry reached for his parang. "Maori best seamen in world," he said.

The white man raised his hands in mock surrender. "Okay, okay, I meant to say Chinese third best seamen in world after Maori and Americans. And I'll tell ya another thing, you oughta fire that goddamn cook of yours. The bugger couldn't boil water if he had a volcano to do it with. Bring aboard a Chinese cook. Most of 'em can make shark piss taste like champagne and dog's ass like Christmas dinner."

Terry was reluctant. "We hire Chinese crew, gotta pay off black-man crew and bring 'um back Solomon Islands."

"Nah, just give a small advance on wages. There's a whorehouse over out Cho Deng Creek where all the whores are riddled with cholera. Black fellas go out there, be dead one week."

The brothers were silent for a moment, then started speaking to each other in their native language. "This haole is one mean rat."

"I agree, Whenua, he has the soul of poison." Terry then looked to the American and said in English, "Which way Cho Deng creek?"

Two weeks later, with four hundred and forty-four coolies, twenty new crewmen, five new cooks and something ancient, Terry and Willy let go the mooring lines and drifted steadfastly into the expanse of the Pearl River outbound for Hawaii.

After passing Elubani Point on the southern tip of Taiwan in the darkest of night (to avoid the Spring Scream pirates), the vessel steered toward the gathering sunrise, adjusting her course to have the prow pointing dead to the upper limb of the sun as it broke the horizon. In the daytime, Terry and Willy steered due east by the compass. At night, they used the wisdom of their forefathers and pointed the good ship toward the star Hokulue'a, knowing by legend and experience that it would, like a spirit set free, guide them into the harbor named after pearl divers.

*

It became evident to the family who owned the McWilliam Flax Mill that their profits were exceeding all competitors' by a handsome margin.

The reason for this stemmed from labor stability and a wage rate significantly less than that of the competition. They allowed that this favorable condition was made possible by their young protégé, whose methods in achieving labor stability and wage disparity were ruthless and at times barely palatable to even the most hardened capitalist. What also became apparent was that their protégé's methods were realized by the rank and file. The rank and file was beginning to smell a rat, though a rat would have been an exalted entity compared to the scent they were getting. To give the owners their due, they acted decisively and terminated from their employ the person responsible for the mill's gains.

The boy, who was no longer a boy but a teen, and in these times therefore a man, was told there would be "no severance pay, employment elsewhere in the company, or payment of wages earned that month. Good day." But the wisdom of fighting was deep and eternal within him. He told the fossilized owner of the mill that a parcel outlining his own methods of labor control, as well as the industrial operating practices and output were ensconced handsomely in a barrister's office in Hartley Pool, and should he come to no good or find himself otherwise unfavorably situated, copies of the parcel would be sent to all the mill's competitors, as well as every union in England and the British Industrial

Controls Board. The old man, grievously unused to threats, raised his hand for The Ring to pounce, then hesitated to look into the eyes of the person before him. He felt his soul being pulled into this boy, a nonphysical motion, alluring though thoroughly frightening. His head swirled and instinct told him to withdraw, that he was being pulled into dangerous territory, though his thought structure disintegrated and he no longer felt his body— only an increasing heat around him. In panic, he tore his gaze away as though a somnambulant would wake himself from a nightmare. His speech unsteady, he said to the boy/man, "What is it you want?"

A commission in the British Army was arranged, and as was agreed upon beforehand, colonial service in India. The Colonel's military career had begun.

CHAPTER SEVEN

India. In an era of colonial adventure where the world's mysteries were being opened for the first time on a daily basis, India was an event, entity, and mystery unto itself. It ranged from the unimaginable heights of the frozen Himalayas down across the equator through deserts, swamps, boreal forests, and jungles to the tip of Ceylon where cities thousands of years defunct were only now being discovered.

It was a place where famine, generational in scope, and wealth incomprehensible in scale, lived side by side. Where the most beautiful of humanity soared and where the worst of it festered.

And the very worst currently sat in an officer's club in Calcutta sipping a gin rickey. Another man, heavily built and well-dressed, appeared at his side. He motioned to the bartender for a drink, pointed to the gin rickey, and sat down. "What did you think of the plantation country, Colonel?"

"Darjeeling in the summer? Why, heaven on earth, of course. Not like this place." He waved a hand, indicating the entirety of the outdoors. "Calcutta is positively dreadful this time of year. Heat and stench, what."

"Too true," replied the other. "Any good word for our masters?"

"Only good words," he said with forced irony and a smile. "The tea crop will make it out uninterrupted."

"I say, old boy, that IS good news. How did you ever pull it off? I thought a strike was imminent."

"Was, I should say. However, I had a talk with the pickers and balers." The Colonel sipped his rickey. "All up in that region are Hindus, to the man. I let it be known to their wallahs that if the tea did not make it off the vine and out, the tea barons would be broken."

"Should've thought they'd love that."

"Quite. However, I informed the lads that the barons would, in the following season, be forced to pay Muslim workers from the valley at half the rate of the Hindus."

"Brilliant, old man, brilliant." He grinned. "Bet they swallowed a cobra when you told them that."

The Colonel passed a hand over his smooth pate and nodded sagely. "Quite. Hell is, with famine being so near, I might recommend they do it anyway. Muslims would take less than half."

"Yes, quite, Right man we have for the job. What's next, then?'

"A chat with a member of parliament."

Curious, the man asked, "One of theirs, or one of ours?"

"One of ours, I should say. Know the bloke whose son's off to Cambridge this fall?"

"The blighter who's agitating for coffee trade with the Yanks?"

"That's him himself. Seems his son's has a bit of a penchant."

"Small boys?"

A silent nod from the Colonel.

"But I heard the old man had a 'penchant' himself."

"Quite," replied the Colonel, "but the old man, when he's done, leaves the boys alive."

"Ah, good show. Another one in our pocket, then; quite rightly, too. And after that?"

The Colonel reached for his glass. "A jaunt down to Goa to let the Muslim factory workers at that Portuguese mill know that the owners are lubricating the machine with pig fat."

"But they're not. No one's that bloody stupid."

"No, certainly not, but the Muslims don't know it, and we should get at least a few days riot out of it."

"Whereby…"

"Whereby our team picks up the slack in cotton production, and therefore, sales."

"Right man for the job we have. Right man, indeed."

And so it went. The Colonel was dispatched to Germany to addict munitions workers, specifically chemical munitions workers, to the heroine. He sold guns to Mexican revolutionaries and Algerian rebels fighting the French. Wherever stability prevailed, he brought instability; wherever light prevailed, he brought darkness.

*

As seen from a distance on the high ocean, it appeared to be little more than a paper-thin crack running horizontally on The Wall of Pali. Closer in, it became obvious it was an addition to the landscape, though manmade. An eye seasoned to Pacific sights and structures might have guessed a plantation boardwalk for inspecting a new cargo of slaves brought ashore. Coming in closer, though, landward of the surf line, one could tell this was not the malignant terrace of the blackbirder, but something different, something… helpful.

75

Father Damien walked the length of the boardwalk, inspecting its integrity. He was proud of its primitive progress. He, with the aid of Jeemo, scoured the shore for old dunnage and waterlogged timber. A supreme bonus fell to them in the form of the masts of an old schooner made of teak and still stout. These would be used as the pilings for the floor of the structures.

The latrines and showers were built as tiny cabanas as one might see on the English seaside. Jeemo had already dug a long ditch and sluice gates at the base of one of The Wall's many waterfalls to control the water to wash the effluence out to sea. It was a thoroughly satisfying start.

A foundation, though skeletal in appearance, was taking shape. When the small amount of lumber and nails that had been ordered from the Church arrived, it would only be a matter of time before they could commence building at full pace.

*

Overall, Major Jack Tanveer was happy. He had sailed into Pearl Harbor three days ago with his top secret cargo and was already at work. "Best goddamn job in the Marine Corps," the roaring wind heard him say. And for a guy like him, it was.

Major Jack Tanveer was the black sheep of an aristocratic Ohio family. All the Tanveer brothers had attended the Groton school, then Harvard and Harvard Law and became scions in the burgeoning automotive industry.

For Jack's part, he was busted out of Roxbury Latin School for gambling and "consumption", and was banished to the Albany Academy in upstate New York. There also was a brush with expulsion for fighting and "consumption", but a generous donation of crewing shells (a fleet actually) allowed him to graduate.

For four nail-biting years, the family followed in regal tension, anxiously awaiting their son's expulsion from the Naval Academy, an expulsion which never came.

Such men are prone, even drawn, to the unique and severe discipline that such institutions offer. Jack excelled at Annapolis, scoring high in navigation and history. His less delicate tendencies found outlets on the Navy Boxing Team, where his victories (particularly over Army) allowed slight leeway for extracurricular activities.

To the shock of the family, he graduated summa cum lade, an honor that allowed him to choose any position in the Department of the Navy he so chose. The Tanveers had aspirations of their son becoming an admiral, or at least secretary of the Navy, but were shocked once more when Jack chose, as was his right as first in his class, Marine Corps lieutenant.

"The Marine Corps!" his father exploded. "Have you lost your mind? Do you want to be rendered a zombie in Haiti in service to the United Fruit Company, or perhaps you prefer syphilis in China? You fool! You could be a U.S. congressman in ten years, but you're chucking your life away!"

Jack walked to the old man's sideboard, poured himself a generous shot of his bourbon, and said, "It's my life to chuck, Pop. Don't boil over it."

But what really drew Jack to the Marine Corp was almost completely unknown to outsiders and to the great majority of regular corp members.

And that secret was that the Marines were the first to test experimental equipment. Often dangerous and life threatening, but the thrill was unequaled. And Jack had been selected to try out the government's new flying machine. Created years before the Wright brothers invention as a special project by the army corp of engineers, if successful it would give the United States the ultimate secret weapon.

With many inventors in many countries closing in on the secret of manned flight, they knew their secret weapon wouldn't remain a secret all that long but for now, it was their's and their's alone and they had no intention of revealing it to the public.

*

The cloth airframe of the newly created aeroplane he was piloting felt nimble. Nearly overwhelmed by the experience of flying over the ocean, Jack thought, *Hell, I could die right here and now and still be the happiest sonuvabitch who ever lived.*

Jack had been dispatched from San Diego to the newly created secret Marine Aviation unit at Pearl. Jack's first mission was simple enough. It was to provide an aerial and meteorological survey of the outer islands.

Like any good navigator, the new major had memorized the charts of Lanai and Molokai for his two-day survey and recognized the isosceles spit of the Kalaupapa peninsula. During the survey, he had one mail bag to drop on Molokai, to see if it could drop bombs the same way in the future..

The winds were favorable, a slight southerly breeze blowing off the island about five to ten knots, visibility unlimited. Jack decided on a mid-altitude approach at the apex of the peninsula for a preliminary lineup on the drop, then bank left out to sea, drop altitude, and come about for a fifty-foot above-deck drop.

The mailbag next to the cockpit were secured with cotter pins on lanyard. He need only give the lanyard a yank nose up, and the bag would drop to the beach. Easy as pie. After the turn and coming in low, the plane lined up on the spit. He moved the stick back and forth for a little roller coaster-like fun.

"Okay, 'nuff fun now, boy. Don't wanna auger in on this fuckin' rock." He saw a figure on the beach look up and stare in slack-jawed astonishment and cursed himself for allowing himself to be seen.

Damn it! This part of the Island was supposed to be deserted this time of day!

Figuring what was done, was done, he came in a little lower for a softer drop. He pulled the lanyard, nosed up, looked behind him and saw the mailbag punch the sand softly, and the man wave in continued wide-eyed amazement.

As a salute, Jack dipped his wing left, then roared off. Over the sea, the pilot thought to himself, *That didn't look like a leper.* No, the man was healthy looking in a nice white suit. *Ah well, doesn't matter. No one ever leaves that Island anyway.*

Jack stared at the controls and made a checklist. *Okay, course 242 degrees to Lanai, forty-five minutes out, mail drop there, bank zero eight nine degrees to Pearl, take those two cases of Wild Turkey I won from that shmuck Waters, shave, shower, and go "visit" Martha, the renowned ninety-nine-cent whore of Honolulu. Ninety-nine cents, and with me getting paid thirty-four dollars a month. And just think—my two brothers are stuck in some office in Detroit going home to their fat wives and I'm getting paid to fly around the South Pacific and whore and drink in my spare time. Good livin'.*

It was at that precise moment his oil pressure dropped. It was then the fact that his aeroplane was experimental truly sank in.

*

Damien sat cross-legged on the sand smoking a cigar, writing in a small notebook and calculating where he was going to stow the barrels of nails and which end of the boardwalk he and Jeemo could start planking. He made a few more notes about future needs for nails and tools, then placed the notebook in his pocket, allowing himself the luxury of finishing his cigar, envisioning the completion of this project with unvarnished glee.

As Damien finished the last puffs of his cigar, he saw a lone figure walking in the east. Burying the cigar in the sand, Damien got up and took a casual stroll to meet his friend.

"Aloha on the beach, Father."

"Aloha yourself, Sean. Good to see you."

"Likewise."

"What is it you have there, my son?"

"Mail, Father," He didn't mention that Jeemo told him it had been dropped from a flying machine. If the government had created such an incredible device, he was sure they wouldn't want word getting out about it.

"Were you praying, Father?

"No, just lost in thought. I was thinking of how and where I was going to store the building supplies I requested from the Church."

"Ah, well then, you'll be pleased to know you've received one post from France and one from the archdiocese in Honolulu."

"That's grand. It's likely the bishop confirming my request. Would you consider it rude if I opened it now?"

"Not a'tall."

Damien ripped open the envelope with the anticipation that his mission here was on the precipice of real success.

Dear Father Damien,
I open with a light heart in meditation
upon your work amongst the poor lepers of
Molokai, a divine mirror of our Savior.

Coming to you soon, when repairs of the steamer are complete, will be one case of merlot wine, a gift from the Franciscan Brothers in California U.S.A. There will be a new meerschaum pipe, a gift from the monsignor, and new linen vestments from your former parishioners on Kauai. I will also be enclosing some current books, magazines, and catechisms which I'm sure you will put to good use in your loving ministry.

We have received your most humble request for supplies made, as we are sure, in the sincere spirit of charity and giving. We have likewise contacted the Honolulu Board of Health concerning this matter as it is entirely outside the purview of the Church. The letter which we received from them, which we will quote to you, states in part, "The issue of one pair of pants and one cotton shirt for the males, and one cotton dress per year for the females, is deemed to be sufficient to the needs of the settler/patient." The Board went on to recommend [That] "Upon a patient/settler's ultimate demise, said garments of the deceased should be laundered and issued to the newest inmate/arrival, or some such other settler/patient in need."

I trust this addresses the concerns of your previous and most welcome letter. Myself and the entirety of the Church pray for you daily and rejoice in your most worthy missionary efforts.

In Christ's love, I remain...

"Something amiss?"

Eh? Oh, ah… yes. Or no. Maybe. I'm not sure. The archbishop mentioned something of donations, but penned not a word concerning my requests for building supplies."

"Nothing?"

"No, not a word."

Sean looked up at the sky and breathed deeply. "Father, during your meditations this night, I'd like you to ponder something." The priest gave a quizzical look, but Sean smiled. "I'm a businessman, Father, and one of the most important things I've learned in business is to pay close and particular attention to that which is *not* said. Not saying no means they are considering it yet."

Father Damien nodded and thanked him for his optimistic observation. He did not have the heart to tell him that neither the Church nor the Board cared enough about their health to send anything at all. Not mentioning it meant they weren't considering it at all. Their silence was a firm no.

*

Jack remembered that an oil pressure drop might just be a temporary slug in the line. Nothing to worry about. Just a glitch to report once I get back to Pearl.

He decreased the mixture and increased the revs to try and dislodge the slug. No luck. He did an invert, then a steep dive in an attempt at a line blow.

Nothing.

Now he began to worry.

Taking stock of the situation, he calculated sixty-nine miles over to Lanai, which had a long concrete pier and a hard-dirt plantation road to land on. It made for a good runway, but he feared he would never make it if he lost the engine. Ditto the eighty-four miles back to Pearl. He could ditch in the sea, but the swells would probably break up the airframe, sinking it, and even worse, the two cases of Wild Turkey. He could fly back to

Molokai, aka Leper Land or "The Island of the Creeping Crud" as the sailors called it. Another good choice, if he didn't worry that his face would fall off in his rotting hands and his nuts wouldn't swell to the size of medicine balls.

The only chance he knew—the only chance he had—was to reverse course, head toward Molokai, and try to make it over The Wall of Pali to Topside Molokai. Its sheer size and incline kept the lepers from scaling it. That part of the island was uninhabited dense jungle with a long sand beach on the south side. He could do one of two things: bring the plane to a slow stall above the jungle to crash-land in the treetops and wait for a search party to find him nestled high in the coconuts, or he could make it to the beach and try for a similar crash-landing. That would be preferable. He could gather enough wood, douse it with aviation gas, and build a bonfire big enough for Admiral Callahan to see on the golf course at Pearl. He could even break out the Wild Turkey, shoot a wild pig, go for a swim, and have a little party for himself.

The beach it was.

He turned and banked back for Molokai, hoping the oil pressure would hold till he sailed over The Wall. He was developing a powerful thirst, but the Wild Turkey would have to wait until he was on the ground.

*

After anchors aweigh, Terry ordered the helmsman to steer the *Roratunga* toward the white church spire on the hill. He would come in at about five knots, and right before it appeared, he would ram the customs pier, order all sails struck, and bark the command for a hard left. The forward momentum dampened by the turn would slip the big brig, pretty as you please, alongside the pier in an elegant display of Polynesian seamanship.

Willy scratched his stomach with his hook contemplatively. "Hey, brudda, mebbe me thinkin' we just get money for these coolies, let go lines, and sail home. Mebbe we stay there."

Terry was surprised not so much by what his brother said, but that he was thinking the same thing himself. "Same thing me thinkin', Whenua. Take boat, sail her to our own islands, catch whale, catch oyster, trade with our own people, teach boys navigation." At the thought of teaching the ancient art, they both smiled inwardly, contemplating the gift of the stars, the winds, the currents, and the high seas. "I think yes, we do that," said Terry. "Offload coolies, get money, load stores, GO! No more fucking Solomon Islands; no more fucking haoles!"

"Sounds good, brudda. Mebbe ask Chinee cooks to stay?"

The older brother belched meditatively, remembering last night's teriyaki bonito. "Yeah, brudda, I ask cooks to stay!"

He smiled and thought of home.

The Roratunga made fast all lines along the customs pier. A gangway was lowered for the customs officers, six in all, such that they could board and inspect the necessary documents and "cargo to be offloaded."

A chain was placed across the gangway stanchions to prevent any departures until such time until the health and contraband inspection could be completed. Four of the armed officers descended the ladders down to the holds while the two senior officers strolled to the fantail to greet master and mate, Terry and Willy. The two officers took note of the facial tattoos. They had learned over the years to treat the Maori people with kid gloves, for they were known to agitate quickly and kill even quicker.

"Mahalo Aloha" said the taller of the two officers. "Welcome to Hawaii."

"Mahalo," said Terry, handing him the crew lists and cargo manifest. As the senior officer read over the list, Willy handed the junior officer a bottle of "South Seas" whiskey and a box of Sumatran cigars, the customary baksheesh for officers in these parts.

After being thanked, Willy bent down and scratched the inside of his left ankle with his hook. In so doing, the sun caught the left side of his face. The junior officer was at first fascinated by the markings, then horrified by his ear—it was grey and leathery.

Willy stood up and asked, "You like cigars? You like whiskey?"

And though the other man's testicles had frozen and his bowels seized, he managed to smile and say, "Yes, thank you."

Over the years, having inspected the vessels of smugglers, traffickers, and scalawags of every sort, the two customs officers had devised a series of codes to avoid danger on suspect vessels. If one were to remove his cap and wipe his brow, it was a signal to the other that he suspected there was harmless contraband aboard like kava or tobacco. Were he to ask one of the crew for a drink of water or rum, it would mean he thought the vessel carried something significant, such as guns or gold. Were he to light up, or ask for a cigarette or other smoke, it would mean, "We're in trouble."

"Say, Lieutenant, what say we light up one of these fine Indonesian cee-gars?"

The lieutenant, without missing a beat, smiled and said, "Damn fine idea, Hercules. Clip one for me and get it going."

The younger man turned away from the wind and coincidentally from Terry and Willy, put the cigar in his mouth, and made a bombastic show of lighting it, letting the flame from the match rise and fall with the starter puffs. Between exhales, he spoke out of the side of his mouth. "See the big bastard?"

The lieutenant smiled in frustration. "They're both big."

"The big bastard with the hook for a hand. The one you wouldn't want giving you a hernia exam."

"Yes."

"Well, sir..." puff puff... "the bugger's got leprosy. Left ear, a week or so away from falling into his soup."

"Seen any others aboard?"

"Nope, but maybe I best inspect the holds. Younger hands might panic were they to see the signs on others."

"Good, God. I'll take that smoke. You put one in your pocket." Then in a whisper, he added, "I tell them I'm going to clear the vessel with no duties payable. After you inspect the coolies, meet me at the gangway."

The younger man saluted, gave Terry and Willy a broad smile, and while walking away murmured, "Give the hook a wide berth."

The small breeze gave way to dead air. Even the seagulls soaring the thermals grew weary of the effort and swooped lazily to the dock, concerning themselves with little outside the world of seagulls.

"Something's not right with dat haole," said Terry.

"Which one? The one that smells like ass, or the bugger?"

"Both."

"What you thinkin'?"

"Don' know. Don' think they steal Chinee; don' think they steal ship, but something..."

"Fucking haoles. Always something." Willy used his good hand to scratch under his loin cloth. Terry sat back on the gunnels, careful to keep a smile on his face.

*

The colors of the Colonel's delightful waking dream were muting as he watched what was happening aboard the ship from the veranda of the consulate—the soft shapes starker, the scene more real. He was too long in the game, too experienced a provocateur, not to realize the dynamic had changed.

The young customs corporal emerged from the darkness of the hold to focus on his lieutenant at the top of the ladder well. He still had one foot on a rung and one on deck when he reached for the smoke in his top pocket. He missed twice. On the third try, he forced his trembling hand into his chest and grabbed the cigar fist-like. The lieutenant took note. "That bad?"

"Light first." The lieutenant struck a match and held it to the cigar. The corporal sucked in with all his might, filling his lungs. "Like two pages of the Sunday news." It calmed him down enough to speak. "At least twenty."

"Twenty?!"

"Maybe more. It was dark."

"Crissakes, you didn't touch any, did you?"

"Nope, stayed cool, but I'll tell ya, I'm so scared right now even if I could piss, I'd piss a bucket of dust."

"All right, keep puffing that goddamn rope and keep smiling, I don't want those two kanakas smelling a rat."

"Lieutenant, those two could smell rat fifty fathoms deep. I think we…"

"Brudda, you want me to go below and retrieve our rifles?"

"No, Whenua, those two white-shirt haoles see things as we do. If you leave the deck, they know why. Let us go forward. Trouble starts, take belaying pin, smash the head of the little haole, and hook the big one, I'll finish off rest with harpoon and knife."

"Corporal, quietly get the men on the dock and raise the quarantine flag. I'll follow and call the Navy from the dock box on the pier."

"Navy's never helped us before, sir."

"When I tell them we got a ship full of lepers they sure as hell will."

Terry and Willy approached the gangway. At first, they thumped slowly with deliberate ease, then as tension grew on both sides, their pace increased, bare feet pounding like two angry elephants charging the customs men. Willy eyed a gaff used for shark fishing; Terry, a harpoon.

Only one of the five customs men on deck took sharp notice of the two Polynesians thumping their way down the deck. The boy was a new recruit, a simpleton from Dallas. But as he noticed the corporal raising the quarantine flag on the dock, he surprisingly put two and two together. "Shit! Fire!" he bellowed. "Goddamn if they ain't got plague aboard!" The horror of disease and the big Maori coming at him full blast caused him to fall back on his Texas upbringing and do what he was bred to do—shoot anything that moved.

Terry heard the shot, and out of the corner of his eye saw the shoulder of one of the Chinese explode in a spray of blood. Terry tumbled, rolled on the deck between the hatch and gangway, and unlashed the harpoon from its slipknot.

The Colonel's mood lightened "Ah, some sport," he said to himself as the spectacle on deck commenced. He sipped his gin and raised his binoculars, the pleasant dreamscape returning.

The Texas boy shot three more Chinese. The lieutenant charged him with the intent of pistol whipping the lad and throwing him over the side to save his life, but before he could, Terry let fly, and in a stroboscopic instant, the harpoon designed to pierce the six-inch skin of a baleen whale travelled through the Texan's sternum, heart, and spine, impaling him to the teak mast at his back. The boy did not die in a rage as would the whale, but with arms and feet flailing like a panicked and stabbed starfish. For a moment, everyone on deck—the white-shirted customs men, the tattooed Maori, the terrified Chinese—stood still, paralyzed in horror and fascination... and in the next split second, as though by theatrical prompt, the players re-engaged in the mayhem.

The lieutenant, like his enemy on deck, was also used to chaos. "Higgins, stand on the pier and sharpshoot anyone who tries to go over the side for a swim. The rest of you bastards hit the pier, form two rows at the bottom of the gangway, rifles at port arms. Do not, I repeat, do not fire indiscriminately. Shoot only those attempting to disembark. Look 'em in the eye; let 'em know."

Eight Chinese were killed or wounded on the gangway, with twelve more shot in the harbor before the message became clear. The coolies stilled, the crew murmured, the captain frothed. "Hey you..." his brother spoke at his side. "Tangata, mebbe I just go get rifle. Shoot off fucking face of haole."

"Not yet, Whenua. There endless supplies of haole; kill us all dead for sure. Other ways to fight." Then to the man on the dock, "How come you do this? We weren't hurtin' nobody. This no blackbird cargo." His voiced pitched. "They peaceful people—want to work, want to eat, want to live, same you and me." The rage bested him, and forgetting the words to his brother, he unlashed another harpoon from the starboard rail.

"Captain, NO!" came the voice from the dock. The lieutenant held up both his hands. "Captain, you have plague aboard."

"Eh, plague?" He lowered the harpoon, touching it butt to the deck, barb upward like a spire. Terry well remembered the cholera at Soochow Creek and the influenza outbreak in Port Moresby. "What kind plague?"

"Chinese sickness—ma'i Pake."

"Separating sickness!? How you know this?"

"We saw it on the coolies. Bunch of 'em have it. So does your first mate. Look at his left ear."

"Whenua?" He cocked his head. Willy slow-thumped the few steps to his brother. "The white-shirt haole say you got it. Turn to me." His brother did so, a giant grinding wheel turning slowly on its axis. Terry inspected his brother's ear. It was gray and leathery, but there was only one way to tell. Terry ripped the shark tooth off the thong that was hanging from his neck. Slowly, deliberately, he pushed the pointed edge into the lobe of his brother's ear. "You feel anything, brudda?"

"No."

On the inside, Terry died a small death. "You got it, Whenua."

"Fuckin' haoles."

"What you wanna do?"

"What dat heesus haole say in Solomon Islands? Ear for an ear?"

His brother nodded. "Yeah, ear for ear. Okay den, we wait for ear."

There was no more terrifying sound to the ear of the white Hawaiian bureaucrat then the clarion call of random leprosy.

The Navy did come, and it came fast and nervous. When the militia arrived, customs officers had already secured the pier. All two hundred coolies were on the dock, sectioned into eight groups of twenty-five coolies, each such that they could be more easily handled.

90

The suspected were to be marched to an as-yet-unfinished asylum where they all would be examined for the separating sickness. All were unshackled, as the white officers were afraid to touch them. Instead, a length of rope, lasso-like, encircled each group. Sailors with fixed bayonets stood at each quadrant of the circle. The march toward the asylum began down Enterprise Street, where at the end, they would be examined by a Navy doctor who would decide their fate.

Viewing the parade from the balcony, the Colonel was concerned, but not worried. *They can't all have the disease,* he surmised. Besides, there were still enough syphilis-infected coolies on the Sanford Plantation to bring his plan to fruition. This last bunch was mere icing on the cake. The Colonel ordered another gin stinger and was delighted by the suggestion from one of his compatriots that they descend to street level as the coolies passed for a better view of the white man's burden.

As the circle of sailors and the roped coolies approached the consulate, the Colonel and his associates were already on the street, cocktails in hand.

The sailors were nervous. They knew if the coolies chose, they could easily slip the rope and simply disappear inland. Their only hope was to bluster and prod with the bayonet. One of the sidewalk drinkers taunted, "Hey, Yanks, frightened of some yellow rice devils?"

The ensign in charge of the militia, barely holding his composure, barked an order to one of his men. "Martinez, silence that man." Martinez did not know who shouted the taunt, so he randomly chose one of the onlookers and cracked him in the head with his rifle butt. The man collapsed unconscious to the sidewalk. "Sailor," ordered the ensign, "pass that man into the cordon, have the coolies carry him, and if any of those bastards move or say a word, shoot them."

"Aye, aye, sir."

*

In darkness he never expected and in depths he never knew, the Colonel encountered a diversion. A voice spoke to him. A basso rasp, ugly and ancient; a voice he had only heard twice before. *There is a new enemy emerging, a powerful one.* The Colonel knew a reply was not necessary or requested. *The existence of this foe cannot be tolerated. Engage as before.*

As the captain maneuvered the stern of the cattle boat toward Kalawao Cove, the Colonel, refreshed and invigorated, stood up. *Time to check out the new digs, I should say.*

*

The beach was empty, except for the man and his skeletal structures. Damien was oblivious to the mewing gulls and the pounding surf. He paced off lengths and calculated widths and dimensions in that part of his mind that held the carpenter.

He walked east along the crude markers he had laid out, then west to double-check them, then east once more to re-calculate. *Perfect,* he thought. *The baths and showers will face the sea for a calming effect, and The Wall of Pali behind for comfort and security. It's almost a perfect location, if only...*

"Father?"

The smaller man jumped, lost as he was in his hammer-and-nail reverie. "Oh, Sean, it's you. You gave me quite a start there."

"Sorry. Didn't mean to frighten."

"Not at all. You just have a gift for appearing without me ever taking notice."

"Well, it's grand to have a gift," Sean said with a smile. "Construction coming along, is it?"

"Nothing built yet, as you can see. Just the benchmarks. Come, take a walk. I'll be having all the showers and paths on a sort of boardwalk that can be reached by stairs at both ends. I'm planning an open cistern at the east end to gather the falling waters off The Wall, with culverts beneath to cut to the sea to wash out the wastewaters with the tide." He beamed at his friend, but Sean put a cautionary hand on his shoulder.

"Father, I don't mean to be a thief of joy, but there's something to tell."

"Oh?"

"There were seven last night."

"Seven? I treated four patients yesterday, and it seemed they had days left."

"Ah, well, afraid not, Father. Those four passed, and we lost Mr. Stanley and two young children."

"Seven?" The question, not really asked, went unanswered. "Allow me a moment please." The smaller man fell silent. He now heard the mewing of the gulls and the pounding of the surf and became one with them and the departed. After a moment, he lifted his head. "Sean, there is plenty of light left in the day. If you help me build the coffins, I'll dig the graves. Some of the kokua can help us bury them. We'll have services at sunset."

It was the taller man's turn to be silent before speaking. "Well, enough. There's other news to tell, maybe some a bit happier."

"That would be welcome."

*

Major Jack Tanveer breathed a sigh of relief as his aeroplane crested over The Wall. Trouble was, it was still early in the day, the ground hadn't time to heat up enough for the warm air to give him lift, and he fell in close to the treetops, though still above them.

"Fuck a duck!" he said aloud.

Deciding that he was not going to reach the beach on the south side, he planned for the slow stall to drop him on top of the canopy. But he didn't plan fast enough. The oil pressure dropped radically, the engine sputtered, and the plane slid in altitude just enough for a thousand-year banyan tree to grab his tail.

Holding the fuselage firmly in place, the tree watched impassively as the plane ripped in half. The nose dove up while he pushed desperately on the stick to get the remainder of the craft to level. It spun up, then gave way to gravity. It momentarily rested on top of the jungle canopy. He saw daylight for an instant and thought, *Maybe I'll have that bonfire after all,* when the plane reinitiated its descent and was engulfed by the canopy as though it never existed.

*

It is a long and melancholy labor manufacturing coffins, more so when finished wood is in short supply and the carpenter must scour the beach for old dunnage or driftwood. Father Damien also found it difficult digging a proper grave in volcanic soil. For the first three feet, the pure ash kept re-filling the hole after every shovelful was discharged. He had to hack the next three feet with pick and hoe as it had formed volcanic rock. But difficult jobs get done, even if delayed, and at sunset, Father Damien began the eulogies, seven in a row.

"I knew not this woman, for she had begun to enter God's kingdom when I arrived…"

"I knew briefly Mr. Stanley, our brother in Christ. He was a fine man…"

"These two sisters were banished to this island for thirty years. They had only the love of human kindness…"

"Maree, Heekolay, and Kati now walk as children should, in the bright light of eternity…"

"E nomine patri et filii e spiritus sancti…"

The gulls soared overhead but did not mew, as if observing their own moment of silence. They rose on the thermals, barely flapping their wings, and glided out to sea. Damien watched the kokua shovel the dirt and volcanic ash on the little girls, the man, the women and the sisters. Tiredly, Father Damien finished his prayers for the souls of the departed and realized that his efforts to save the bodies of the living would have to wait another day.

*

First are the sounds. The jungle in the morning is a symphony. Cicadas, slow to wake, buzz like slowly rolling maraca. Parrots and toucans flutter furtively, and monkeys cry out more in yawn than communication.

Next comes the light. As the sun rises to the meridian, it penetrates the canopy in radiant flitters, bouncing off the low plants and grasses, then in great rays as though streaked through the green stained glass of a cathedral. It was such a streak that caught the corner of Jack Tanveer's closed eyes.

He didn't understand why hundreds of canvas rags wrapped around limbs were pointing rigidly to the sky. Like the frozen viscera of some long dead avian monster, the shreds were everywhere, always pointing up. It was puzzling. He tried to turn his head to look behind him and felt a dull ache in his ribs. He turned his head to the right and noticed his flight jacket. The wrist cuff was wrapped around a branch, and it, too, pointed rigidly to the sky. *God dammit.*

As consciousness and common sense gained, he realized he was hanging upside down. He tried to take stock. He'd done enough boxing to know the pain in his side was caused by at least two broken ribs. Not good, but not too bad either. Feeling no other immediate pain, he did as he was taught and prioritized his steps.

Reaching between his legs, he felt a comforting familiarity. *Good,* he thought, *all downhill from here.* Next, he tried swinging side to side, ignoring the pain in his ribs, to ascertain just what it was he was hung up on. Feeling a compression on his shins, he turned his gaze to look up at his legs. He was caught in the crook of a huge branch. He thought it a miracle his body hadn't snapped in half when he fell.

"Chalk another one up to clean living," he said aloud.

The branch that held him was massive, three times the width of his body. He remembered his father once telling him that the thickest branches in a tree were closest to the ground. With that comforting thought, he tilted his head up to look down at the ground.

"Thanks, Dad." His father's advice, though sound for the family hazelnut orchard in Ohio, did not quite apply in the tropics. The tree he was suspended in never knew a dying northeast winter or prevalent frost. This tree was ancient before Genghis Khan learned to ride a horse. He reckoned he was at least one hundred feet in the air. The only way to free himself, he realized, was to swing his torso up in a sit-up-like position, rise to the vertical, and unhinge his legs, then shimmy down the tree. Easy enough. He tightened his stomach muscles and swung for glory.

When his midsection passed the horizontal parallel to the ground, the sudden pain in his ribs electrocuted every nerve ending in his body, shocking him into unconsciousness. The shafts of sunlight remained in his eyes, and the canvas shreds still pointed mutely to the sky.

It was now late afternoon in the jungle. The ground had begun heating up, and the warm rising air caused the broad leaf fauna and limbs in the trees to sway gently. Two things awoke him this time: his own movement in the swaying tree and a creaking noise from above. He opened his eyes and brought his head down toward the sky. At first he was frightened by what he saw, then calmed by its familiarity, then frightened again at realization.

It was a human skull wearing a silk top hat. Clenched within a bony smile was a cigarette in a lacquered holder giving death's head a jaunty air. Originally, there had been a half-naked woman in its place. He remembered the military, iambic pentameter tongue-lashing he received from Colonel Nelson: *God - dammit - Tanveer, the - fuselage - of - Marine Corps aero-plane - is - not, I repeat - not –a - billboard - for - your - whoring. RE-MOVE it off or I'll ship your ass to Twenty-Nine Palms!"*

Fearing the dreaded transfer, he paid that fat ass Flanagan $10.00 to paint over it, then another sawbuck to paint the skull. *Goddamn extortionist bastard!* And though it didn't look as good as Martha's shiny orbs, he had to admit it somehow fit. Now, as though mocking him, skull and fuselage swayed like a hula girl in resonance with the tropical tree that held it. Seventeen hundred pounds of severed government aircraft was suspended precariously in the jungle canopy above. Within that torn-in-half fuselage were a flare pistol, an as-yet-unexploded fuel tank, a medical kit, a pack of nude broad playing cards, and two cases of Wild Turkey bourbon.

Realization now embedded itself more deeply.

Being a good pilot, and therefore good weatherman, he knew that as the afternoon progressed, the wind would pick up and possibly shake the contents (if not the whole fuselage), loose from the tree and dump it on his face. Not good. But at least he had till sunset to figure a way out of the tree. Good. But in his dazed condition, he forgot his hours of unconsciousness. The wind was already picking up.

Not good.

CHAPTER EIGHT

As the sun was now low on the horizon, it shot its beams horizontally into the jungle. Jack was startled to see two flickers, one after the other, right in front of him. Then another and another, then nothing. He heard a slight whish, then a flicker, this one slightly slower. He saw that it was a playing card from his deck that must have somehow opened itself in the crash. He looked up at the ground, following its descent. It was turning over and over—nude broad, three of clubs, nude broad, three of clubs—all the way to the jungle floor. A few more followed, nude women tumbling over, ace of spades, queen of hearts, king of diamonds, jack of clubs. He thought himself descending in the royal realm. He heard a clunk and looked down toward the sky. With a quick twist, he managed to avoid the tumbling flare pistol.

"Would have fucked me up for sure" he said. A few more cards wisped out, some flickering against him, one caught under his chin. He swung his hand up out of dumb curiosity: the Joker.

"Ha ha," he said to the trees. But before the irony could grind in, the loud screech of a dying artificial bird forced Jack to look down to the fuselage above. The unclear lettering became more readable at the increasing, infinitely slow pace…

Wild Turkey Bourbon

Product of Kentucky

81 Proof

12 Bottles per case

He did the math. One quart of liquid plus glass weighs about six pounds times twelve bottles equals seventy-two pounds, plus the weight of the wooden case…*"Strange"* he thought, *to be doing a physics problem at a time like this."* Then, when the lettering became imposingly clear he said, *"Oh, sh…"*

*

The Colonel adjusted his eyepatch and said, "Ask them how they are progressing."

Terry spoke to the older of the two Filipino boys. "XXX aba pagsunod sa mga order Colonel's?"

"Oo."

"*Paano?*"

"Araw-araw na nagtatrabaho kami, nakawin naming supply, maytapon, ng mga ito sa dagat."

"Walang notice?"

"Hindi, nakawin lamang ng kaunti pari ay dapat itigil any trabaho dahil walang supply."

"He say priest good carpenter. Take too much all together, he mebbe notice. Steal very little. He no be able finish. Mebbe give up all same."

The Colonel knew exactly what they said. He'd never heard, nor spoken Tagalog before, but he understood every word. He thought a moment, then spoke aloud to neither of the three. "No, a man such as he will not be felled by so simple a blow as frustration. But," he allowed, "it is a wound, the first of many." Then to Terry, "Instruct the little simians to carry on as before."

*

Damien maintained his residence under the Pandanus, or as the Hawaiians referred to it, the Puhala tree. He received an offer from Sean to stay with him, and another from some of the Catholic inmates to construct a shack or lean-to till proper building supplies could arrive. He politely refused both offers. He wanted to resist the temptations of comfort and warmth, and adhere, as strictly as possible, to his monastic vows.

Some of the inhabitants of this island lived in caves, under palm trees, or in the lee of boulders. Others lived without walls, without limbs, without life. For him to live otherwise would be a sin. He would greet and live amongst the lepers as did the Savior. He would feed them, clothe them, and dress their wounds. He would not be a priest if he lived otherwise.

But it was difficult. He found it nauseating to breathe the cadaver stench from their open sores. His skin crawled and his eyes screamed to be shut as they watched the maggots feast on the burst pustules of the living dead.

God give me strength.

Damien found the roots of the Puhala tree almost as difficult and unclean. The roots were gnarly and tall, and were home to lice, scorpions, and centipedes, all of which Damien swept out three times a day. He had learned to live with the lice (almost), but felt the scorpions and centipedes to be a greater evil, one that could debilitate or kill him. What a failure to his church and his charges if were he to be struck down by a minor vermin ascending from a minor hell.

Recalling a camp protocol he learned from the Legionnaires in Algeria, he made his way to Sean's house to borrow a can of kerosene.

Returning to the Puhala tree, he once again swept the living filth from beneath the roots. Opening the can, he poured a perimeter outside the overhanging roots, making several passes to allow the fuel to penetrate deeply into the soil. The Legionnaires told him such a perimeter, once ignited, would deter the entry of vermin for weeks at a time.

Satisfied with the circle, he entered, struck a wooden match against the tree and lit the circle. With a whoosh and a thump the fire rose to waist height, a perfect wall of circular flame. He sat in the sand, his back against the tree, and gazed out at the Pacific, limitless and blue beyond the wall of red and orange.

As the fire died, he contemplated the ocean now behind shimmering waves of heat. In a manner more Hawaiian than Christian, he thanked the sea and the sky for their beauty, and as the flames left the surface, he dozed contentedly, thinking of the greater evils to be purged.

*

Her name was Margaret. She came to the islands over forty years ago from Iowa and hadn't returned to the mainland since. Outbound from San Francisco aboard the *Hawaiian Endeavor,* Margaret befriended a shipping executive for that line, and the man, impressed by her manner and professional appearance, offered her a job in Honolulu upon arrival. She gleefully accepted.

In forty years' time, Margaret rose from secretary to assistant pay clerk to head paymaster for the line, paying people cash in hand every Friday. Over the years, she got to know every dock worker, chandler, seaman, and mate employed by the line, as well as most of their sons and even some of their grandsons. She never had children nor married, and as such, became an extended family member to all the employees and their families. In an era where segregation was mandated, she, a white woman, mixed freely with Hawaiians, Chinese, and Filipinos, and without prejudice amongst the gentrified white business community. She attended baptisms, weddings, and graduations. Little boys who once carried her groceries or eaten her cookies had risen to positions in the community such as shipmaster or legislator. Margaret was as welcome in Hawaii as the cool trade wind.

It was at a company picnic at Diamond Head that her troubles began. Pony rides had been provided for the children. One of the Shetlands had been innocently fed a piece of roast pork that had been spiced with too much pepper. His reaction was abrupt and rude. He kicked and snorted like a mule gone mad.

Most people leapt quickly out of the way, but Margaret no longer moved that quickly and was kicked from a shoed hoof directly in her right thigh. Knocked down and shaken, she was rescued before she could be stomped. As the pony was subdued, the company doctor rushed to her side and helped her up. Her arm over his shoulder, she limped to a picnic table.

"How do you feel?" the doctor asked, examining the nasty bruise.

"I'm fine." It was the reply he expected. He knew if Margaret's head had been severed from her shoulders, her answer would have been "I'm fine."

"Nonetheless, this is an angry bruise. We need to get you home, but first we'll stop at the ice house on the docks. When you get home, I'll show you how to apply the ice, and you'll be just fine."

Ordinarily, Margaret wouldn't have left, but the doctor had one of the few automobiles on the island, and she thought it might be fun to ride in one. "That would be fine," she said.

But by Sunday night she wasn't fine. The bruise was now as large as the pony's hoof, and was purple and yellow, dark and swollen, though that was not what alarmed her. Having been raised on a farm, she had received similar bruises, the difference being that those injuries hurt. This bruise didn't. Certain it could mean but one thing, she composed two notes: one to the assistant payroll clerk and one to the company doctor. Walking in no pain whatsoever, she headed down the wooden stairs of her apartment next door to her office and left the envelope on the clerk's desk.

She next walked two blocks to the doctor's office and slid a similar envelope beneath his door. On Monday morning, for the first time in forty years, Margaret missed a day of work.

"What makes you think it is so?" the doctor said.

"Just a feeling," came her reply. The doctor examined the entire leg. "Hmm, it fits, but it could be something else. You are of a certain age."

"Doctor, I do hope it *is* age."

"Well, there is only one way to tell. I'll have to take a small skin sample. I'll just give you something for the pain."

"There is no pain. That's why I'm here."

"Yes, yes… I'm sorry." He was short of words. He only hoped she thought it was from professional embarrassment and not his medical suspicions coming to the fore.

After the results, she sent a heartfelt letter to the shipping company thanking them for forty wonderful years in their employ. She wrote a similar letter to the *Honolulu Post-Star* and the *Ka Nuhou*, thanking all her families and friends for making her life on the Island so memorable. She wrote a third letter to the governor general asking him to make arrangements for her for passage and settlement to the leper colony on Molokai.

The reaction was massive. Men whom she had known as boys offered to pay her passage to Japan where leprosy was more liberally tolerated. The Church offered her sanctuary in one of the monasteries in the hills, or transportation to Louisiana, where there was a colony and hospital more preferable to the one on The Island.

Two ship's captains approached her and offered to spirit her away to Korea or Brazil. But she was adamant. She had known children and adults over the years who had been banished to The Island, and she considered herself no less Hawaiian than they. She considered it the right thing to do.

Margaret pulled hard at both oars, her back to the land, her face to the sea. The ocean swell was large, and when the small craft descended into a trough, one or both of the oars would stroke at air only and she would lurch forward. Twice she struck her forehead upon her steamer trunk.

She was luckier than all others banished to the "Tomb of the Living Dead"—they had been cast into the sea with nary a fare-thee-well and left to their own devices. The shipping company she had retired from built, both as a mission of mercy and a gesture of supreme friendship, a small Curragh, a double-ended rowboat to spare her the fate of the thousands exiled before her. Her arms strained, though she ignored the splinters in her palms. She pulled again and caught no water, only air, but caught herself before being pitched aft. *I'm getting the hang of this,* she thought when CRACK, then slam, the wind rushed out of her lungs and the boat split in half upon the shore.

She knelt upon all fours gaining her breath, stunned that she was alive, but as her lungs took hold and she looked up she wasn't sure…

Margaret could not discern if they were men or women, or even if they were human. Several of the creatures stared at her though there were no eyes in their heads. Some wore tattered robes to hide their forms, but a skeletal hand or bloody stump would emerge hinting at the horror within. They were the residents of the "Leper

Colonies' Leper Colony," the farthest along with the disease; the most damned of the doomed.

They stood in waves, the stench a chimney from hell. She tried to summon courage to speak, but only choked. She tried to raise a hand in peace, her limbs refusing, her mind closing the distance to madness. The wave of the dead began to shuffle and murmur. *Are they advancing to rape or murder?* she wondered.

Near the middle of the wave, two of the creatures stepped aside. Margaret viewed a form between them, an intact form, a human form, a man. It approached her and spoke to her in a soothing tone. "Miss Hansen, I am Father Damien. I'm here to make your second emigration to Hawaii as pleasant as your first." She was never able to remember how she stood up that day; she only recalled falling into his arms.

With her savings and a comfortable pension, she established a large home. It had five rooms, a front porch, and a large working kitchen where she would bake cookies for the children and stews for those who could not cook for themselves.

She found a kindred spirit in Father Damien. They would occasionally take tea on her porch, or she would bring a kettle out to the Puhala tree. They would discuss matters of the island, most particularly his plans to build a restorative sanitarium for the inhabitants.

The bacillus began to run rampant within her, making its way to her extremities and soft tissue. One day, holding a pot of tea in the crook of her arm (as she felt no pain there), she dragged herself and her unfeeling left leg out to the tree to see the priest.

"Damien," she said (she never addressed him with the honorific "Father," and he felt so comfortable in her company that he never noticed), "time will eventually pass until I am no longer alive. I have a significant savings and a comfortable home. I would like to bequeath them to you."

Damien smiled, "My child, that is most kind, but such offers are usually made directly to the Church. I'm not sure I can accept."

"I will not offer it to the Church. Only to you."

"Margaret, I do not think…"

"Damien, I know business. My home and monies will be placed in a trust, a simple business entity, assigned in your name and managed by Sean. The Church will have no say. All components will be disbursed for projects on Molokai only. You can use my home for an office or residence, or tear it down and build homes for others. The final say is yours, but it is yours alone."

"It is as if God has brought me an angel," Damien said.

She eyed him. "God has brought an angel to Molokai, but it's not me."

Margaret sent a note to Father Damien the following day explaining that she would be missing their afternoon tea. The next day, just after sunrise, she passed away quietly in her sleep.

Damien did as Margret suggested. He had her house disassembled by the two Filipino boys under the direction of Jeemo. Of the contents, he gave a bed to a couple who were currently sleeping in the dirt, chairs to those who could no longer walk, and clothes to the unfortunates donning rags, or nothing at all. There were many books which he asked Sean to store for future use, and interestingly, a collection of postcards, thousands of them sent to her from seamen and businessmen who had traveled the world over. He planned to donate them to the island's post office to be displayed inside, so that people could see something of the outside world.

The components of the house were brought piecemeal to the beach to construct the latrines and showers. Till then, work had been brought to a standstill. Lumber had run out, and nails depleted. Sean had the necessary tools, and Damien realized that Margaret's refusal to donate to the Church allowed him to circumvent it.

He measured and inventoried every stick of Margret's former home. There were doors (ten in all), floor planking clapboard, paneling shingles, and delightful windows. He estimated he could build five showers and five outhouses upon the boardwalk. The windows could be used as skylights that could be louvered both for ventilation and sanitation, whereby water from above could be used to scrub them down, sanitation being what he believed to be the first reconcilable component to good health. They would also detract from a closed-in feeling, allowing people to look up at the blue sky during ministrations, important for a people whose culture so interacted with wind, sea, and sky.

Jeemo had lost speech as a toddler. Leprosy attacked his soft palate, incinerated his vocal cords, and caused his tongue to swell monstrously, almost causing him to suffocate till his father crudely removed it. Then, with the same suddenness in which it attacked him, it went into remission

Every morning, just before sunup, Jeemo strolled to the "Other Side" of Kalaupapa—the darker side where the Colonel and his minions lived; where the other castouts lived unencumbered by society's laws or morals. Jeemo padded through the compound, past the ghost stones, the tiki idols at the men's club, and into the bunkhouse where the Filipino lepers resided.

He prowled through the darkness into the filthy warrens and into the room where the two boys slept. Quietly he would sit on an orange crate in front of the lice-ridden and smile. He did nothing more. The boys in their bunk beds would be dead asleep, oblivious to his presence, but he kept smiling. Eventually the boys, feeling a presence, would stir. In their deepest slumber, they felt kindness and peace, something they were unused to. They would stir a bit and thrash some, but the feeling deepened. As they reached the light of day, guilt overpowered them and jolted them awake...

...Where they would see Jeemo sitting and smiling. It was a strange motivator.

Before arousing the two Filipino boys, Jeemo would swoop down to the Kalaupapa post office, where the Chinese postmaster would have ready a pot of rice & mahi and a pot of tea. Jeemo would pay the little man (out of his own earnings) and cart the breakfast out to the worksite and set it on a slow fire. When Jeemo and the boys arrived, they ate before commencing the day's labor.

The young Hawaiian supervised the two young boys by instruction and example. Silently he would smile and put twenty nails in his mouth, lift five planks for the boardwalk, lay the boards across the vertical pilings, hammer two nails in each end for each board, then repeat. He showed them how to lap a smooth board atop a rough one so as to pattern a smooth cut for the latter.

The boys caught on swiftly, seemingly diligent in their efforts while at the same time burying handfuls of nails in the sand, making "accidental cuts" that rendered a board useless, or, when Jeemo left the site to confer with Father Damien, they would throw a small amount of building materiel into the sea. Thus, by proxy, the Colonel ensured the work would continue but never quite get done.

Damien kept to a strict regimen. Before the sun rose, he would walk to the shore and bathe. The water, too rough for swimming, allowed him to stand only knee-deep, where he accomplished his ablutions by splashing and getting soaked from the salt spray. Returning to the Puhala tree, a small cook fire would heat tea and rice while he knelt in the sand and recited his favorite prayer, "Hail Mary, full of grace…" ten times, followed by the Lord's Prayer a further ten and a scripture or two that he had memorized depending on this thoughts when he awakened.

Nourished by a handful of white rice and warmed by two cups of Russian Caravan tea, he allowed his day to begin. The first order of business was a stroll across the entire length of the peninsula. He walked by every cottage, every lean-to, every shack. If there a black rag, hibiscus flower, or wreath of flowers placed on a door or fence post, it meant that someone had passed away during the night. There were always several. He jotted names in his small notebook so as to plan for coffin-building later that morning. A visit would be made in the afternoon to confirm the name and offer condolences. The stroll ended at the eastern shore, where the out- and bathhouses were being constructed.

Admittedly the boys were doing good work; the boardwalk upon which the structures sat was almost complete and the trenches to carry the water away were likewise near finished, but not quite. *Always not quite.* There was always this delay or that, this lack of material or that. God's work progressed at its own speed, he realized.

Walking to the spot where The Wall of Pali met the sea, he kicked the sand about, hoping to find some more artifacts like those he found his first day upon the island, but no joy. Sitting in the sand and removing his sandals, he faced east and let the sun's rays, just now breaking the horizon, envelop him. He closed his eyes, concentrated on the glow, and settled into his morning meditation, as necessary to him as his administrations were to his charges.

Now refreshed and recharged, Damien started the second evolution of the day: a visit to the post office. Besides Sean, Jeemo, and himself, the postmaster was the only other early riser. None of these men discounted any other resident as slothful or lazy, for Molokai was a crepuscular place, a twilight existence where one might very likely greet the new dawn with death or misery. Why hurry to meet it?

The priest tipped his hat. "Good morning, Mr. Mah."

"Ah, good morning, Father Damien. How are you?" He said, not looking up from the mail he was sorting.

"I am well, I think. And you?"

"Very okay. Yes."

Damien pushed the glasses on his nose up a notch. "I see that you displayed Miss Hansen's postcards."

The postmaster at last looked up. "Yes, all very nice. Come look. See this wall? All cards from Europe. This one America, this one Asia, this one Pacific. All four walls, all four corners world. Very nice, yes?"

"Indeed. Very nice." Damien could see a black-and-white photo of a tall vertical building in New York, the Eiffel Tower in Paris, a sepia-colored card of the gardens in Kyoto, and a watercolor of Diamond Head amongst the hundreds of others. "Beautiful, Mr. Mah."

"People come in, look at cards, they get happy even for small time only."

Damien held his hand over his heart in thanks. "Mr. Mah, I have some mail for the steamer."

"Yes, steamer come tomorrow all fixed, two months late, okay anyway. Much mail arrive."

111

"Mr. Mah, do you have my rice?"

"Yes, Father, no problem. I think maybe I have better idea for you. Every day I soak mahi in lime water, wrap in banana leaf. I give rice, banana, mango. You eat rice and tea morning, mahi and tea day time, fruit and tea suppertime. Eat like Chinese person. More strength, more understand island. Same price, maybe little more, all same no problem. Ready every day—you only need cook." Damien thought perhaps it would be a good idea. It would free up some time, and he could eat as the people do. Yes, a good idea. "Mr. Mah, I would like that very much."

"Okay, have ready tomorrow. Pick up when pick up mail."

Walking the two steps to ground level, Damien literally bumped into his friend, knocking some parcels from his hand. "Sean, my word, please forgive me."

"Not a thing, at all. Top of the morning to you."

"And to you."

"Father, I have a wee bit of postal business inside, but if I may, may I have a precious few minutes of your time? There are some things I need to ask."

"No trouble. I'm starting my morning rounds. Do you mind speaking as we go?"

"That would be grand. Till then, you can get started on this." He produced a slim brown cigar from his pocket. "From Brazil," he said. The smaller man smiled.

It was Damien's practice to visit every day every patient/settler on the island who would receive him as guest. He heard confessions, said mass if requested, picked up letters to be delivered, dressed wounds, or gave last rites. On rare occasion, he engaged in tea or happy conversation.

After Sean finished his business at the post office, he joined Damien on his rounds. "Father, there's a thing I need to ask…"

..."Sean, I'd like to ask you something," replied Damien, as though he hadn't heard his friend speak. Sean deferring, nodded his head. "My first day here was quite a whirlwind."

"It's quite a whirlwind for me, and I've been here five years."

Again, as though not hearing, "You showed me a terrible place."

"The one where we buried my friend Anne?"

"No, though I do want to discuss that place. No, it's the place where you said the lepers were not even human."

"Aye, I know it." Sean kicked a centipede oozing across the trail.

"I'd like to visit the place."

"Visit?!"

"Yes."

"Ah, well, Father, I'm not sure a man 'visits' such a place as descends into it."

"I am unafraid."

Sean shook his head. "Father, for that place, it's best to *be* afraid."

"Even the people there deserve redemption."

"I'd debate you on that, Father, but for the moment, I respectfully recommend that you concentrate on the lives and souls of those outside that compound. As time goes by, perhaps you can address yourself to the souls in that compound, with my aid and assistance, of course. If you like, I'll walk you by there today, so you at least add them to your prayers. Who will you be visiting this morning?"

"The Fong family, the old-timers, the Kanikaus, and Mr. Oyata."

"After you visit Mr. O, I'll take you over. It'll be a small jaunt into the Wailau Valley."

"Thank you, my son."

At the Fong's, Damien changed a bandage on one of the children he had wrapped up the day before. He dropped some dated newspapers at the dwelling for old bachelors and said mass for three young Hawaiian women whose disease was very far along.

His last stop before taking lunch was Mr. Oyata's. "Sean, I may be a moment within. Yesterday, I noticed Mr. Oyata's thumb was in distress. It might require some attention."

And within sat Mr. Oyata, his left hand in the later stage of the disease. Four fingers were distended to a hideous three times the normal length, each knuckle and joint cracked and oozing, most exposing bone and sinew. Mr. Oyata was waving his hand slowly back and forth, a disgusting metronome, "To keep it cool," he said aloud. Damien noticed two things when he entered: a broken window and that the thumb he treated yesterday was gone. Only an oozing hole remained.

"What happened to your thumb, my son?"

Mr. Oyata, eminently polite, replied, "So sorry, Father. I know you work very hard in dressing. But thumb get too big overnight. So sorry, but I break glass, hack off thumb. No problem now." The sight of the hand stunned the little priest, but the casual admission of removing a thumb because it was "too big" numbed him to the core. He was speechless. "So sorry, Father."

Jolted back to the here and now by the staggering politeness, Damien said, "Not to worry, Mr. Oyata. You said you were hot?"

"Yes. Hand hot; body hot."

"Let us take a look at that hand." At once Damien knew the source of the heat. The hand was badly infected, swollen, about to burst. The infection traveled up the wrist and into the arm. The heat was fever. In an

114

even tone, he said, "Mr. Oyata, I'm afraid we are going to have to remove the hand."

"Okay. Hand no good anyway." Again the terrifying calm. "You take."

Damien, his horror barely contained, asked Mr. Oyata to rest his arm on the table before him. Sean fetched a pail of sea water with which the priest cleansed the hand and the area of circumcision about the wrist. He felt the lice crawl in waves up his legs and down his neck, even though there were no lice present. He made a small incision to start, shortly finishing with scissors. Upon cutting, the skin burst through with liquids, forcibly venting. Green and black and red, almost alive, a foul vermin departing. Damien could not swallow from the fear. "Mr. Oyata, I will be cutting around the wrist. Please tell me if you feel pain."

"Okay, Father. Feel nothing yet." Damien cut, snip, snip, snip. The thick liquids turned to blood, and the surgeon paused to tourniquet the wrist. "Mr. Oyata, I have completed the cutting. I must now reach into your wrist to find the joint. Please let me know if you feel any pain."

"Okay, no pain. Still hot, though."

The small priest reached in, feeling for bone and muscle, but strangely, felt something else. The tentacle of a monster gripping his hand, gripping his soul. It began to overwhelm him, growing in blackness and horror. The man before him became a monster, too, eyes golden, teeth sharp, its smile obscene as it hissed, *Let go, Damien, let go. Monsters are not worth saving.*

No! he cried. *All are worth saving.* He grabbed the wrist harder and found the bone.

Momentarily recovering from his struggle, Damien calmly spoke to his patient. "Mr. Oyata, I will now sever the hand from the wrist." The monster hissed again, *Let go, let go the tourniquet. Join me in peace.* Damien tried

115

to swallow, but could not. At last he forced his own hand to remove that of the man before him.

After suturing and prayers with Mr. Oyata, Damien returned to the light of day shaken and exhausted. He wearily approached his friend. "Sean, would you have another of those cigars from South America?"

"Aye, I do, but I'm thinking there might be something else for ya." He removed a metal flask from his coat. "Here, Father, try this. I use it when horseback riding. For some reason, it seems to soothe the saddle sores a bit." The priest accepted the flask graciously.

Sean and Damien gained the trail just outside Mr. Oyata's house. After the stench of poor hygiene, poorer housekeeping, and festering pustules, Damien was glad to get a good draught of fresh and a stout stretch of his legs.

"Sean, I don't recall walking this far the first time to the compound."

"Trick of the eyes and of the moment, Father. Last time we came from Kalawao Cove and followed The Wall of Pali inland. We had The Wall to our left, and hillocks and jungle to the right. Not to mention it was your first day, and forgiving me saying so, but I think you were a wee bit overwhelmed."

"Indeed, a wee bit. Not likely a day I shall be forgetting."

"*No* days are forgotten on this island, much as I'd like it so."

"So we will not be passing through the Village of the Deceased?"

"No, Father, that 'village' is close to The Wall. We must head away from it, into the Wailau Valley"

"Sean, I've been meaning to ask—concerning the Village of the Deceased…"

"Aye."

116

"Well, I've been here a month and a half already. I consulted my journal yesterday and noted that we bury at least three people a day, sometimes as many as ten."

"Aye, Father, and sad to say there are more not being buried. There are people in the jungle and the caves who are simply left out for the pigs and the crabs to consume. You saw that in the leper colony's leper colony, the Village of the Deceased."

"Sadly, yes. That vision has plagued me since the first day."

"Tis no sin of yours, Father. Tis the way of things here. Till you arrived, precious few souls were properly interred."

"And that is what I'd like to change."

"Tis a mountain of a problem; one I see no way around. Besides sunshine and ocean, dyin' is the only thing we have in abundance here."

"There is a way. Back home in Belgium, and in France, and if memory serves, your homeland, there were burial societies."

"Burial societies?"

"Yes, it was a pride amongst villages to provide as best could be done for the departed."

Sean stared vacantly for a moment. "Aye, in Buncrana, things were especially lively during the time of the evictions. If memory serves, the spinsters sewed up shrouds, the widows cooked a sup for the mourners, and the farmers and fisherman constructed caskets and served as pallbearers for the dead. Afterward, there'd be a touch of music and some drams. It brought the village together during a time of loss. A great comfort it was."

Damien snapped his fingers. "Exactly so! My thoughts are that some of the less-ravaged could assume the duties you mentioned, and the Kokua could assist with the more burdensome burial chores." Without realizing it, both men quickened their pace.

"Aye, it could work, and grandly so. The Hawaiians believe their people to be an extended family—they've just had so little to motivate them in this place. I think they'd happily embrace your proposal. It would give them a sense of purpose. As for the Kokuas, I think they, too, would jump at such a thing. Give them another reason to help. Grand, grand idea."

"Thank you, Sean, and God bless. Perhaps before my rounds tomorrow, we can speak to the postmaster. He can talk to some of the Chinese and Tokinese, as well as the Hawaiians, to gather their feelings."

Sean and Damien hiked the middle of the Wailau Valley. The sand trail gave way to packed dirt and lava scree. Low brush surrounded both sides of the trail, and The Wall narrowed into the distance. "Seems like it goes forever, Sean."

"Appears like it, but no. It gradually comes to a complete stop."

"There are no breaks or other valleys?"

"No, that's the t'ing of it—a massive wall enclosing everything and everybody."

"No one has ever made it over?"

"No one, Father. We occasionally see mountain goats about half way up; we've even found some of 'em on the floor that have tumbled to their deaths. Some have said that they've seen mules at the top, but I never have."

"Mules? Forgive me, Sean, but where there are mules, there are usually people. Didn't you tell me once that Topside Molokai was uninhabited?"

"Aye, I did. But there have been rumors."

"Rumors... of people?"

"Aye."

"Then how did they get there?'

"For a long time there's been talk of secret caves. Caves hidden in The Wall, and caves that expose themselves along the seashore during the lowest of low tides, but I…"

"Aloha on the trail!" a voice boomed. Both men were startled and spun round, Sean reaching into his sleeve. "No need Irishman," came the voice. "Besides, I could slay you with my pen any day."

Sean relaxed and slid his hand from his sleeve. "Mahalo Aloha," he said.

Sean and Damien stood fast while the man on the trail caught up to them. He was a large Hawaiian dressed as a California cattle baron—denim vest, watch and chain, gray linen jacket, and ten-gallon stockman's hat. "Nice to see you again, Sean," he said, shaking hands.

"Nice to see you, too. Judge Lae, may I introduce Father Damien of Belgium. Father Damien, Judge Lae, late of Honolulu."

"Father Damien, Aloha a'uiala"

"Aloha a'uiala Kau hana ho' ohahohano"

"Ah," the big man beamed, "I see you're learning our language."

"I spend an hour a day with the books, then practice speaking on my rounds. The people have been most helpful."

"Dey like it when you try. Most white men force their language on us. Locals like it when you try to speak Hawaii language."

"Just a courtesy really."

"People like courtesy."

"Judge," said Sean, "looks like you've come from the peninsula?"

"Dat right. In to get mail; out to reach home and tower."

Sean smiled broadly. "The tower?" The tower usually meant good news for the island.

"Yeah, when in for mail, boy tell me he see sails on horizon, ship hull down."

"Hull down?" said Damien.

"Yes, Father, it's a sailor's term. It means the ship is still below the curve of the horizon, and thus still far off, but you can still see the tops of the masts and sails," Sean interjected. "I can see by the look on your face you're curious as to why we care."

The judge explained, "No ship can arrive in Honolulu with beef, pork or chicken. Must be dumped prior to arrival. Sometimes it can be thousands of pounds that go overboard, all to the benefit of the sharks and barracudas. American captains aware of our plight here navigate close to shore and dump stores for us before heading to Honolulu."

"Dump it into the sea to be washed ashore?"

"Yes," said the judge.

"But won't it be contaminated by the salt water?"

"Some," replied the judge "Some in casks. We dry out everything, then give to the needy. Sometimes just a little bit; sometimes big numbers. Everybody happy."

"As for the tower," Sean added, "every time we hear about a ship, he climbs this small tower he built and uses his spyglass to see if it's an American ship and whether it's inbound for Pearl Harbor. If 'yes' to both, we gather the hands and head down to the beach and wait for the discharge."

"I must say I am confused. Is not the Territory of Hawaii responsible for the lepers whom THEY banished here? Isn't an allocation of food supposed to be provided? Why is it the people of this island have to rely on the detritus of passing ships?"

The judge and the planter looked at each other each slightly flushed. Judge Lae spoke first. "Well, Father, there are certain, ah, 'complications' with food coming here."

The eyes of the small priest narrowed, and Sean took over the explanation. "Here's how it be, Father.

The Honolulu Board of Health provides food for the 'settlers' as they call them. Each person is allotted one-and-a-half pounds of beef and one-and-a-half pounds of poi per week." Damien's eyes narrowed a touch more. "The beef comes pickled in barrels, the poi in jars, and both are supposed to arrive on the monthly supply ship. The problem is…"

"The problem is," continued the judge, "it never arrive."

"Eh?'

"Never. Stolen by dockworkers, ship's crew, and corruption. The Board indifferent; it never comes. Never. I been on dis island four years, never seen it once. How about you, Sean?

"I've been banished for five, and I've never seen it either."

"And nothing is done about this?" Damien's face turned red.

"Oh, aye. We've petitioned the Board for years. They write telling us they allocate the food stuff, but their responsibility ends with the delivery at the dock. Myself, I believe it to be part of the Board's disease-eradication policy."

Damien, now flush with anger, asked, "How does not providing sustenance eradicate leprosy?"

The Judge looked at him with years of exhausted frustration. "Starvation eradicate the carrier, thus eradicating the disease."

*

The pilot touched the limestone with his fingertips, then swept his palm across the cool surface. The limestone was set in a series of blocks with lichen growing out the cracks, and reminded him of the walkway of the Anglican cemetery back in Ohio. *Oh, shit*, he thought, *I'm dead. Fuckin' case of booze musta*

cut my head off, now I'm floating around this stiff farm.
Pop sure had the last laugh.
Major Joseph T. Tanveer
USMC
Beloved son
Killed in Action by descending case of bourbon
Rest in Peace, dipshit

Before he laid his head down again, he wondered where he was buried.

But he wasn't dead, or more accurately, he wasn't sure he was dead. Upon waking, the first thing he felt was the coolness of the limestone against his body. *Cool is good,* he thought. *Cool definitely means NOT hell. Which, if I were dead, is the place I would most certainly be.* He rolled onto his back and sat up, a grinding pain searing his ribs. *Balls, pain can't be good. No one feels pain in heaven.* He felt his ribs; someone or something had packed them in mud. His shirt was gone, as were his boots and socks. He wore only his dog tags and khaki pants. In front of him, though his vision was blurry, stood a wall made of the same giant limestone blocks he was lying on. Ditto on looking left, then right.

Okay, Tanveer, let's see if you can live life vertically. He tried to stand, but his head swooned and he flopped back to a seated position. *Well, Jack, you still have one wall to check out.* Crabbing himself with his legs, he spun the one-hundred-eighty degrees to his rear. He was greeted with soft light, a keen and tropical scent, and a vision—the engine sans propeller, from his aeroplane draped in flowers and lit candles as though it were an altar. He figured out where he was. Pain, blurriness, no fire, nice-smelling flowers, airplane parts,—must be purgatory. "Purgatory? I'll take that," he said out loud, enormously relieved that he beat the odds yet again.

But the major had miscalculated. He heard a thumping, a deep pounding like a bass drum. Looking into the light, his vision improving slightly. Two torches, one on each side of a large, still blurry object. Some motion to his left caught the corner of his eye. It was people! Rescuers? Natives? Cannibals? The forms approached, the larger one to the front. He could hear no slapping of shoes, only the slight wisp of bare feet on stone. They approached slowly, almost without movement. He felt winter change to spring, spring to summer, summer to fall, yet they only got a touch closer. He closed his eyes, embracing the cool air with its inviting scent of tropical flowers. After an eternity, Tanveer opened his eyes. The two were much closer.

CHAPTER NINE

Even though the air was dry and beginning to cool, it was still thick with tension as Sean and Damien continued their trek to the insurgent leper colony. Since the beginning of their stroll earlier that morning, Sean had been meaning to bring up something with the priest, but was unsure how to broach the topic. He thought the little man would either be ass over teakettle in love with the idea, or as immovable as stone against it. Damien's reaction to the Board's supply (or lack thereof) of foodstuffs made the tall man all the more unsure.

The two walked for half a mile, the only noise the crunch of gravel beneath their feet and basso pound of the surf in the distance. The incessant rhythm of the waves comforted Sean and gave him the courage to go on. The sea stood eternal no matter what obstacles it faced. "Father, I have something to ask of you."

No reply—only their footsteps. Sean wondered if he should ask again. The little man continued in silence. "Father, what I need to ask might be a tad difficult." The gravel crunched, the wind rustled the scrub brush, and the sun fell further behind The Wall of Pali, but still Father Damien did not reply.

Of course he's angry with the Board, thought Sean. *Does he think WE are not? Does he think the judge and myself and the postmaster—men of means and influence—have NOT written thousands of letters to territorial governors, senators, and church groups that all refer us back to the goddamn Honolulu Board of Health? Does he NOT know the goddamn Honolulu Board of Health does not WANT us alive? That they want us all dead, so bankers from San Francisco and New York can play golf on this godforsaken island? That they want us dead so that the Board can proclaim, "Hawaii is free of leprosy. Let us build hotels in Honolulu! Let us strip mine on Maui! Let us denude the teak and monkeypod forests on Lanai and Kauai for furniture on the mainland so the bloody bastards can make all the islands a playground for their goddamn mistresses and trust-fund brats." Doesn't the man know this?! God damn it all!*

"Sean, I apologize for my silence. What is it you have to ask?"

*

Major Jack Tanveer's vision improved. He looked clearly into the eyes of the massive man before him. They were black as coal and staring right through him a thousand yards distant. A warrior's topknot crowned the man's head. From his ears hung two hoop earrings, one in each ear, made of turtle shell. Allowing his gaze to travel south, Jack fixed on a one-foot-thick tattooed band—a blue border on the top, red on the bottom—that ran around the man's entire torso. *A perfect warrior,* thought Jack, *and a bone to be chewed should I have to engage him*, a notion that was beginning to take hold.

With his eyes now in full focus, he pushed the anticipation of combat aside and took in an entity to the warrior's left. Her dark hair, long and over the shoulders, practically absorbed light. It framed a face of perfect cheekbones and mysterious almond, epicanthic eyes, the irises radiating different colors off the reflected torchlight. Jack breathed in deep and took in the rest of her. She was wearing his flight jacket and beneath that his uniform khaki shirt, and... nothing else.

Mother of ten erotic sea devils, he thought, *would you look at this? A woman like that is kept from me by a man like him. Perhaps this is hell after all.*

He marveled at her perfect proportions; her skin tone café au lait and blemishless. Forcing himself back to the here and now, Jack looked into her eyes and began to speak. She cocked her head slightly, the motion of a china doll, and put a finger to her lips. It gave him great comfort to see this simple gesture, one recognizable and calming, a mother wooing him to sleep. She reached for the pot by her side and knelt before him, his open jacket and shirt revealing another depth to her beauty. *Jesus,* he thought, *let this be my heaven. You could make no better angel.* From the pot, she lifted a spoon, and with the motion of the weightless, fed him. It was either crab, or chicken, or maybe beef. *Who cares? I'd chew cat shit if this woman were feeding it to me.* After a few mouthfuls, she stood and smiled. He noticed his dog tags between her breasts twinkling in the ambient light. *This must be heaven.*

She knelt slightly, grabbed the wire handle of the iron pot and swung it into the pilot's jaw. Between that ever-so-brief period between impact and unconsciousness, he thought *Nope, definitely not heaven.*

*

"I apologize again, Sean" said Damien. "Please don't take my silence as an expression of anger or disinterest."

"No, Father, I would never do that," replied Sean, though he had been doing that just moments before, his friend's silence bringing his own rage to a boil. "I'll do as you teach, Father, and forgive."

"Thank you, my son."

"There is something else I wish to discuss, however." He stopped walking and put a hand on his friend's shoulder.

"What is it?" asked Damien.

Sean whispered, "Just around the curve ahead is something rooting in the scrub brush."

"Could be a pig."

"Aye, or maybe a wild boar. They're foul-tempered this side of the peninsula. We're upwind of him, so he won't smell us. Let him come to us along the path—safer that way."

The two men stood quietly. They were far enough inland that they could no longer hear the surf—only the cawing of nearby crows and the pig ahead. Sean reckoned it would emerge on the trail thirty yards away. The sky above the eastern Wall of Pali was growing dark, morphing into twilight. The sun had passed below the western Wall, painting the horizon blood red. They stood and listened. Both watched as the brush parted and the creature appeared, much closer and certainly not in the form Sean anticipated.

Damien said, "I've never known them to grow so large."

"You've seen one of these before?" Sean whispered.

"Indeed I have. Hyenas are quite common in Algeria, where they scavenge the dumps at the Legionnaires' forts. They're brave in packs, but cowards when outnumbered, especially by man."

"If I told you what these buggers are fed, you'd not be too sure of that." The hideous dog eyed the two, its jaws—the most powerful in the canine world—opened and closed threateningly, a rope of drool descending from the lower lip and mooring the slime in the dirt below. "Father, please forgive the desecration of one of God's creatures, but reverence has no place with these brutes."

He drew the pistol Judge Lae had discreetly given him and aimed it between the hyena's eyes. The dog, no stranger to human firearms, turned tail and darted off, its speed defying its broken-back-like lope. As it rounded a curve and headed for home, it let off one its ghastly laughs, mimicking the cry of an insane woman.

Completely unperturbed and slightly distant, Damien said, "Sean, I did not realize hyena were indigenous to Hawaii."

"They are not, Father. In fact, Molokai is the only island in the chain that plays host to their foul lot."

"Oh?"

"They came here as trade and barter commodities."

"Trade and barter, you say?" Sean kicked at the gravel beneath his shoes. He was flushed and once again embarrassed, ashamed. "Sean?"

"Ah, well, Father, it's a wee bit difficult to explain." He wondered if he should lie to the priest for the second time today.

"Sean," said Damien, "I've seen precious little on this island that is not difficult, so please go on."

The tall planter wavered and wondered. *Would it not be a kinder thing to render a false story, to turn around on this path and suggest that the holy man forget this part of the island all together? No, Damien is here in the name of God to better the lives of living beings, if living is what you'd call us. If he wants to see this side of the peninsula, so be it. I'll explain everything for better or worse. The little man is strong. The only danger will be his reaction—and that could prove fatal by day's end.* "Father, the hyenas came here aboard ship, a Senegalese whaler. The crew kept them as pets. The vessel anchored outside Kalawao Cove and rowed ashore. They offered the hyenas and a few casks of rum in exchange."

"In exchange for what, my son?" Sean kicked the gravel again and swallowed a few times. Damien repeated a little more sternly, "In exchange for what, my son?"

"Children. Little girls mostly; a couple of little boys." Silence between the two, not even the whisper of a wind. After a moment, Sean spoke with venom. "The ship stayed for three days. Then early on a calm tropical morning, the Senegalese crew dragged the children, who were shrieking in terror aboard the longboat, and rowed out to the ship. The vessel sailed calmly, quietly, into the rising sun, an idyllic tropical scene."

*

Jack Tanveer had had enough of being unconscious. The little bonk that crazy, beautiful, Hawaiian china doll gave him was enough to turn out the lights, but only for a minute or two. He decided to use a trick he learned in boxing. After a particularly hard shot, he'd let his muscles droop and half close his eyes, letting his opponent think he was either out or easy to finish off. When his opponent came in for the kill, Jack would burst awake and let him have it with all he had. Worked every time. As soon as he felt the pain in his jaw, he knew he was coming to. *I'll play it cool. Keep the muscles relaxed, eyes closed, as if I'm still out. When the time's right, I'll blast the big kanaka in the throat with a haymaker, cop a feel on the broad, and hightail it into the jungle. The Marines taught me well. I can live off fungus and spiders and shit. No worse than the grub in that whorehouse in Diego, till the goddamn Navy sends a search boat or a shore party to find me. Twenty-three-skiddo, that's what I'll do.*

It was not meant to be.

*

Sean and Damien noticed their path sloping downward. They also noticed the scent of occupation: cook fires, palm oil, animal excrement, and human grease.

Rather than being carried on the wind, the smell hung upon them like foul rags, entrenching their clothes, their palates. Sean spit. "We're getting close." The two men rounded a turn and nearly choked on a strong sulfur smell. The scrub brush had all been burnt to a cinder, the ashes mixed with black volcanic lava dust. The blackness flowed down half a mile and surrounded the entirety of the so-called insurgent leper's compound.

Sean spied a new fence around the men's club, as well as a new fence around the livestock and drying barns adjacent to the kava field. *Curious,* he thought. He also noticed six more ghost stones—four-ton slabs of carved granite shaped like doors lying on their side. "Now where in hell did those come from?" he wondered aloud.

"What's that, Sean?"

"Oh, sorry Father. It's just that I noticed more ghost stones since last time we were here. Tough things to be creating and draggin' about in so short a time."

"Yes, those stones. You mentioned the locals believe if their shadows fall on the stones they will die."

"Not just die, but die and become a ghost, one that never leaves this island."

"And they actually believe this?"

"Oh, aye, they most assuredly believe it." His mind began to wander again. *It simply is not possible that these stones were carved and dragged here since last we visited. Worse, there isn't an ounce of granite ON this island.*

"Sean?"

"Oh, sorry, Father. Lost in thought."

"You mentioned a colonel?"

"Ah, yes, the Colonel. If I may inflict you with some British understatement, the Colonel is the 'unifying force in this... this pen." He swept his arm contemptuously across the compound.

"If you recall the day we met, I mentioned the goings-on in the early days of the colony. Vessels chartered by The Board and known as hell ships would anchor outside Kalawao Cove. Colonists would, without prejudice to age or gender, be whipped and prodded over the side to swim ashore. In those days, it was only lepers who were very far along who were transported here. They had been rounded up throughout the islands by special deputies appointed by The Board.

These were people who were already blind, missing limbs, and unable to feed themselves. They were hunted down, corralled aboard the bloody hell ships, and dumped here. The rule of tooth and nail prevailed. There was violence and murder to obtain food, clothing, sex— the lot. Violence and murder made the sun shine and the wind blow. The barbarism made the Huns and Visigoths appear as though the Christmas choir at Notre Dame. But unlike the Huns and the Visigoths, this hell spun unknown to the world."

"No one knew?"

"Oh, there were rumors. In fact, a young naval lieutenant named Mortimer Mortimer—I recall the name because it's so unusual, sailed a schooner to the cove and landed an armed shore party. What he saw so sickened him he had twenty of the worst murderers, rapists, and slavers lined up on the beach and shot."

"And did word get out then?"

"I wish. No, the Board maligned the facts and accused the officer of murdering innocent Hawaiian citizens 'living peacefully on an outer island.' The Board wanted him tried and hung."

"Was he?"

"No, the Navy, having read his report and speaking to some of the sailors in attendance had Lieutenant Mortimer transferred to China, way up the Yangtze River on gun-boat duty. Never heard from again."

"And the Colonel?" Damien prodded.

Sean spat once again. "Ah, yes. Legend has it that the Colonel was sent to Hawaii by the British government as an agent provocateur to destabilize the increasingly powerful American coffee, sugar, and pineapple combines. How he ended up on this island is a mystery to all, though I have a feeling he has another master."

"Why would the British do this?"

Sean gave a knowing smile. "Ah, Father, I envy you your lack of acquaintance with the British. The Brits believe Hawaii rightly belongs to them. In fact, the first white man to land on these islands was a British naval Captain named James Cook."

"Did he establish a colony here?"

"No, he was grossly unable to do so, owing to the fact of his sudden demise."

"Died?"

"Murdered by a Hawaiian chief who claimed he could see the future."

"Can I assume the British government did not take kindly to this?"

"Ordinarily your assumption would be correct, but by the time Cook's vessel returned to England almost three years later, the Brits were otherwise engaged in uprisings and mutinies in some of their other colonies— India, Malaya, and Northern Ireland. In the meantime, the Yanks came in the back door and established shipping and agricultural empires second to none in the Pacific."

As they entered the realm of the lost and insurgent lepers, Sean stealthily slipped his gun to Damien. "You can give it back when we leave." Seeing the anguish on the priest's face Sean begged, "Please, Father, I know what I'm doing." Settled for the moment, Sean took notice of the Kalawao Kove Men's Club, the so-called "seat of power" for this side of the island. He also took notice of the new clapboard of the building and the shiny new nails holding it in place.

In an instant, it dawned on him. *Bastards! That's why the outhouse baths never get quite done.* The Filipino boys were looting from the project. Not enough to be noticed outright, but enough to stockpile for use over here. His anger began to rise, but he held it in check. This was the Colonel's domain, and there was little he could do here. At most, he could remove the Filipino boys from the project when they reached the safer side of the island.

Sean's teeth clenched for the briefest moment as he directed Damien toward the men's club. Moans came from within—moans from the dying and insane, moans of malignant rapture and abuse. The building itself could have been an Outback sheep station, or a bunkhouse for cowboys.

Hanging from the roof and swaying gently in the breeze read a sign painted in tar: *Aole KANAWAI ma rei wahi*

Upon the porch sat various forms of human. A leper with no ears, lips, or nose rocked slowly in a chair. His teeth gleaming, his eyes wide, he appeared as a skull leering at Damien and Sean.

The creature next to him was completely black with rot, his face a blob without angles. He loudly slurped kava from a dolphin's bladder, which he brought to his lips with his remaining arm.

On the other end of the porch stood two figures seemingly untouched by the disease, one ominous in bulk, the other confidently shifty, as though not even light could touch him. In the center, framing the door, stood Terry and Willy, casual and defiant. Sean walked up to the front gate and redundantly rang the bell announcing his presence. It was the first slap. "Aloha Willy, Aloha Terry," he said, ignoring the others. "Grand day it 'tis."

Terry was the first to respond. "Fuck you, haole! What you doing this side of valley?"

"Oh, just out for a stroll with my friend, Father Damien." He swept his hand back to the man behind him.

Terry's defiance dropped a notch. There were rumors the little priest could speak to some of the gods. "Dat haole okay," he said. "You go home, fuck dog."

"Ah, Terry," he said, ignoring the taunt, "this be a fine new fence you and the lads have. Fine new clapboard, too." He scratched with a fingernail at the strake of the picket, "Fine, indeed. Tell me, Terry, have ye found a way to raise pine trees on this island to produce such grand wood as for this for this fence?" There was silence on the porch. Some of the lepers shifted or stood, but Terry and Willy remained still, defiant. Sean pulled at the strake, then pulled a little more till it broke off.

He broke off five more, such that six lay in the dirt, the same number as men on the porch. The dynamic of the situation dawned on Terry. He spoke with the same rising yet controlled anger of Sean. "Don't speak the white man's speak, haole."

"Ah, Terry, I'd be happy to oblige you, so I'll say it straight. I think you stole all this good wood. I think your brother and those two Philippine monkeys stole from the little man behind me." Silence. "No reply, eh, ya fooks?"

Sean wanted them angry. He knew if the two Maori engaged him with clear heads, he'd be dead in the blink of an eye. "Fact is, that's all Maori people can do is steal. They can't sail ships, they can't do battle, and a retarded crow with one wing can navigate better than any of 'em." Terry inhaled deeply, while Willy tensely passed his hooked hand across his own chest, drawing blood.

"When the British came to your islands, you ran like girls, leaving your women and children behind," Sean said with disgust. Terry's eyes closed to slits; Willy's glazed over. Sean backed up a few steps toward the ghost stone, its shadow just behind his back. "Truth is, even Lono think the Maori are dogs. That's why he allowed the British to burn the land and rape the families."

Willy leapt from the porch and landed in a crouch, fine black lava dust rising from his feet as though he ascended from it. His cry could be heard throughout the valley. "RHOO-GAH!" He remained in the crouched position, his eyes wide and white. He extended his tongue; it was serpentine and long, and he waved it obscenely from side to side.

Sean had seen it before. It was the beginning of a Haka, the ancestral dance and war cry of the Maori people. He knew, contrary to what he had just said, that the Maori were the fiercest and bravest people in the Pacific. This Haka was the Peruperu Haka performed to invoke the war gods, stir the soul of the warrior, and frighten the opponent. Sean knew that it worked. He had seen white soldiers and constabulary in New Zealand flee in terror at its mere invocation. He also knew that during the dance, Willy would be in a deep trance. Still crouched, Willy shifted his bulk to the left, elevating his right side. After a moment, he stomped down, raising more lava dust. In Maori, he screamed the scream of a maniac: "I am from a warrior race! I am noble and shall kill my enemy!"

Over his shoulder, Sean said, "Damien, if this man kills me, run and shoot everything in your path. Try to make your way to Judge Lae's house."

"Surely, Sean, fighting is not necessary."

"Father, in order for one or both of us to leave this valley, someone must die. I'm hoping it's him."

Willy shook his arms violently in the air, his hook glinting in the sun. "My enemy will die! I will eat his heart; I will burn his soul."

"Father, step well back. The Haka is almost complete. When he comes out of it, he will charge. Now, remember what I said."

The warrior stilled for a moment. His topknot began to vibrate, the circular tattoos on his face pulsated, and the shark tooth about his neck leaped off his chest as though fleeing a terrible heart. Then slowly, very slowly, his breathing calmed and his good hand reached for the Patu in his loin cloth. He held the round, bladed green jade club firmly, prepared for close combat.

As Willy returned to the here and now, Sean stepped back a pace and into the shadow of the ghost stone. There were gasps heard from the porch and for a split second, even Willy had doubts about this fight. *Does this haole have some magic that he does not fear becoming a ghost?* Still, he was committed now, unable to control the frenzy coursing through his veins. He charged, his large, lumbering legs pounding the ancient lava, the perfect Polynesian storm descending.

At the charge, Sean leapt deftly upon the ghost stone three feet above the ground. As Willy advanced, Sean stood, and with greatest calm, unbuttoned his pants and began to urinate, laughing out loud as the stream commenced.

Willy had counted coup on hundreds of men across the Pacific, and there was no one he feared or weapon he could not best, but the absurdity of what he saw stopped him in his tracks. Sean shouted to the world, "I piss on you all! I piss on this settlement, and Willy, when you die, I shall piss on your grave." At which point, an unseen knife, a double-edged bayonet, appeared from his shirt. Oblivious to that which was in the wind, he leapt forward and plunged the knife into the giant's shoulder. There was no reaction from the brute, just a momentary huff, and Sean thought, *Christ, the disease! He doesn't feel a thing.*

Though Willy felt nothing, he did react. Aiming for Sean's head, he brought the Patu down with murderous force. Hearing a swish of wind, Sean cocked his head and the green jade connected with collarbone, the crack resonating throughout the village. The air left his lungs, and he dropped to one knee. Willy raised his hand for the kill strike. Sean caught the blow coming out of the corner of his eye and shot through the warrior's legs, rolled, and slashed his knife across the back of Willy's thigh, hamstringing him. Muscle and blood exploded outward like broken tension wire. This Willy felt and let out a terrifying bellow.

From a hillside behind some rocks, the Colonel gazed at the conflict with detached amusement. He was certain of the outcome, but nonetheless chose inaction. *If the giant dies, his brother will react.* This might lead to the little priest shooting Terry with the gun he thinks no one sees. The Colonel realized he could afford to lose Willy—he was almost dead from the disease anyway— but Terry was his most powerful minion. The Colonel whistled a whistle that no human ear could hear.

Sean surged as Willy swung his hooked hand and arm in a blind backwards arc, catching Sean just below the eye, tearing off a part of his cheek. He backed up a step, inhaled through the new hole, and crouched, waiting for the warrior to face him.

In their lair behind the social club, they awoke to an unheard command. Four of them stretched, then began a slithering lope. Two went to one side, two the other. And like the black ooze they were, they converged in front of the building, eyes and snouts focused on the smaller of the combatants.

As Willy spun, Sean leapt and thrust the bayonet beneath the monster's chin, a death stab for any man. But the blade did not pierce the spine or windpipe or brain—it tore through the soft tissue of the upper and lower palates. Willy was still alive. His eyes, wide again, blood frothing from his mouth and nostrils, the matador's mad bull at its most dangerous.

The hyenas advanced as one, jaws clicking, low growls rumbling. Damien saw them first and sensed their intent. He moved toward Sean.

Willy also advanced, one foot pounding the ground slowly, another step, the blood from his nose spraying Sean's shirt.

The hyenas closed, and within a fathom from Sean, the first one leapt. Damien cried out, "Sean, FALL!" Which he did. The leprous dog sailed above Sean and struck Willy, knocking him to the ground. The scent of Willy's blood overwhelmed the beast, and forgetting his unheard orders from the Colonel, tore into the giant's throat. The other three circled Sean. Before they could pounce, they were dead. Damien, with great calm, shot each one in the head, and with a mercy he didn't really feel, shot the dog making a meal out of Willy. Without a word, he returned the gun to Sean.

CHAPTER TEN

Major Jack Tanveer's feint at unconsciousness and counterattack was short-lived. He kept his eyes closed and his muscles relaxed. As he braced to attack, his breathing increased. At the same time, he felt a powerful hand on his shoulder. He looked around and saw the huge Hawaiian behind him. The hand was calm upon Jack's shoulder, but seemed weighted as the mountains. The young Marine felt a holding force through his shoulders, down his spine, into his butt, pinning him to the stone, immovable. "I hate being predictable," he said to no one out loud.

The beautiful Hawaiian china doll once again put her finger to her lips to silence him. In response, and to avoid a crack against the jaw, he gave an elongated, "Okaaaay, me be good Marine."

She smiled as though she were happy with, or indulging a fool, and motioned for him to look ahead. He had forgotten the aeroplane engine at the front of the chamber. Awash in flowers and torchlight, it had been scrubbed clean of grease and oil. Tanveer made the assumption, correctly, that the locals weren't going to be giving it back to him.

The pressure in the room dropped perceptibly—*a passing storm, or an open door*. He could still feel the giant's hand holding him to the floor. There was a wisp of bare feet on stone. Several pairs of bare feet. The feet moved slowly in unison, as though in procession.

Three men entered the chamber without the pomp and circumstance of retainers or toadies, but with the solemnity of wise men of an ancient order. They stopped as one before the engine and turned as one to face the china doll, the pilot, and the kanaka holding him to earth. The three men were fit and clear-eyed. They had fresh, bright tattoos similar to the man holding Jack. Their hair was long and silver, and each was burnt brown as oak and weathered by the sea. Age was indeterminate but ancient.

In a dialect not spoken anywhere in the Pacific, the chief in the center spoke as he pointed at Tanveer. "This is the man that fell from sky to earth."

The chief to the left spoke next. "Maybe he came not from sky, but from hell, a devil to plague us."

Then the third, "Perhaps not from sky, or hell, but from god as messenger to warn." All three bowed their heads, interlaced their fingers, and let their hands fall to their waists in silent contemplation.

After a time, they raised their heads, and the center chief exhaled as though refreshed. "In a time before we remember, the Polynesian people rose from the sea. We settled on the islands and became friends with the birds and the creatures of the land. For us, the sea provided. We sailed beyond the horizons and lived on other islands. We were a people living in unison over the vast distances, with each other, and the world around us. Our culture grew. We studied the stars and surf, and we healed our sick, guided our children, and provided for the old. We were happy.

"No one knows where the first white man came. Some say the island of Nu-Gunu, some say others. But they came, and they did not come in kindness. They took people from Nu-Gunu and made them slaves. On Tonga, they killed the Maori just to steal their trees for ships. Here in these islands, beneath the star of the Houkele a', they brought forth disease to punish those who would not work their farms. For many years, we have not been happy." He lowered his head. Raising it again he spoke slowly, an octave lower. "No, I think neither messenger, nor devil. I think entity of white man sent to plague."

A slight sea breeze fluttered the torches within. After a moment, the second elder spoke. "I have thought much upon the arrival of white men, and I have hoped against hope that they were neither messengers nor devils, but like us—people of the sea and sky come to live in peace upon Oceania. But I cannot be lied to by my own heart and eyes. I have seen the white man come and go, creating destruction where he stays, leaving destruction when he departs. I, too, believe this man from the sky a plague."

"It cannot be otherwise," replied the third elder. "But what to do with him?"

"We can send a warning to the white men," said the second. "We can bloody him and impale him to a piling off the beach. We can pray to the shark god Ukupanipo to devour him and send a message to all the sharks of the sea to consume all white men."

"That is wise," said the eldest chief, "but things are new. Till this white came to us, they all arrived by ship. Had we thought earlier, we could have prayed and had the whales destroy the ships and consume the white men. But it is too late. The whites now come by sky."

"Can we not kill him outright? Stake him to the beach and let the seabirds consume him and drop his foul remains on other whites?"

141

Another contemplative silence amongst the three, this last proposal intriguing them. Finally, the eldest elder spoke calmly, his eyes distant. "This is how it shall be."

He spoke till the torches burned to the last, the flowers on the engine drooped, and the air became humid. Everyone in attendance was stunned at the wisdom, at the simplicity of what he said. Everyone except Jack Tanveer, who understood not a word.

The three men departed and Jack waited, still anchored to the cold stone floor by the huge Hawaiian behind him. The beautiful, petite china doll of the Pacific turned and, with wispy footsteps, approached him. A delicate smile crossed her lips, a sensual light in her eyes. When she opened her mouth, she spoke in English in a manner that would have made a cockney boson proud—the whiskey gravel of her words, the bass of her tone. "Aye, matey, har har har. I think ye be right and properly fucked."

*

The moon was waning gibbous, just enough to light his way. Sean had told him through gasping breaths, "Father, it's best we split paths. If the human hyenas and their hyena dogs follow, they'll smell the blood and follow me. You travel the main trail and make yer way to the judge's house."

"Sean, I can't leave you. You're seriously injured."

"Hurt or not, I can move like the wind. Tell the judge what happened. He'll know what to do. Now go!"

It seemed to Damien only seconds before he heard the noise, a low, throaty growl. *The hyenas*, he thought. He had given Sean the gun and now stood defenseless.

"Hail Mary, full of grace, our Lord is with thee…"

The growling became deeper, more threatening

"Blessed are thou among women…"

The creature came swift and deliberate…

"…and blessed is the fruit of thy womb, Jesus."

…and stood before him.

In the moment before one's death, clarity is achieved. All things are understood in the split second between life and annihilation. But Damien did not understand what was before him. Instead of the drooling, life-snapping dark hyena, a tall, white dog radiating serenity and empathy presented itself.

In near-collapse and shock, Damien realized that it was the same dog, the giant Borzoi that saved him from the wild boar his first day on the island. The dog nuzzled him in the chest, and then turned, loping down the path. The enormous hound paused and looked behind him. Damien felt the words…

Follow me.

Damien did so, trusting this voice as much as the one he heard first thing every morning. Minutes later, he and the beautiful dog reached Judge Lae's house, where the priest was greeted by a firmer, more commanding voice.

"Who come to my house?"

"It's Father Damien. I need help."

"Come along, then. I am just around the bend."

Damien looked to the dog to pet her in thanks, but she was gone.

The priest related all that had transpired in the valley to Judge Lae. The judge nodded, "Yes, I heard the three shots, then much later, two more. I thought you were dead for sure. You two not be the first never return from dat viper's nest."

"Yes, but now I'm concerned for Sean."

"Me, too, but not so much. You know he was a policeman Boston town?"

"I knew he was a miner in New Zealand, but a policeman? No."

"Before dat, he and family burned off farm in Ireland by British haole. He kill many Britishers, escape to America, den escape to Maori people's land."

"You mean New Zealand?"

The judge shrugged. "Yes. I think Sean be okay. He know to come here if trouble. We wait. You sit down, we drink rum, talk about God, wait.

Sean didn't come. The night passed into day. Damien became distraught, unable even to meet his charges. Deep into the second night, the judge, sensing Damien's pain, said, "Father, you wait inside. I go out for little while, just in front of house. Please no come out till I come in."

Damien chose a chair by an open window. It was a large easy chair of rattan construction. It had wide armrests and comfortable cushions depicting tropical scenes. He sank in gratefully, letting the offshore breeze easing through the window wash over him like a gentle thought.

He momentarily forgot the wounds he had to bandage and the people he had to bury. His breathing became regular and the aches in his body subsided. He noted the scent of flowers on the breeze, hibiscus Molokai, coconut oil in the judge's kitchen, and jasmine from somewhere else. He picked up a sound of scratching, mice most likely, and the flutter of thatch atop the roof. He heard something else, something slight—a whisper, or a whispering of whispers.

His mind tuned in and Damien recognized the judge speaking a few words in the Hawaiian language. It was not a secret conversation between two people, or a prayer or plea—more like a request. Damien closed his eyes and let the words flow over him, melodious and friendly and comforting. Over time, he felt the rising sun on the side of his face and fell off to sleep. After what could have been five minutes or five hours, he opened his eyes. Before him stood Judge Lae.

Damien was neither startled nor surprised. "Is Sean here?"

"No, but maybe best you go make up room in back. Sheet there, pillows there."

Damien did as requested. The sheets and pillowcase were starched clean. He made the bed in best seminary fashion—tops of blankets turned up four inches, sheets tucked in at forty-five degree angles, pillow dead center. Satisfied, he turned to leave, but as he did, he lost his breath. A woman stood in the room with him, the door closed behind.

"Your friend come soon," she said.

Her hair was stark white, tied in a tight bun with a lavender ribbon. She wore the classic Hawaiian lady's frock: white cotton to the floor, puffed shoulders, and ruffled blouse. What stunned the priest even more than her undetected presence was the color of her eyes— bottle green with black lava pupils. The white hair indicated advanced age, but her complexion indicated something else, something calm and smooth. She might have been seventeen or sixty.

A light knock came to the door followed by a slow opening. The door creaked on its hinges. Damien wondered why he hadn't heard the sound when the women entered. The judge appeared in the frame, giving a smile. Having no lips and little muscle beneath his nose and above his chin, his smile was tall and wide. Rather than being hideous, it was engaging, making those around feel a touch happier, a touch brighter.

"Come, Father, I explain everything."

They left the woman in the room. Judge Lae went to his sideboard, took out a tall glass, and filled it with cane rum. He drank it off in one swig. He filled it again, took it into the kitchen, dropped a chunk of coconut in it, and handed it to Damien. The priest took a sip and nodded for the judge to continue.

"Dat woman a Kahuna woman."

"Sean mentioned something of the Kahuna to me. They are priests, yes?"

"No, Father, dey not priests—dey like you."

Damien didn't understand and was slightly embarrassed. "But Your Honor, I am a priest."

"No, no, no priests. Dey persons like you—healers; people who speak to God. People with more *spiritual* gifts, deeper moral insight."

Damien without pride or insolence knew this to be true about himself, though he was a little taken aback to be compared to the Kahuna woman, a personage most whites referred to as "witchdoctor."

He recalled his seminary classmates being beaten by the Brothers for even acknowledging Protestants or Jews existed. "The faith you study is the one true faith!" It was drilled into him by rote and martial discipline, but even as a boy he wondered, *If there is but one God, what care he of different faiths' definitions of him? The one true God cares only of love.*

Damien had chosen the Catholic Church as his spiritual instructor because it simply was the faith at hand. He recognized in himself early on that spiritual truths replaced material facts. When he prayed, he was refreshed; when he meditated, he was enlightened; when he taught or comforted the sick, he was enraptured. Yes, he was a Catholic missionary, but ultimately he was a missionary of God.

"Dis woman," the judge went on, "she have power. When she pray, she push sickness from people most times, just like you. She pray to keep the demons from rising from the lava dust; she pray to Pele' to keep typhoons off this island. Maybe prayers not always work, but most times, yes. She known as Kahuna Pui'

146

okaoka—she can heal, and she can comfort, just like you."

Without thinking, and in words that would have had him excommunicated, Damien said, "Yes, I am like her. I will work with her for the good of the people on this island." He was surprised that he was unsurprised at these words, but before the semantics could be welcomed or debated in his heart, a thud came from the wooden porch. Damien and Judge Lae rushed out. There they found Sean facedown, naked and bleeding, trail ravaged, still clutching the Navy colt revolver.

It was bad. While on the porch, the Kahuna woman and Father Damien examined him closely. The hole on the left side of his face had torn, leaving a jagged slash from the side of his mouth to the ear. The wound on his shoulder was worse, the jutting collarbone cracked from the blow by Willy's Patu. It had turned black, the remains of his shirt stuffed into the wound to prevent bleeding now gaining tropic mold and causing the infection to multiply and migrate with extreme prejudice down to his pectoral. He was ashen white, dehydrated, and in shock.

Damien and the woman washed him from buckets of water Judge Lae brought from one of the falling rivulets off The Wall of Pali. Once cleansed, the three of them hoisted his bulk into the back bedroom Damien made up earlier.

With Sean lying inert atop the clean cotton sheets, Damien worked to cleanse the wounds. With a soft towel, he cleaned the wound on the man's face. Next, he used a toothbrush to scour the rot from the exposed bone and expertly lanced the skin to drain the infection. After the cleaning, the Kahuna woman re-set the bones, thankful the man was unconscious, and applied a poultice of crushed mangoes, cool water, and sea salt to the wounds. The judge placed cold compresses on his friend's forehead and trunk. Damien silently said a prayer, and being the last one out, quietly closed the door with every intention of routinely checking on his friend.

The small priest sat in the chair he had before, Judge Lae and the Kahuna woman in chairs opposite him. Without preamble, she said, "When his eyes open and when he speaks, give to him a measure of rum and kava. This make blood flow less furious. When his color regains, give him much water, and to eat, mangoes only. When he can sit—tea, water, and papaya. When he can stand, feed pig liver, then heart, then pig meat."

She smiled a friendly and knowing smile and walked out the screen door, Damien assumed to wash from Sean's administrations. Wherever she went, she didn't return.

The judge and Damien alternatively sat watch over their friend, carefully attending to her prescriptions. After several days, Sean came around. It was no disoriented twilight awakening. He boomed into consciousness like night into tropical day. "Top of the mornin' to you, Father. I see you left the valley alive and well."

The smaller man smiled, and aping his friend's Irish brogue, said, "Oh, aye, a damn sight finer than you, I might add."

Sean laughed. "A bit of a brush-up, aye, more than I'm used to, but less than that which could put me down. Father, there are some things which I must tell you, but I'm wonderin' if you'd hear me confession first."

"Of course, my son, go ahead."

"You'll forgive me if I don't kneel."

Damien grinned inwardly. "Of course, my son."

"Bless me, Father, for I have sinned. It has been six years since my last confession."

"Tell me your sins, my son."

148

"Father, you're going to have to find two more carpenters for the bathhouses…"

On the day Sean began to walk, his two friends prepared and fed him the pig's liver. The pain from the stitches around his mouth made it difficult to eat, but he managed, having not had a true meal in nearly a week. Unable to finish it, and having had a bit too much rum, he pushed it aside and went to sleep. His "nurses" retired to the porch, where the judge handed Damien a tall rum with a papaya slice in it. "Father, you been away many days now—your people, your duties. You return dat side of island; I bring back Sean when he okay. He out of danger now."

It had been a growing concern of the priest's. There were still so many to heal and pray for—so much to attend to—he was relieved his new friend had noticed. "Thank you, Your Honor. If it is square with you, I should like to spend the night and leave before sunrise."

"'Dat okay…"

*

The Colonel looked down at Willy, who had been laying for days in his own blood. *Shouldn't be long now,* he thought. The giant was brutally mauled following combat with the Irishman and the errant hyena. His left thigh was severed at the hamstring, now resembling a forty-pound bowl of pasta. The stab wound through his chin and tongue had just penetrated his upper palate, causing him to snort blood like a blowing whale. And his leprotic immune system would soon deplete itself, unable to fight a two-front war against the wounds and the bacillus. *Damned Irishman got away, what?* The Colonel looked upon a ghost stone and watched the reflection of his enemy's escape. He watched the man crashing through bush, torn on agave, slashed by hog, and set upon by the dark dogs. And yet, all but dead, he had limped away.

The Colonel sighed. All his minions had failed him. His one eye gazed again upon the stone as Sean collapsed on the law leper's porch, only to be attended to by the priest and that woman. Damned priest and his "mission". These Catholics had been a damned nuisance for over nineteen hundred years. He wondered if the two Russians had any thoughts on the matter. *Maybe I'll drop in for tea,* he thought. Then aloud, "Time to turn up the flame."

*

Major Jack Tanveer was propped up in a soft bed as a slight breeze blew through the window. It wasn't really a window—just a rectangle cut in the thatch wall next to him. Outside the rectangle, sitting as comfortably as Jack, was a huge Polynesian man. Legs and arms dark and powerful as oak, the man stared unswervingly at Jack's "window".

There was also a door cut in the thatched room, and outside that sat an equally massive brute staring at Jack. *No way through those two*, he thought. Maybe he could hurtle himself through the thatch wall to the left, but then what? Like any good pilot, he had memorized the charts of the Hawaiian Islands. In his mind's eye, he could see the long, low spreads of beaches on Maui's north and south shore, Lanai's flat coastal plain, and then Molokai. To the south sat high coastal cliffs running the full length—no way to get down those. Inland lay deep, dense jungle, then the impossible Wall of Pali leading down to the peninsula inhabited by the lepers, the isosceles jut of land sticking out into the Pacific. His only hope was to escape and survive the jungle, which that didn't seem likely.

Jack heard a clomping of boots somewhere inside the structure. The steps drew closer, and he heard pottery smashing, furniture being overturned, cursing. Cursing!? The curses were in English. *Goddamn,* he thought, *it's the Marines!* He jumped up to enter the fray, but the guard outside his door rushed in and pinned him to the bed. He was about to shout, "In here, boys!" when he heard another voice.

"When I tell ye buggers I wants a cask a rum, I wants a cask a rum. If one bain't here by six bells, they'll be throats a-cut and balls to be keelhauled." The voice stopped and the clomping continued in Jack's direction. He tensed a bit, and his captor gave him a don't-move look. Jack's heart beat faster. If it wasn't leathernecks, maybe it was another white man friendly with these people. Maybe he could get a message out to Pearl Harbor. Maybe the Marines would save him after all. At this point, he'd even settle for the goddamned Navy.

The first thing he noticed when the clomping entered his room was the blue color of a Marine Corps dress tunic. In less than a split second, his heart skipped a beat in joy. Then, reality, as it seemed to do to him lately, stepped in and offered its latest disappointing and bizarre twist. It was the beautiful Hawaiian china doll. She was wearing his tunic, as well as his polished leather Sam Brown belt, where she had scabbarded a rusted and cracked cutlass. She wore her hair tied tightly back in a ponytail and sported two large hooped earrings. There was no sarong or pants upon her— only a pair of full-length, calfskin sea boots that extended up to the tunic. She offered him a delicate smile, but spoke in the boson's voice. "This be the bad one for ya, lad."

Jack never really gave a damn about children, but now he was captivated by two little boys, both naked and engaged in a mock swordfight. A peck of little girls placed garlands in each other's hair, shrieking with delight. He would have liked to smile at this bucolic scene, but was unable. His chin was flush against the dirt, a result of a metal band placed at the back of his neck, each side with a stake driven through a hole and into the ground.

Similar arrangements were in place for his wrists and ankles. As the little girls delighted in their handiwork, one of the little boys delivered the "Killing blow!" with his stick. The beautiful Hawaiian china doll entered his field of vision from stage right. She was wearing only a sarong to the waist, Jack's dogtags twinkling between her breasts.

Mid-range, she slowed her liquid gait, then stopped to look at the pilot, giving him a non-committal glance before gliding out stage left. Jack drew neither assurance nor threat from her presence. What concerned him was the clanging of iron and the increasing heat from a fire nearby.

The elders agreed—their epic began in the sea, and so should this story. It was simple enough. The branding would commence on Jack's right, working up to the shoulder. The first burns would mimic the aquaform of Pacific coral—the barrier reefs, the fringing reefs of the atolls. The iron used for this was little more than pins, red hot to be sure, and piercing, but after the first sear, Jack reckoned it was something he could stand, though never recommend.

When the first scald of the bonito fish was imprinted on his bare flesh, Jack's muscles convulsed. When he was burn-stamped with a small school of tuna, then, higher a marlin, he bit through his upper lip, but still managed to defy them and demand, "Another!"

Rising to the surface, a white-tip shark—in life, six feet in length; here the size of a child's hand. Above the shark and to scale, the giant cirran octopus, tentacles

152

poised with an eye toward predation. The kanaka administering the brand had to push much harder and hold it longer into the burning flesh to ensure the detail of that mighty sea monster. Above this, and starting to see sunlight, the pelagics: herring, barracuda, the beautiful sargassum. Breaking the surface was a flying fish ascending, its leap to blue sky unnoticed by Jack Tanveer. He had passed out when the octopus descended upon the shark.

Darkness became his friend, though he did regain consciousness briefly during the branding of the land creatures of the Pacific. Seared into him were a wild boar and a Javanese tiger locked in ferocious battle as if representing Jack's dubious battle with his sanity.

There was a stay in the mapping as dirt and flies began to accumulate, entrenching and infecting the burns. A pause was necessary to clean the wounds and save the man's life.

The heavy sea of oblivion gave way to a gentle swell that rolled easily onto the beach that was the mind of Jack Tanveer.

A quiet tropical village began to morph and rise, its perimeter tinted in gray and aquamarine. Out beyond, native Polynesians worked a rice paddy beneath the shadow of a blue-green guardian mountain. Jack watched their industrious efforts with a calm, painless interest. Men and women of every age worked side by side beneath a subtly starched sky.

It was a different treble from that of the small waves lapping the shore before Jack knew what he was seeing—the oars from six different boats cutting into the sea in unison. Beyond the boats lay a clipper named *Brigand*. As the boats glided to shore, the men within replaced the oars with cutlasses and guns. With fervor, with ferocity, the landing party rushed the village, the paddy, clubbing or shooting the villagers. Men were killed and women carried off to the boats. One by one, they shoved off, back to the *Brigand.*

In the stern of one of the boats, Jack's mind saw a girl bruised and beaten. She was young and beautiful, with delicate breasts and almond eyes. A fragile doll...

The burns drawing the physical life out of him floated through Jack's mind in the painless bliss that is near death. No single thought would hold, but he was comfortable, care-less.

Like a leaf falling to earth, the falling gave way to spinning, faster and faster. He could again feel the conscious shackles of pain. His eyes fluttered, and he began to take stock. Every internal nerve blasted him. The once exquisite blanket that had been his skin had been deformed into a crude, demented map of Oceania. Beside his bed, a candle flickered, casting a tropical shadow play on the thatch wall. The light swirled and hardened, taking on edges, borders. Finally the pilot beheld a square of light on the wall, flickering as though controlled by a projector:

THE VOYAGE OF THE BRIGAND
Continues across the South Seas!

The scene, in sepia, shows a five-masted ship sailing gently on a rising tide.

THE CAPTAIN IS ANGRY!

The scene switches to the deck of the *Brigand.* There are no colors, though the sepia has faded to black and white. The beautiful Hawaiian china doll of the Pacific, still a teenager, bursts from the Captain's quarters. She is barefoot and bare-breasted, wearing only filthy seaman's trousers, which she holds up with one hand. The Captain, thick-browed, malevolent, blood streaming from his cheek, noiselessly roars:

"THE WENCH HATH BIT ME!"
"BOSON!"

The boson rushes in.

154

"YES, CAPTAIN?"

The onscreen images switch from Captain to Boson as they argue.

"SHE SHALL KISS THE GUNNER'S
DAUGHTER!"

"CAPTAIN, SHE IS BUT A GIRL!"

"SHE SHALL KISS THE GUNNER'S
DAUGHTER OR
YOU SHALL HANG!"

The beautiful Hawaiian china doll is lashed to a cannon on the vessel's starboard side. She cries as the boson approaches.

"I'M SORRY, LASS."

The boson swings the horrific cat o' nine tails, tearing and flaying its thirteen lashes. When at last it is over, the girl is unlashed from the cannon. She is doused with seawater and faints. The Captain issues a silent order:

"TAKE HER TO MY CABIN!"

Once inside, the ravages continue.

Jack was nauseas, but he had no water or bile left to vomit. He wanted to cry, but there were no tears—only pain in his eyes. He tried to utter, "What horror this?" but the words choke. He prays to float away, but the bright flickering lights draw him back to the thatch...

MEANWHILE, BACK IN THE GOOD OL' U.S.
of A...

Jack stands on a street corner, handsome and smiling in his Marine Corps, Class A uniform. Behind him reads a street sign: Atlantic and Clinton Avenue.

A WHOREHOUSE IN BROOKLYN!

Jack drinks bourbon and pays two dollars to fornicate.

A WHOREHOUSE IN PENSACOLA!

Jack drinks whiskey and pays a dollar fifty to fornicate.

155

IN SAN FRANCISCO!
HAVANA!
VERA CRUZ!
HONOLULU!

His ruttings evolve from "Boys will be boys" to exotic to decadent to disgusting, a farm beast without joy.

NO FUN AFTERALL!

Jack tries to look away, but cannot. He hangs his head in shame.

AND WHAT OF THE WOMEN?

In darkening shades of gray, Doris of Brooklyn pushes a needle into her arm and dies from heroin. Collette in Pensacola is beaten to death by her pimp. The scenes flash at faster and faster tempo toward the climax. Mona in San Francisco commits suicide; Susie dies on the streets of Vera Cruz. All the women Jack paid to perform nature's most beautiful act are dead. He realizes the savagery of a business he perpetuated and sustained. He wishes death upon his soul, but it is not to be.

The ancient Polynesian looked down upon the near-lifeless body of Jack Tanveer. The chief was frozen in grim contemplation, like one of the massive idols of the island to the south. Contrary to his appearance, he was satisfied, pleased even.

His people had just completed the final cartography and "storytelling" upon the white man's body. He studied the left side, a perfect map of the Pacific, starting with Eas-tah Island in the southeast, up through Hawaii and Midway, south to the Line Islands, then swooping west and south to the Marquesas all the way to Van Diemen's Land. All islands and atolls were burned into the pilot in perfect scale and shape. Also seared in (and the welts rising nicely, he thought) were current directions, wind directions, and coral reefs. Excellent! The maps would make a Maori navigator proud.

He looked at the man's right side. The burnings portrayed the Polynesian people's migration throughout Oceania—the great longboats, the storms, the island settlements, culture, and law. All the fish of the sea were branded in, as were the flora and fauna of the islands. The active volcanos were mapped on his biceps and forearms.

Not an inch of skin, save the soles of his feet, the palms of his hands, his face and his testicles, lay unmapped. The chief was glad he did not have this man fed to the sharks or impaled by a gannet. Now he would be seen by all haoles. Now they would be warned.

They would see the power and potential of his people, and they would be afraid. Of this he was sure. With the warning so issued, he knew it would be but a matter of time before the white man would vacate the Pacific and leave the Polynesian people to live in peace forever.

But there was a problem. The beautiful Hawaiian china doll of the Pacific whispered into the ear of the chief. He gave a stern look and barked commands. Four of the island men seized the pilot from the ground and carried him to the hut.

"What do you mean near death?" the old man bellowed. She whispered again in his ear. "No, no, he must live. He must give warning! You have ghost of haole doctor inside you. Bring forth; make the white man live!"

And in a frightening instant, her posture changed, her back straightened to ramrod, her movements formerly weightless and feminine became rigid and robotic, a field marshal in the body of a goddess.

"Ja, ja," she said. "I vill cure him." She put two fingers on Tanveer's neck. "His pulse is papery." She put her ear to his chest, "Breathing is shallow. Zis is no good." Jack's eyes fluttered open when her face rested on his chest, then closed, returning him to darkness.

Though he was completely sure he was dying, Jack remained unafraid. His soul was buoyant, his body unencumbered by pain and fatigue. He wondered if he could watch another movie. In thanks for his serenity, a silver screen appeared, not upon the thatch but simply floating in the mystic.

THE LITTLE CHINA DOLL OF THE PACIFIC
IS BROUGHT TO HOWLAND ISLAND
TO BE SOLD

The *Brigand* docks, the gangway lowers, and the teenage girl is led down by the Boson. There is a slim man on the dock. He is healthy, wearing a white lab coat. The Boson silently speaks.

"THE CAPTAIN SAYS TO SELL YOU THIS
ONE FOR FORTY DOLLARS."

The man in the white lab coat looks her up and down.

"HAS SHE DISEASE?"
"NO, BUT SHE CAN BE FERAL,
AND SHE CAN BITE!"

The man in the white lab coat lights a pipe and contemplates the decision.

"JA, I TAKE HER."

Many quick scenes follow:

The girl is left in a small, locked room, withdrawn and frightened. The Doctor leaves food on a table, which she eats with her fingers, wild-eyed. She calms slightly, and soon is allowed to eat with the Doctor, where she learns to use utensils. When he gives her clean white clothing, she marvels at the scent.

At a blackboard, the Doctor teaches her German, English, and Latin. She collects shells with the Doctor and sings a song about an alpine wildflower.

She is happy.

And then...

...the silver screen goes black for a moment before motion returns.

INTRUDERS COME TO HOWLAND ISLAND!

A longboat with a massive outrigger rides the surf to the beach. From within, warriors emerge heavily armed. A leader with a torch in one hand, war club in the other, silently declares:

WE WILL RESCUE OUR FAIR CHILD

FROM THE CLUTCHES OF THE WHITE MAN

The warriors creep across the screen. They approach the building and burst inside. The beautiful Hawaiian china doll of the Pacific and the Doctor are seated alongside each other on a piano bench. The Doctor jumps to his feet.

"VAS IS DIS?"

The chief of the warriors harangues the Doctor.

"WE HAVE COME TO TAKE OUR

POLYNESIAN DAUGHTER HOME!"

The girl stands with infinite dignity and refuses to leave.

"THIS IS MY HOME."

The chief shakes his club, and the words snarl across the screen.

"NO, YOU COME WITH US!"

The chief raises his club and brings it down violently upon the Doctor's skull.

The girl is led to the longboat. She stares vacantly toward the sea, her joy drowning in the outgoing tide.

Jack's eyes opened to find her standing above him. He summoned impossible strength to raise an arm. As he does, the light began to fade. She grabbed his hand, and for a splitting instant, they felt an explosion of mutual

159

empathy. From somewhere in his shattered soul, he reached out to her. *I'm sorry.*

I'm sorry, too…

As seen from sea, The Wall of Pali burst in colors of blue and green. The winter rains had just finished, leaving the rivers and streams of Topside Molokai swollen and angry. The excess water, desperate to roll, flowed over The Wall, joyous in its descent. Exploding columns of mist captured every light in the spectrum— red to blue to purple, and orange to silver to yellow. The rainbows dappled over The Wall from its Olympian heights to its very base.

The people of Kalaupapa saw something different in The Wall. No longer a massive geologic, omnipotent and foreboding, it appeared embracing, a guardian rather than a sentinel. It was springtime on Molokai, and for the people of the peninsula, the first spring of their lives.

CHAPTER ELEVEN

Damien had been questioning the postmaster, Mr. Mah, for days about Chinese burial customs. He was thrilled to learn that the ceremonies were elaborate and tradition-bound. But he was also confused—he saw none of that pomp and circumstance here on the island. "That's because Chinese people here think themselves already dead," Mah said

"For certain, Mr. Mah, things are hard on this island, but there can be dignity in death. If people can understand this, they will soon see there is dignity in life. Will you help me show them this, Mr. Mah?"

The postmaster smiled. "Yes, I help."

Sean told Father Damien, "No, I don't think palm trees will work. They grow fast and are beautiful, but they're not sufficient for wind breaks." Damien scoured the island and raised his hands in frustration.

"What then? There has to be a way to prevent the daily west wind from ripping across the peninsula and tearing up the small vegetable plots of these people. It is one of the reasons they've given up on farming; one of the reasons they starve."

Sean thought for a moment and said, "We could use Norfolk pines or even dwarf juniper. Both were effective in the Kona Valley when we first started planting coffee there."

"Are they hard to acquire?"

"No, Father. In fact, there is a nursery on Kauai that could provide them."

"Grand. We can use some of Margaret's money, may she rest in peace. Can you make an estimate of how much will be needed, and then place the order?"

"Aye, I can surely do that."

In a surprisingly short time, the junipers and pines were planted in successive rows to diminish the impact of the wind on the soil. Even as saplings, they proved effective. The wind, once the ravager of soil and sprouts, was now impotent. The soil began to hold, and crops began to grow.

To lead by example, Damien ordered seed—potato eyes, corn, and melon—and soon tended a garden of his own. And though he still lived beneath the Puhala tree, he tended the small garden as though it were a mighty plantation. The settlers on the island took notice. Lepers in all stages of the disease scraped and sauntered into the post office to ask Mr. Mah how they could order seed.

What started out as an optimistic meeting between Judge Lae, Damien, and Sean about the declining pneumonia deaths turned into a tense, frustrating discussion about an impossible situation. "Has it always been thus?" said Damien.

"Aye, as long as I've been here, and that's over five years."

"I been here long time, and it's happened every year," said the judge.

Damien exhaled. "But I've noticed SOME children."

"Sure enough, but you'll also take notice those children are a touch below toddlers. Their time has not yet come."

"If Job had to live on this island, he would have been a relaxed man."

Damien retired to the shade of the Puhala tree. Although tempted to toil He allowed himself the indulgence of a cigar before conducting business in an attempt to calm his anger. He sat down at his small writing desk and took pen to hand.

> *To the Honorable Archbishop Edrick Wannamaker,*
>
> *Your Excellency,*
>
> *I open hoping all is well within the diocese, and that life on the big island of Hawaii is agreeing with you.*
>
> *I write today to inform you of some minor successes and to relate a matter I believe will be of grave concern to the Church.*
>
> *As you may recall from my previous missives, I was able to instigate a sanitation infrastructure in the form of bathhouses for the inmate/settlers. As Your Excellency may know, most of the settler/inmates do not die of leprosy per se, but from its collateral ravages: blood poising, infection, shock, and pneumonia. Early in my mission, I tracked the causes and found pneumonia to be the primary antagonist.*
>
> *If I could eliminate at least this one horror, light could again be brought to this dark place. I am pleased to say that through prayer and the divine will of our Savior, I*

have been successful. The pneumonia rate has dropped by an astounding forty percent!

Bathing in our facilities allows settlers/patients to increase longevity, allowing them to bathe in the light of Christ's love for a longer period of time. Money for this project was set in a trust from the deceased Mrs. Hansen. Blessed are the ways of the Lord!

I send you another message of joy in that we have been able to wound one of the other great monsters of this island: starvation. One of the internees here, a son of the Church from the diocese of Moville, County Donegal, Ireland, owns a plantation on Kauai. He and I have taught these poor banished people how to retrieve kelp from the sea to fertilize this less than perfect soil. We have instructed them to crush rocks upon the land such that when the sea breezes blow across, nutrients are released to the soil. Of late, we are witnessing the initial raising of corn, taro, and soy. A miracle, it is as though the Savior himself has walked amongst us!

Your Excellency, I must now address an issue that is less than satisfactory. As you are aware, the Honolulu Board of Health oversees the entirety of island administration, from clothing and food stipends to the delivery of mail and medicine. While the goals of the Church and the Board remain the same—the establishment of humane living conditions—the execution and methodology has not always been in concert.

164

Many times the Church and I (as its humble servant) have been rebuked and told these areas are "Not within your purview." I submit to his Excellency a situation that historically has been within the "purview" of the Church—indeed within the purview of all civilized people—that being the orphaning of children.

The horrors and degradation on this island are unique. Even Father Xavier, who wrote about the immoral depravity in his mission along the shores of Lake Huron, and Father Moynihan, who brought to light the unspeakable cruelty of the civil administration in Nagasaki, made note that, even within these terrible environs, systems were in place to care for children. Here, it is not the case. What is most shocking is that this is no fault of the indigenous people—it is the fault of the administrators.

To wit:

Children are conceived and born here as they are in any other community, the difference being every other community is not the leper colony on Molokai. When it is ascertained that a number of children have reached the age of two, the Honolulu Board of Health dispatches the Honolulu Sherriff and his deputies to this island. With the excuse of good intent, that being "Not wishing the children to contract the horrible affliction," the children are removed from their mothers and fathers, at times I'm told most forcibly, and carted away upon the inter-island steamer. During these "goodwill" abductions, families are held at

bay, often violently, by deputies. The
children, I am told, receive examinations at
the clinic in Honolulu, and if cleared, are
sent to work on the plantations or as
domestic staff amongst the wealthy families
of the islands. Contact with their own
mothers and fathers is forbidden. Any
children diagnosed as positive for leprosy
are re-banished to the island.

   Your Excellency, this situation is not in
consonance with humanity or the goals of
the Church. It does not bring people into the
light of God. I beseech thee, with all my
heart, to intervene with The Board to
discontinue this practice. If so persuaded, I
have plans (enclosed) to set up a school for
boys and girls here on the island, such that
if they are uninflected, they may remain
(with precautions) segregated from the
disease but unsegregated and un-rent from
their families.

   In closing, I wish you the continuous
light of Christ's love,
      Your obedient servant,
      Fr. Damien deVuester
      Island of Molokai
      Hawaii, U.S. Trust Territory
                  *

   On the far side of the Peninsula where the Colonel
reigned supreme, the bodies of the dead and soon to be
dead were ordinarily reserved for Sunday sport. On that
day of rest, the Colonel would order all the corpses and
soon to be corpses brought to the jetty. As though
signaling the start of a festive race, the Colonel would
wave a silk kerchief and the formerly alive and half-dead
were dumped into the sea, wherein the sharks would

engage. There would be fanfare and great merriment as the dark lepers watched their former comrades get devoured in an orgy of sea foam and blood froth. But for the past two weeks, these Sunday outings were suspended. The Colonel ordered all the newly and half-dead seated in a circle at the lowest level at the fire pit, then piled atop each other as the bodies collected, several a day.

The Colonel had planned a tête-a-tête with the two Russians, and ever the thoughtful host, wished that they should enjoy themselves.

After a disappointing sunset on a Saturday night, the Colonel ordered Willy to touch the torch to the ignition corpse to set the bonfire a-roar. Willy had surprisingly survived the battle with Sean, though he lost the arm with the hook to the disease. After the lighting, he tossed the torch with his remaining arm into the inferno and thumped into the darkness, hatred and anger swirling about him like a foul cloak in the wind.

The Russians were impressed. The one with the hircine beard pointed with glee to the popping entrails and crackling bones of those lowest in the fire. The one with the spectacles now tinted red in fiery reflection nodded favorably, most impressed with the wide-eyed gazes of the burning departed. Braking the reverie, the Colonel drawled, "So what do you think?"

"Da Colonel is most good."

"Da, da," said the other. "Impressive fire architecture."

"Sorry, old chums, I was referring to our problem with the diminutive priest and our possible solution thereof."

Without a pause, the beard said, "Da, I see his work is taking hold. Dis is nothing new. He will spray the great opiate of blue skies to these savages, and they will believe it." He reached for one of the sticks stacked against a rock. The Colonel thoughtfully had some rats skewered for roasting. The Russian began to toast it over a roaring femur.

The other Russian removed his glasses, his eyes retaining the tint of red. "Colonel, as you know, our troubles have always been with the lesser humans, the believers. In contrast, the 'greats', the leaders, have always belonged to us. A simple transaction involving the trade of souls for worldly goods and power has allowed us to control the believers through control of their 'leaders'."

"Da, it has perpetually astonished me that it has always been so easy."

"Yes, Levantiny, our Master works in mysterious ways." He finished off the rat, now quite well done, with crunches and slurps. "Not to fear, we will soon show the little priest the error of blind faith."

*

What was once an empty beach now had a skeleton boardwalk with a ditch beneath. Upon the boardwalk stood outhouses and showers. Later, they were whitewashed, and louvered sky-lights (old window panes really) installed in the roofs. At the outset, the "complex" lay dormant, unused, seemingly abandoned before even occupied.

The first leper to use the outhouse was a former US Navy sailor who had contracted the disease in Honolulu. In truth, he missed the forced sanitation of the service and later told one of his friends, "I was tired of the filth on this rock, so I said what the hell." His right arm was taken by the bacillus, as was his left hand, so in the perpetual slight breeze of the island, he wavered up the steps to the boardwalk.

There is little romance surrounding human ablutions; waste discharge and hygiene of a gravity-fed shower are seldom things advertised in travel brochures.

But to the old sailor, they may have well been. He had forgotten what it was like to be lice-free and un-encrusted. He returned every day, then every day at six a.m., in a routine similar to his time as an engineer's apprentice aboard the cruiser *Indianapolis*.

In the shower, he would whistle; in the latrine, he sang *Anchors Away*. Curiosity grew. Leper settlers came down to the bathhouses to see what he was up to. He told a few of his friends that being able to use a box toilet and overhead shower was like "being reborn."

The less skeptical indulged and they, too, were "reborn." A few more of the bachelor lepers arrived, showered, etc., and soon made it their daily routine. Word spread until people in all states of decline arrived, and the decline began to stall.

Damien stood on the edge of the beach watching the patients use his humble creation. A daily line formed to get up the steps. Some of the settlers had informally volunteered to help the less ambulatory navigate the stairs and plumbing. He noticed other groups sitting about on the sand, ladies knitting and gossiping, men playing cards or cribbage. The detachment and self-loathing incurred by the disease was reversing. Instead of perishing independently in filthy warrens and hovels, the colonists were coming together, slow to be sure, to fight the ravage. Rather than waiting to die, they were learning to live.

Lost in contented thought, Damien was less startled than usual when his friend came up behind him. "Top of the morning to you, Father."

"Ah, yes, and good day to you, Sean."

"Care to make a good day better?" He held out a Quintero cigar. "Another from Hispaniola."

"You know you'll never have to ask me twice." After the ritual of the light, the little priest said to his friend, "And how are you feeling these days?"

169

"Father, the American cowboys have a saying: Rode hard and put out wet."

The priest thought for a moment. "Ah, an allusion to the life of a horse on the trail!"

His friend beamed. "Correct and correct again." A short silence between the two followed, one inhaling, the other exhaling, a cigar. "There were three passings last night."

"Only three?" Even through the sadness of hearing of three deaths, he was stunned and (almost) pleased by the low number. In his first months on the island, the daily toll was, at least, six and as many as twenty. He built coffins for every one of the departed souls till the wood ran out. In desperation, he sewed shrouds, then doused them with kerosene to keep the pigs and dogs from rooting out the newly entombed. "Who were they?"

"Yvonne Dupruis."

"From New Orleans?

"Aye."

"Who else?"

"The mother of Seamus Quinn, from Brooklyn. I understand the boy is taking it quite hard."

Damien nodded. "And…"

"The elder Loy from the Loy Ho Kok family."

"Well then, three different burials, three coffins to build. I best get to it."

"Father, if I may, I'd like to help in the building. Give me a chance to stretch my sore bones. And me and Mrs. Quinn sometimes spoke of home."

The older of the two smiled and put his hand on his friend's shoulder. "Come."

Just after sunrise the next day, the procession for the elder Loy commenced. Mr. Ho Kok Loy had been a prosperous dry cleaner on Oahu before being banished for leprosy. He was a pillar in the Chinese community.

As such, there was a large funeral with many friends and professional mourners wailing unto the heavens. And though Father Damien was not of the community or the faith, he was welcome, as much a part of the burial landscape as the sea and sky as were part of the landscape of Molokai.

At the gravesite, Father Damien said a few words from the *Tao Te Ching* (which were translated by a mourner), deeply touching those in attendance.

Toward midmorning, the wind stilled and the sky clouded over. The waves crashing to shore was the only sound. It reminded Sean of the lonely autumn days in Killybegs when he was a boy.

Fitting, he thought, as he walked arm in arm with Mrs. Quinn's son amongst the handful of the present version of the Irish diaspora—tattered and deformed, banished from one merciless island to a new merciless island. Before the poor woman, now gone home, was lowered into the ground, Damien spoke from *Revelations*, and having heard of the strong Celtic history of the family, *The Book of Kells*. The family retreated from the site in mourning, but comforted.

There was only one other person of French ancestry on the island besides Mr. and Mrs. Dupruis—an Acadian from Gaspe in Quebec. In uncomfortable coincidence with Mr. Dupruis, he, too, lost his wife and his left leg to the disease. When the two men walked behind the coffin, they walked in military cadence, their pegs swinging out to the side, then back in perfect cadence.

As the sun set and the services closed, Damien shook hands with the two and said something quietly to them in French.

It had been less than half an hour since the mourners left the beach shack. Seamus Quinn had been stirred from his sadness by a sound he couldn't quite figure coming over the hill from the Dupruis lean-to. It confused him. It was either the sound of a distressed farm animal or a musical instrument. After a couple of blasts, he realized, *Of course, ye eyjeet.* It was a trumpet. He recalled that, before losing his lips to leprosy, Mr. Dupris had been an avid player piping out the soulful melodies of his home state. The horn had been silent for a long time.

Still stinging, even more so at hearing the attempted laments, Seamus took his bow and case for a wee stroll over the hill. A few dozen yards from the Dupruis' place, Seamus uncased his fiddle and drew the bow across. The strings caressed the night with a dirge from his own home. The lament of *Oh, Danny boy, the pipes, the pipes are calling ye* could draw tears from a stone, but it was also one of hope, bidding farewell and beckoning onward, the chords touching the souls of the bereaved and the departed. *From glen to glen and all the fields again...*

Mr. Dupruis stood stone still, first with grief, then with love, as the melody walked his wife to a happy goodbye into the mists. When he was able to move and collect his thoughts, he approached the boy and shook his hand. After a muted conversation, he pointed to another dwelling just down the road. Seamus nodded.

A few minutes stroll on the stone-and-shell path brought the two to the home of the Ho Kok family. Seamus brought the fiddle to his chin, but withdrew the bow at the wave of a hand by Mr. Dupruis. With his other hand he brought the horn to his face. *Merde,* he thought with determination, *this will happen.*

There is no more powerful and evocative funeral song than the American military ballad *Taps*, its chords and themes evolving from sadness and agony from the time of Napoleon. In the silence of the Molokai night outside the home of the grieving Ho Kok family, Mr.

172

Dupruis, through his own sadness, commenced rendering into the clarion the opening notes:

Day is done, gone the sun...

The family within stilled, then emerged through the symbolic moon gate of the door of their home. They stood mesmerized.

....From the lakes, from the hills, from the sky...

The song itself, short yet seemingly infinite.

...All is well, safely rest,
God has begun,
God has begun...

And from the streams, the hills, and the sky, the dirge whispered down upon the peninsula.

Damien, just finishing his cook fire, cocked an ear and listened. Others came out of their huts and hovels, lean-tos and caves to hear the melancholy promise of the ballad. Damien took note of this, as well. He could see the leper villagers standing, some swaying, mesmerized. He inhaled deeply, surprised—the settlers here never came out at night. They held the darkness as Ka Lua Kupapa'—corpse, pit, tomb.

After *Taps* faded into the night, people remained out of doors. There was a calm on the promontory. Conversations rose, a hum of confidence gained. *A miracle*, thought Damien. *Death has given birth to humanity. God has begun.*

When the Kahuna' Ana' ana woman awoke, she knew she had two tasks to accomplish. It was told to her in her dreams. She did not know the details of either task—she never did—but she would undertake them anyway.

She was one of the most powerful Kahuna women in the islands. Her aunt was a Kahuna Ho' opi' opi' o, one whose power lay in counteracting sorcery by sending back the malevolent and life-taking energy to he who sent it.

Her mother, a Kahuna Kilokilo, read the clouds and birds and translated messages sent to the human world from the sea and sky. The Kahuna woman did not recall a moment in her life when her aunt and her mother were alive. They tutored her in the arts as she dreamt, her dream world as real and viable as her waking world. Her own spiritual gift, that of the Ana'ana enabling her to pray an enemy to death, was innate, untaught.

She stepped down off the porch and gazed into the sun, closing her eyes. Childlike, she enjoyed the light play as the golden orb dappled behind her lids—mauve pink and gold when facing the sun; blue and turquoise when her head turned to the sea. She opened her eyes and gazed up at The Wall. High above the peak, a small flock of frigate birds played in the wind. Though they were almost a mile high, she could see them as clearly as though they were perched on her forearm. One of them, a small female, broke off the play and sailed toward the crater Kauhako, located near the center of the peninsula. *Ah*, she thought, now knowing the first of the two deeds to be done. She set off for the post office at Kalaupapa, her gait a mix of sensuous teenager and wise dowager. The island would be a better place today. Her mom and auntie would be proud.

It was Steamer Day! The monthly steamer from Oahu was due just past noon, and the whole island was abuzz. This was the day the inhabitants received mail from kin on the other islands. Mr. Mah would receive stamps and parcels to distribute, and with any luck, Damien would receive blankets and beef allotments for his charges, though the beef did not usually make it past the pilferage of the Honolulu docks.

It had become an informal practice for Damien, Sean, Judge Lae, and a few of the more ambulatory elders to meet at the post office well in advance of the steamer's arrival.

Out behind the office, Mr. Mah had built a small patio of oyster shells surrounded by a small floral garden of lavender and hibiscus Molokai. The men sat drinking tea, the conversation light and buoyant, happy in anticipation.

The judge and Damien engaged in a friendly cribbage game, while Sean and the elders interjected with strategy, advice, and good-natured ribbing. Mr. Mah brought to the table more tea and fresh mangoes. As he set them on the table, a giant pillow of a cumulus cloud wallowed overhead, momentarily blocking the sun. When it passed, the sunlight resumed. As Sean reached for a mango, he saw the Kahuna woman standing behind the judge. Startled, he said, "Christ, woman! Sorry, Father. When she shows up like that, I jump out of my skin. I'm not taking the Lord's name if vain, I'm just looking for comfort."

She gave but the barest of smiles, then whispered to the judge. He looked up at her. "And what will be there?" A silent reply. "Hmm," he mumbled. "Gentlemen, it seems we're to take a short hike."

"Where?"

"To the Kauhako crater."

"What about the steamer?"

"Not even on the horizon. It will be hours yet."

Damien asked, "Your Honor, what will be there when we arrive?"

His lipless face beamed his famous smile. "I don't know. This woman, she don't know. Only know important we go."

The cone of the Kauhako volcano was a hushed place. Not because of silence, but because of the roar. The wind rolled up the coast and to its peak. The gusts tore through vegetation and crags and swirled down the cone to the tiny lake, said to be bottomless, below. Because of the battering wind, one could not hear another speak. One could barely hear oneself think. Denuded of speech, one was forced to observe. It was a lonely and terrible place more ancient than any other on this ancient island.

The volcanic rock, gray and black, grasped at the wind. The vegetation was scarce, a disallowed life even in this tropic landscape. Damien and Sean sensed an ominous presence, something frightening they couldn't put their fingers on.

Judge Lae and the Kahuna woman knew the basis of the fear. The volcano and the bottomless lake were the lair of the Hukai-Po, the Night Marchers, long-dead Hawaiian warriors who roamed its environs. The woman and the judge had not revealed this to the outsiders, not wishing to cause their companions any further discomfort.

All four were gazing out to sea when the woman turned. She squinted her eyes and placed a hand on the judge's shoulder. He also turned, then stared, his smile incongruous to this barren landscape. Sean and Damien turned next and joined in the reverence. What stood before them was more corporeal than apparition, more astonishment than reality.

The mule didn't move. It didn't nick its ears or swat its tail. It stood as gray and motionless as the volcanic rock, its burden likewise inert. Strapped across the mule's boney back was a person, or the remains of a person. Its feet hung lower over the burro's right side, balancing the hands over the left. The person was naked save for a tattered pair of khaki pants and a small chain that hung from its neck. The Kahuna moved the moment she noticed a slight rising and setting atop the mule.

Respiration.

As his chest rose and fell, so did she notice the depicted rising and falling of a "Tide" burnt into his chest. She noticed the air, sea, and land creatures of Oceania singed upon his body, including the great migrations of Polynesia. In an instant, she understood but was silent. The eyes on the body atop the mule fluttered for the briefest moment, then were once again still.

The "corpse" was alive.

She hurried to its side, followed by the other three. Sean lifted the body from the mule and lay it down in the volcanic ash. He screamed over the roaring wind, "It's a white man! He's alive!" He bent on one knee and looked at the chain about the man's throat. "He's an American officer!"

Damien then bent over the man and put his ear to lips. The man's breathing was shallow. Damien spoke to the Kahuna woman, and she nodded. The little priest motioned for the man to be set back upon the mule, then yelled into the wind, "We have to get him down to the settlement!"

The Kahuna woman took the lead. She picked the trail that was not the smoothest, but the quickest. It was the trail of the Night Marchers.

The mule did not flag as it carried its burden down the valley. The party was now entering the path along the cemetery on the outer edges of the small village known as "The leper colony's leper colony". Sean noticed that more ornamental trees had been planted, and colorful wildflowers had replaced the scraggy native scrub atop the graves. There were no pigs or jackals rooting—the only creatures were seagulls and white terns whirling in the sky. The mule snorted twice, then

177

stopped. The Kahuna woman turned and silently beckoned Damien forward. He trotted to the mule and the pilot. "He's trembling, and his throat is closing. He needs water now!"

Sean, remembering his visit a month ago, ran to the nearest inhabited dwelling. He knocked, then knocked again. The wind blew dry and dust devils rose, spinning on the dirt road. The door, whitewashed and worn, scraped open. For a moment, Sean was speechless. Before him lay the worst manifestation of leprosy he had yet witnessed. Half the creature's face was without skin. The cheek bone, jaw, and orbital bone surrounding the eye were bleached white, a skeleton impossibly alive. There was no skin on the hands—only sinew and bone, and maggots crawled along the crevices. Hardened by the mines, war, and famine, Sean still stood terrified. He managed to creak out, "We need water."

"Why give you water? For who?" Sean a little surprised and angered by the terse response, nodded his head toward the inert man on the mule. "He's dying."

"Yeah, so? Everybody here dying."

Sean bristled. "Listen, laddie, we just need a few cups of water."

"Why give you anything? You haoles give us this." He raised his skeletal hands and pointed to his skeletal face.

Though admittedly frightened, Sean thought he'd be damned if he'd be denied water for a dying man. He roared, "I have this curse, too! My body may rot like yours, but my soul never will!" His fear and anger fueling him, he thought he might just kill this bastard and take the water.

The Kahuna woman suddenly stood between the two. The skeletal leper did not know who she was, but instantly knew what she was. She motioned for Sean to step back. Though no words were spoken, the leper in the doorway nodded his head and disappeared inside. After a moment, he stepped out again. From behind the building, two other forms emerged entirely cloaked— faces, limbs, skin unseen. They set up two carpenter's sawhorses six feet apart. Next they laid a plank atop and set up a crude awning above it. Finishing, they withdrew inside. The skeletal creature then hissed at the Kahuna woman, "Lay him there, then depart." The three men did as told and stepped back.

Damien pressed the woman, "They looked terribly afflicted. Will the man not catch his disease?"

She turned to the judge and smiled. He answered for her. 'No, Father, he won't. He will never get it."

And so the pilot remained.

By the time Damien, Judge Lae, Sean, and the Kahuna woman returned, most of the hubbub of Steamer Day had died down. There were still some hangers-on at the post office, and some lepers lazed at the landing trying to sell shell necklaces to the sailors who floated cautiously in the longboat. Sean collected a few parcels and headed quickly home, hoping to compose a letter and get it to the crude mail launch before the steamer set sail.

Damien entered the cool of the post office to await his turn on the receiving line. He noticed Mr. Mah was tired from the day's labors, but also happy. He smiled when he glimpsed the small priest. "Hallo, Father, how you?"

And though the thought of
Tanveer, John, J
691318
Blood Type: O
Religion: M

was foremost in his mind, Damien did not wish to appear rude. "It's been a delightful day, Mr. Mah, and I see a busy one for you."

"Yes, yes, busy same all time, nevermind. You see new postcards?" Damien hadn't noticed, but was happy to see Mr. Mah had indeed hung more cards from Margaret's collection. "Look," said Mr. Mah, "from different parts world." Some were hand-painted, some were black-and-white photographs, and some were photos with touches of color. Damien saw the waterfront of Alexandria, minarets in Constantinople, tall palms in Mandalay, and rice steps in Pondicherry.

"Lovely," he said. "Just lovely."

"Many more to come. Many boxes. You see cards now and for rest of life."

"I'm looking forward to it, Mr. Mah." His mind now on happier thoughts, he asked, "Did I receive much mail today?"

"Okay, yes. Parcels plus envelopes." The postmaster reached behind him to a large cubbyhole marked Puhala tree, Kalaupapa, Molokai and removed Damien's receivables. "Here you go."

Within the bunch, Damien spied a letter from the archbishop. Giving way to the anticipation of an important reply, he asked Mr. Mah if he could read one or two of his letters on the patio. "Okay, sure, Father. Later I bring tea."

Damien's hand shook slightly while opening the letter from the archbishop. He was thrilled a reply came so soon and was looking forward with boyish enthusiasm to his superior's approval of the proposed projects.

Dear Father Damien...

The priest read through the usual salutations, still excited by what was to come. After the first paragraph, he was mortified. After the second, stunned. He paused and re-read to make sure he was not getting the wrong impression. After the third paragraph, resentment mounted; the fourth brought shame. "No," he said in a whisper. His hands visibly shook as he dropped the letter. With the self-loathing and shame brought on by betrayal, he staggered toward shore, tears in his eyes.

The Kahuna woman and the judge were just bringing tea to the patio when they saw Damien rise and lurch away. Judge Lae had seen self-destruction in the little man's eyes, while the woman sensed a soul torn asunder.

The judge turned to follow his friend, but the Kahuna woman put a hand on his shoulder and shook her head. Both then saw the object of the man's distress. Falling, than rising slightly in the breeze, the letter fluttered as though threatening to take off. The judge, ordinarily a man of discretion, knew he must read the contents. It might help him save Damien's life.

Dear Father Damien,

I am your prelate, your confessor, and the spiritual authority of the Church in all matters extant in the Territory of Hawaii. I have had the pleasure of interacting with hundreds of missionary priests and have engaged in the spiritual endeavors of hundreds of communities in the South Pacific. Having spoken thus, I must relate to you my extreme anger and disappointment concerning your administration of the Leper Colony Molokai.

You are far enough along in your tenure as one of God's servants to understand the role of Priest. That you have acted in any capacity other than Priest beggars the imagination of this office, unless

(As the abundant rumors in Honolulu have informed) you have succumbed to alcoholism or one of the numerous native venereal diseases prolific in these islands. For your soul I pray.

If it is that you are sound of mind, let me relate: 1.) You are NOT a physician, 2.) You are NOT an agronomist teaching the heathen to farm, 3.) You are NOT a member of the Bleeding Heart Society tasked to administer to the welfare of wayward children, and finally, 4.) You are NOT a financial officer of the Church. This last is the most disturbing to this office. By your own admission, you have received funding for your "projects" from the estate of one Margaret Hansen. As you are aware, Mrs. Hansen was not a member of The True Faith. As you are aware, all fiduciary arrangements must be authorized by and channeled through the archdiocese. You have facilitated neither. All though it shames me to ponder, I must ask if these lapses had cause stemming from a relationship with yourself and the departed woman. In conclusion...

The judge finished reading, himself shaking with rage. He looked to the Kahuna woman. Strangely, she was smiling. She now knew what her second task of the day was to be.

*

The Colonel sat alongside the two Russians on chairs made from erratic driftwood, drinking something that could have been mistaken for merlot. The Colonel put down his crystal goblet, adjusted his eyepatch (today's version made from hyena gut), and said, "Shan't be long now."

The Russians sat next to their host, between them a crude chessboard atop a rough beach stone. Absorbed in their match, they paid little attention to whatever was coming soon. "Levantiny, it is your move."

His opponent licked some blood off his finger tips and said, "Bishop takes pawn." He smiled at his friend, hoping his friend understood the elegance of both the move and the entendre. The man across the board grinned in return. The two were locked in mental combat. The Russian with the hircine beard had the one with the blood eyes in check.

*

There was lightness in the heart of the Kahuna woman. She swayed slightly as she walked, occasionally brushing away a wisp of hair as the wind played through it. Her footsteps did not kick up any of the fine volcanic ash as she approached the Colonel.

To the wind the woman whispered, "Wa hei moe." Neither of the Russian fiends heard, but "blood eyes" felt his body go limp. His face crashed down upon the board, striking the sharp crown of the white bishop, the impact driving it through the left lens of his glasses and into his eye, stabbing his brain into darkness. The beard sat bolt upright, watching the blood ooze from his companion's eye. He could not give aid, nor cry out. His vocal chords snapped like tension wire. He felt warmth then heat, then fire in his chest. He couldn't conceive that he could die from a burning heart. As he crashed upon the chessboard, black smoke billowed wildly from his mouth.

The Colonel immediately felt the deaths of the two. "NO!" he roared. Not even bothering to put an eyepatch over his hollow orb, he sailed down the black lava beach, the darkest angel avenging. He came to the two dead disciples and froze.

The Kahuna woman stood there, more still than time. Before he could lash out, a gust of wind displaced a lock of her hair. She playfully tucked it behind an ear and grinned, turning to walk calmly across the black lava dust. As she drew away, she would, at intervals, glance back and give the Colonel a come-hither smile. He dared not approach.

*

In a tidy office at the naval station in Pearl Harbor, the admiral dropped a letter on his desk after quickly reading it. "Goddamn! Tanveer's alive. Ensign Roberts!"

A buffed and very junior naval officer raced into the room, unsure of what he might have done wrong this time. "Yes, sir?"

"Get me a line to Cincinnati. If no operators are available, get me a horse or car to the telegraph office."

"Yes, sir."

"And Roberts..."

"Yes, sir?"

"Get me Colonel Wessinger at Marine Corps."

"Yes, sir."

"And Roberts..."

"Yes, sir?"

"Keep your mouth shut about this."

"Yes, sir!"

*

In a large and expensive Honolulu office, a powerful man considered the information he had just been fed. "Kristan, this report says there may be thirty children available."

"Yes, give or take."

"That seems a bit high from times past."

"Well, there's a reason."

184

"And that is?"

"The life expectancy has risen on Molokai. Adults are living longer, giving them a chance to breed."

"Not exactly how we had things worked out. Why are they living longer?"

"The priest has made some changes in uh… health and… sanitation."

"How much has this cost us?"

"Almost nothing, and with an unexpected yield in children."

"Ah, yes" he said smugly, "Progress. At least the growers association will be happy. Pass me the order to the sheriff's department." With a rough scratch, he signed the document. "Now get this going—harvest season approacheth."

*

Damien stumbled through the wilderness. He supposed it was from bleeding feet. He had lost his sandals somewhere in the scrub brush, the bottom of his trousers frayed, torn, and soiled. He reeled breathlessly across the scrub brush. His mind, his morality, his ethos torn asunder by a lesser man and lesser force than himself. How could his holiness have berated him so? How could he have accused him of immorality, erosive pride, and the breaking of vows?

Damien had offered up his health and his innocence only to be repaid with words meant to crush his spirit. He knelt down to pray, his only recourse, but no prayer came. There was no first word or thought to catch. He raised his arms to the sky, but there were no heartfelt questions for God, only profound anger at the Church.

Damien attempted to rise, lowering his hands to push himself up, but then thought the better of it. The sun was at its zenith, the anvil of its heat beating his skull. The pain was liberating, as if a deserved punishment for his failure to coerce others to his mission. He laid down on the scorched earth as hot as hell's furnace. It might, at last, bring him peace.

*

The Colonel was not so upset as might be imagined. Yes, he was angry at his defeat by the Kahuna woman, but now that he was aware of her existence, he could plan ahead before she could strike again. Also, the diminutive priest was neutralized, and by one of his own at the Russians' behest.

The Colonel laughed out loud. Truth be told, he wasn't too particularly miffed at the loss of those two Russians. In fact, he had their bodies nailed to a post at the bachelors' club for the hyenas and those beautiful a' ama crabs to feast upon, a bit of cocktail enjoyment at sundown. There were always minions to replace them. He still had Terry and Willy, fierce buggers, furious to their depths for what the white man did to them. "Ah, yes," he thought. "Irony more delicious than blood."

He had received several correspondences on Steamer Day. Primero of the bunch was the letter concerning the Sanford Plantation. It had been recognized, not so long ago, by his lord and master, that American businessmen and plantation owners were the causes of democracy and the advancement of living conditions.

To them, this was good business. Democracy meant stability, while a healthy humanity meant happy workers. However, to the entity the Colonel represented, this advancement meant the advancement of churches, which brought on the advancement of religion, which in turn could bring on enlightenment. This simply would not do. The Colonel and his like had worked too hard and too long to let some newcomers change the balance. One little upstart priest was proof of that. His work had begun to take hold even among the most hopeless on the islands. Fortunately, he would no longer be a problem.

Although time wasn't too all together pressing, the Colonel felt it best to act soon.

"Comfort Women" had been introduced to the Sanford Plantation to provide recreation and release to its thousand workers. The "plantation" wasn't just one massive farm, but a co-op of hundreds of large farms growing pineapples for export to the continental United States. Pineapples were the lifeblood of the Hawaiian Islands, supporting shipping, finance, construction, and just about everything else. If the pineapple fell, so would Hawaii.

Though there were many parts and parties to it, the plan was quite simple: when the Colonel gave the word, the other apprentices of the Master would dispatch letters to mainland America. These posts would outline, in great detail, the 100% syphilitic rate among the Chinese workforce on the Sanford Plantation.

For the uninitiated, the letters would describe syphilis, its contagion, and how it ran rampant amongst every picker, sorter, inspector, and cook on the property. It would go on to describe how every can of fruit and every pineapple currently being served on tables across America was contaminated by the carrier of a venereal disease.

The letters, with photos enclosed, would reach stateside newspapers, congressman, church groups, and investors. The all holy pineapple, mainstay of Pacific trade, would go down, taking Hawaii with it. The colony would regain its status as a malarial backwater plagued by tribal warfare and hedonism. The whites would be driven out, anarchy would prevail, and the Colonel would smile.

By pre-arrangement, the British government would step in to "restore order and eradicate disease," even if they had to eradicate the native population to do so. The

Colonel smiled again. The nation of the perpetual fog had always been most helpful to him and his Master.

The Colonel adjusted his eyepatch and sipped a dry gin. *Dee-lightful,* he said to himself. With the snap of his fingers, a one-armed girl appeared bearing a tray with fresh gin, an unidentifiable piece of meat, and pen and paper. Though the mail steamer was a month away, the Colonel wanted to compose several drafts of his instructions. After all, the fall of Hawaii would be his magnum opus.

*

While lying flat on the sand, Damien could read the contents of the archbishop's terrible letter floating in the sky. Wiping his tears away, he felt large lumps upon his forehead. He pressed on one and it exploded. Sun blister. He had been inert under the sun a long time. The hot saltwater cursed the eyes, augmenting his spiritual suffering with the physical.

Wiping his forehead again, this time with a filthy sleeve, he turned his head to drain the burn. Though his vision was blurred, Damien could tell he was lying in some scrub far from shore. He then noticed a dark form approaching. Then another, and then two more. Rubbing his eyes, he realized what was beside him and nearly jumped. Scorpions scurried forward, inches from his face. A fifth and sixth scuttled forth, tails raised. *Ah,* Damien thought, *my pallbearers to hell.* He closed his eyes and prepared for death.

CHAPTER TWELVE

The transition from sail to steamer came slowly to Hawaii. It was not uncommon for the islanders of Molokai to see great clippers pass gracefully on the horizon well into the 20th century. Occasionally the hellish cattle boat condemned from livestock service could be seen dumping the newest leper "settlers" off its decks, leaving the unfortunate internees to swim ashore. And, of course, the mail steamer was a familiar sight, though it only plied these waters once a month.

So, when the superstructure of the battleship broke the horizon, it was no small occurrence. No one on these islands had ever seen anything like it. Indeed, no one in the world had ever seen the like. It was gray and hulking, billowing black smoke from its coal bunkers.

As it drew near, the islanders measured its full aspect. It had two sets of gun turrets forward and two sets aft. The barrels extruding the turrets were longer than the entire length of the monthly mail steamer. It didn't sail over the ocean blue with a gentle pitch and yaw, but cut through the sea with rape-like arrogance. It was typhoon and tempest, eruption and destruction, an artificial sea monster created for one thing: death.

The inmates of Molokai, be they in the hills or along the shore, stared at the beast, wondering if the white man had finally given up the charade of "caring for the lepers" and came to murder them outright with fire from this gray dragon. When Father Damien went missing, their hopes of a good life began to erode. They were sure the end was now.

*

Half a league off Molokai's western spit, the battleship dropped anchor. From the beach, the islanders could read its name; the *Glens Falls*. The smoke pouring from its stacks went from black to gray to white to nothing. A volcano dormant. The lepers exhaled.

The mighty ship rode quietly on her anchor, flags in the rigging flapping in the light breeze. To the vessel's stern and unseen to islanders, a boat was lowered with a coxswain to steer and two Marine officers as passengers.

The motion of the sea had a more pronounced effect on the little boat. Two men stood at the bow, adjusting their stance with the movement of the swells. "Do you really think it's Tanveer, Captain?"

"Difficult to say, sir," said the other with a slight brogue. "My man's letter only read they were caring for a white man, but he enclosed Tanveer's dog tags. Won't know till we get there, General."

"Damn lot of good getting there's going to get us. We've got orders not to land. How will you be able to examine him?"

"See the long lava ridge that makes up this coast? There is a horseshoe-shaped curve about five yards across. We'll ask the locals to bring him down." There was silence between the two, both observing the land as they approached. They inwardly marveled at the aquamarine heights of The Wall of Pali, the black lava coast, the thundering waves upon it.

The general was the first to speak. "You've been here before?"

"Aye. Long before I was a naval officer; long before I was a doctor."

"How bad is it?"

"Remember Haiti, sir?"

"Trying to forget."

"Though I've heard some things have changed here, I'd say Haiti is a fountain of paradise by comparison." As the boat drew within earshot of the shore, a tall white man at the horseshoe break called out to them. "Hello, Tom!"

"It's Lieutenant Cavanaugh, ye West-Cork-muck savage!"

They both smiled. The man on the beach said again, "Hello, Tom. What brings you to my side of heaven?"

"Sean, this here is General Wessinger, USMC. He knows Tanveer and wants to see him. I'm here my own self to examine him."

"Tough to do from a boat." The doctor gritted his teeth in embarrassment.

"Orders is orders, Sean."

It was Sean's turn to be embarrassed. Damien was gone four days now with no sign of coming back, and the Irishman's temper was wearing thin. "Aye, sorry for that. Apologies to you and the general."

The Marine doctor nodded. "What's Tanveer's condition, Sean?"

"If it's him, he's not well. He's been burned."

"How was he burned?"

"He was branded."

"Branded?"

"Aye, tortured; branded over most of his body."

"Tortured!" The general's eyes went wide. "I will shell this fucking island into the Stone Age!"

191

"Ah, then, General, don't you know you'd be doing us all a grand favor. But it wasn't us what did it. We don't know who did, and the man hasn't been well enough to speak."

The doctor said, "Sean, can we see him? Can he be brought to the beach?"

"Dunno. Maybe. Take a while, no matter. Why don't you two steam back to the wee gray boat and load up some hardtack and beef. Chewable meat with nothing moving in it would go a long way. The people takin' care o' yer man don't eat so well. Let's figure back here at six bells."

*

It was colors, staggering luminosity, and colors. There were no visions of the natural world, nor any of the manmade world—only colors from a spectrum never witnessed, never alight. Through a depth of refined delicate density so deep it was only a whisper, Damien thought himself ascending.

He rose through the layers, inhaling with great exertion, then exhaling as though pushing his life out. The conflict and contrast of unknown colors faded, and ones from the world he recognized began to hue. From blue to gold to red hot.

Damien's breathing was labored, and he turned his head groaning in agony. The scorpions faced him unafraid, all stingers poised. Then, shadow, a cool darkness upon him. Darkness upon the serpents in human form, a foot crushing the vermin to sand. A voice, "Father, we come to help."

The man raised water held in a shark's bladder to Damien's lips, but he could barely breathe, much less swallow. He could, however, see, and through his dry, gritty eyes, he saw a giant and a man—a wounded man, a leprous a man. It was Mr. Puha from Damien's first night on the island.

Damien, had carried water for this soul and his dying wife from The Wall of Pali. But the man's wife didn't die. The elder Hawaiian bent to one knee. He slid his hand under the priest and lifted him to a sitting position. It was an act of kindness and embrace. He nodded toward the larger man. "This man, my son. He come as kokua for me and his mother. Now you." The giant hoisted the priest over his shoulder and started off for home. Damien recalled the man's hovel, a wall made from an old wooden box that said: PROPERTY U.S. NAVY, MACHINE PARTS, MADE IN TOLEDO OHIO, and though bouncing on the giant's shoulder like a tuna bought at market, Damien closed his eyes and let full darkness engage him.

*

A sailor scanned the shores of Molokai with his binoculars from the bridge of the *Glens Falls*. Three forms appeared heading for the beach: one tall white man, a young Hawaiian male, and what appeared to be an elderly invalid. The sailor put down the glasses and hand-cranked a phone on the forward bulkhead. "Captain, you wanted to be notified when anyone approached the shoreline."

"Very well. Notify the General and the ship's doctor and have the launch waiting."

"Aye, sir."

When the launch came within hailing distance of the shore, the doctor spoke first. "Ahoy, Sean. Is that the man between you?"

Sean and Jeemo helped the barely conscious man on his feet. "Aye, 'tis him, but don't take long. He's not well."

The general couldn't believe his eyes—the man wavering between the two looked to be seventy years of age. His hair was shock white, and he carried a long white beard. It couldn't be Tanveer. "Are you Major Jack Tanveer, USMC?"

With a strained effort, the frail man raised his head. In a whisper he croaked, "Sir, yes, sir."

His words were lost in the wind, and so Sean spoke for him. "He says, 'Sir, yes, sir.'"

Still incredulous, the general shouted, "Where were you born?"

Without raising his head, Jack scratched out, "Cincinnati, Ohio."

Again Sean spoke for him. "He says Cincinnati."

"What sport did you play at the Naval Academy?"

Jack raised his head slightly. "I was a boxer."

Sean boomed, "Says he was a fighter."

"By Christ, that's him! What do you think, Doc?"

"He's in rough shape, that's for sure, but I think he can travel. Sean," the doctor shouted to the beach, "you know we can't land. Can you and your man wade him into the surf and lift him aboard?"

Before he could reply, Tanveer spoke to Sean in a barely audible whisper. "I can't leave."

Sean and Jeemo froze, but remained expressionless. Without moving his lips, Sean said, "Say that again, boyo."

"I can't leave."

*

Damien felt the weightlessness of being lowered to the ground. He felt the cool mass of rock on his back as he sat, then leaned back. Opening his eyes and inhaling deeply, the priest sensed a vague familiarity of place. Before recognition could set in, the giant spoke. "Here, drink dis water. You need it." Damien sipped from the bladder flask, slowly letting the water hydrate him until he could speak.

"Dis water good. From Wall of Pali."

The priest drank again, more deeply this time, and looked around, his head starting to clear. He saw the hovel and the old cook fire. Damien suddenly knew where he was. He said to the son of Mr. and Mrs. Puha, "This is where your mother and father live." The priest looked around. *Yes, this was the place*, yet it appeared long vacant. The MACHINERY PARTS wall was still there, but on the ground and rotten. All the utensils were gone, the outhouse torn down, and the ash from ten thousand cook fires mixed with the sand.

"No, they live here no more."

Damien was confused. "If not here, then where?"

"Someplace better."

*

Sean boomed out to the launch. "Ma'I Ho'oka'awale."

The doctor froze, and the general asked, "What is it?"

After a moment, the doctor said quietly, "He's got it."

"Got what?"

"The separating sickness. Leprosy."

"Christ!"

"Sean, are you sure?"

Sean thought fast "No, we're not. But those what were caring for him were very far along in the disease, and he does have a blotch on his right thigh. There's only one way to tell."

"Sean, I say again, we're prohibited to land. Is there anyone on the island who can take a skin sample from the patient?" Sean noted with disgust his friends too soon use of the word "patient".

"Aye, there's a man, but he's currently indisposed. Way far under the weather. Why don't you and the general head back to the beast. I'll reengage you when there's word."

The doctor considered the options. "All right, Sean, we'll wait on ya."

"See no other way, but before ye' scoot, could ye' roll the hardtack and beef into the surf? We'll retrieve it when it washes ashore."

The coxswain did the hard work and set the hardtack and beef adrift in the waves. He then resumed his position, and the launch turned its stern to the island, sputtering toward the vessel at anchor. The two men on the beach maneuvered their "patient" for the walk back. Sean said to Tanveer, "I hope you know what you're doing, lad."

With a gentle lifting of his head and a soft lilting of his voice, Jack said, "I do."

Sean said, "Jeemo, let's take Major Tanveer back to my place. When we get him comfortable on the porch, run out to the valley and fetch Judge Lae. Tell him it's important."

*

"You feel better now, Father?"

"Yes, my friend. I think I can walk."

"Okay, I watch anyway."

"Do we have much farther to go?"

"Yes, much distance to where Wall of Pali meets ocean."

The elder Puha, his son, and Damien walked to the west longer than what seemed necessary, and to Damien, longer than seemed possible. They saw no other inhabitants, sea birds, or land creatures along the way, but as they approached the junction of sea and mountain face, Mr. Puha bent to pick up something in the sand. "Look, Father, fishhook and lady's charm." He held them in his palm. "Made from whalebone. Very old."

Damien peered at the tiny items. "Amazing. I found objects exactly like these my first day on the island."

Mr. Puha smiled. "I know."

His son motioned to the priest. "Father, you see outcropping on Wall?"

"No, my son, I do not."

"Watch after third wave hit wall."

Damien counted the swells, and after the third breaker crashed then receded, he saw the rock, or more accurately, two rocks shaped like pillars.

Mr. Puha said, "Underneath rock, there is cave. Swim through little bit, dry land other side. We live there now." Damien was confused. "You come with us; see life other side. Very pretty—no Ma'i Ho'oka'awale."

The father and son smiled, but Damien felt small butterflies fluttering in his stomach, a happy anxiety. "I'm afraid I cannot swim," he said nervously.

"Dat okay. All Hawaiian peoples born from ocean. We help you." Damien gave his consent with a smile and a nod, excited about seeing the other side, but worried about the ocean swells.

The younger Puha said, "Father, I hold you when we swim. You inhale, exhale three times deep, then we go." The priest did as instructed, and then, for a change, put his faith in the hands of another and plunged into the deep.

The cool waters enveloped Damien. He heard the bubbles of the dive and the muted hiss of the surf on the surface. The priest strangely felt no fear as the giant holding him dove deeper. In fact, his thoughts pleasantly wandered as his body shed the tyranny of gravity in the weightlessness of the sea. He thought of his family's country home in Belgium where he would chase butterflies in the summer, and of his first thrilling days in seminary. He thought of his long-dead mother and how glorious must her present days in heaven be. He longed to see her again.

*

"Thanks for coming, Your Honor." And without any other small talk, Sean explained to him what Jack Tanveer said on the beach and his idea for a solution. "Would you be up to it?"

"Sean, dis big subterfuge you plan. Take sample Tanveer's posterior. But who gonna take sample?" He nodded to Sean's back room "Damien only one know how, and he maybe not live. He been unconscious two month now."

"True enough, but his body is sound."

"Body okay, yeah, dat true, but sometimes mind can kill body."

"Aye, I'm with you there. Then, let's just wait. Let the goddamn doctor and general and Navy wait."

Judge Lae thought for a moment. "Yeah, let goddamn doctor, goddamn Navy, and goddamn stinking haole ship wait." He smiled.

*

The priest was comfortable with the enshrouding darkness of the sea. He let his head sway with the motion of his companion's swimming and wondered briefly why he didn't feel the desire to breathe. The darkness grew deeper and deeper until he saw a change in shade—dark green to blue green to aquamarine to golden, and as they burst through the surface, the blue of the sky.

The giant boy who carried Damien as they swam, stood. "You done good, Father. Everything easy now." The little priest glanced around him, shaking off the seawater. It appeared he was in a very wide valley surrounded by a mountainous rim. From the rim, thin waterfalls cascaded. The fauna was lush green, and in the hazy distance people relaxed. Everywhere, the tall palm trees swayed in a gentle breeze.

"Where are we?"

Mr. Puha replied, "This a place all Polynesian peoples know how to get to."

A melodic Hawaiian voice pulled Damien away from his first friend on the island. "Hello, Father." Damien turned to the voice behind him and was taken aback. He thought he recognized Mrs. Puha, but she seemed younger. Years younger, and unscarred by leprosy. She wore a white sarong with blue and gold dyed lilies upon it.

Damien stuttered, "Mrs. Puha, I recall you being blind."

"I was blind. No more now." She smiled.

"A miracle."

"No, natural thing. It happen for everybody." Damien stared, open-mouthed. "Father, you stay now forever with us. Everything happy." Her husband and son stood behind her, smiling broadly. The priest felt an overwhelming sense of comfort and peace, but that made him uncomfortable, as if it were too perfect. As if he had more work to do and should be on his way. He was torn between the peace offered here and the practical world that called to him.

"Yes, I'll stay, but if I may sit for a moment." He sat upon the grass, dipping his head between his knees to calm his breathing. As it slowed, he looked up. A thick fog was rolling in.

Kalawao Cove was like any cove in Hawaii—crescent-shaped and sand-lined, its waves forever broaching the shore. Its difference lay in what lived inshore, and what was occasionally deposited from offshore.

The fog wisped and the overwhelming sense of calm dissipated. Damien heard the waves pound the shore and then detected something else; something to seaward and something ashore. As the wind poked holes in the fog, he spotted heads bobbing in the sea. Horribly disfigured bodies clung to floating furniture, rum crates, driftwood. He heard cries of anguish, fear, pain.

As the waves deposited the human flotsam upon the land, Damien saw they were lepers crying out, and he instinctively rose to help them, but to his own horror, he could not move. His body sat frozen on the beach.

From the shore side came murmurings, guttural grunts, and liquid and raspy laughter. As the fog lifted, the island's occupants, the dead of the living, savagely descended upon the immigrants. Women were set upon first, clubbed into unconsciousness and ravaged. Their husbands and fathers defended them, but were beaten off with machetes and clubs, their necks snapped, their bones broken.

The resident lepers stole their possessions, carrying them inland. Children were stolen, too, carried off by hair and limb. The elderly and infirm lay upon the beach, kicked and shattered, left alive only to be consumed by dogs and pigs. To Damien, the gates of hell had swung open.

Damien, frozen in the sand, shut his eyes through the tears. As his courage burned through, he opened his eyes to a deserted beach of white sand and gentle surf. The shore was vacant of horror, and only the wind moaned.

He then saw a form approach slowly and with purpose. Damien, shocked that one of the plunderers remained, rushed to him, his vows forgotten amid the murder in his heart. As he drew closer, the priest saw his opponent not to be disfigured or enraptured with rapine. Rather, the burnt man with a white beard wore a calm smile on his face. Recognizing him, Damien let his rage subside and allowed the man to come within a few steps.

Silence, a puttering of wind, gulls overhead. Damien said, "You're the pilot we found on the mule. You're not dead?" A question.

"No, and neither are you." A statement. "Father, I've been told to tell you you're needed for the children."

It was evening twilight. The chorus of tropical birds began to fall off as they took roost in the koa trees and the banyans. The hum and dim of island conversation stilled as the lepers laid down from work or a day of weary pain. Even the surf morphed from crash to hush to whisper as it approached the shore.

Damien opened his ears to the calm around him as his eyes swept across the unfamiliar room. He sat upright, vaguely enjoying the crisp rustle of starch sheets covering him, noting with mild curiosity that he was wearing an oversized linen shirt and cotton undershirt.

As wakefulness rooted its grip, a powerful thirst overcame him. Damien folded the sheets aside and let his feet hit the wooden floor. The boards squeaked a comforting welcome. Steadily (though a touch lightheaded), he trekked to the door at the far side of the room. Emerging into the next, he noted books upon shelves upon walls; *The Rights of Man; The Golden Bough,* Damien realized where he was and smiled as the flow of awareness and self-confidence swirled within and around him. With a steady gait, he left the room of books and opened a screen door to an outside porch. A flickering kerosene lamp presided over the unsure silence, dancing shadows over the faces of three men. To the astonished looks from Sean and the judge, he asked, "Is there a glass of water about?"

Without hesitation, Sean rose and retrieved cool water for his friend. As Damien drank deeply, Judge Lae finally asked, "Father, you been incoherent almost two months. You remember anything?"

"I recall a letter from the archbishop."

"Yes, we read letter, too. We think letter what cause you to 'depart'."

Damien smiled calmly. "Not to worry. 'Twas the reaction of a mortal man, and as a mortal man, I am prone to err. But that is behind us. We still have important work to do." Sean and the judge smiled, noting the words "we" and "work". Their friend was back.

The judge asked again, "Father, you remember any ting else?"

"Yes, I a recall a visit with Mr. and Mrs. Puha. I met their son, a powerfully built lad. They took me to a lovely part of the island."

Sean and the judge exchanged worried looks. "Please tell us 'bout it, Father."

Damien went on to describe the blissful valley and the happy people there. He told how the husband and wife were cured of leprosy and how their son came from the island of Lanai to live with them in their dotage. Damien paused, and in that pause, Sean gave a nod, slight and hesitant, to Judge Lae. Purposely ignoring the usual honorific, the judge said, "Mr. and Mrs. Puha passed away."

"Oh, I'm sorry. When?"

"The same day you receive da letter from archbishop. Da same day you wandered into wilderness."

"I see."

Sean took up the verse. "Thing is, there was a son; hulking muscular man he was. He came as a kokua, but right before he arrived, his parents passed away. In grief, he climbed The Wall of Pali and threw himself off. We never found the body."

202

"I see." Damien let it sink in. Exhaling, he tilted his head downward. Inhaling, he raised his head and smiled. "I am a most fortunate man. God has given me the greatest gift He can bestow upon His servants." The unasked question hung in the air. *And that is...*

"A vision of heaven." And without the advent of a "Hello on the porch" or a creak on the wooden steps, Jack Tanveer stood before them in the dwindling twilight.

Damien was un-astonished. He stood calmly and took stock. The man before them was white- haired and carried a white beard. He had a sparkle in his eyes, and all his exposed skin, save his face, was horribly scarred by symbols—fish, clouds, maps of islands. The little priest said, "We met at the cove."

"Yes," said the pilot.

"You spoke of children."

"Yes."

Damien sat back down, crossed his arms, and smiled a knowing smile. "I'm not leaving."

"Neither am I," said Tanveer.

Damien was the only one on the island skilled enough to take skin samples. What surprised him this morning was his lack of reluctance in taking these specific two.

Mr. Mah twice dipped the American flag flying over the post office, a prearranged signal out to the ship to send the boat in with the doctor. Sean, along with a still frail Tanveer met the boat at the beach. It held out bobbing in the surf. "Mornin', Tom."

"Morning, Sean. Do you have the samples?"

"Oh, aye. One from his bicep," Sean said, pointing to a bandage on Tanveer's upper arm, "and one from his buttock."

"Do you think he has it, Sean? Do you think he has leprosy?"

"We're not seein' it, but with these samples, it's for your doctors to tell. They're three times wrapped in cloth, canvas, and oilskin. There's cork about it, so it'll float." With that, he heaved the package toward the boat. One of the sailors fetched it from the surf with a hook and tied it to the side slightly above water but most pointedly not aboard. The doctor called to the beach, "Okay, then, boys, we'll either be back to take the major to hospital in Honolulu or back to tell you why we can't. Till then, aloha."

Sean watched the launch sail back to the great ship. He waited till it was raised aboard before he turned to go. He felt a little oozing just below his rear waistline. He didn't want to chance any of the launch crew or the doctor seeing the blood stain emanating from where Damien had clipped him earlier in the day.

*

There is always a reason—and always an excuse for the reason.

It was conceived from the mantra of the day: Commerce. On every island in the Hawaiian chain, the majority of plantations harvest coffee, pineapple, sugar, and copra. The smallest of these employed dozens of workers; the largest many thousands. Disease imported by Captain Cook's crew two centuries before had ravaged and whittled the native population to less than thirty percent of its primacy. The majority of the standing thirty percent were employed on the plantations with precious few left over to support the infrastructure of the plantations—stevedores, road builders, warehousemen, and servants.

The labor shortage held a knife to the throat of Hawaiian commerce. Measures were attempted, including the importation of coolies from China, convict labor, and indentured servants from the Philippines and Puerto Rico. There was even talk of resurrecting the blackbird trade, but the rising missionary class put a hesitant halt to it, though it was still practiced covertly on the outer islands near Midway.

The solution, of course, was children. Native children. They could be taught, at an early age, civility and later English, and how to properly serve canapés. Trouble was, Hawaiian children were not lining up to request employment as house coolies, and the early blackbirders and British press gangs experienced great dismay and permanent peril when they tried to steal children from the Hawaiian families. This led to a different tact: what you can't steal, take.

A meeting was convened in the executive conference room of the Honolulu Board of Health.

"Doctor Fitch, how do you vote?" The man being addressed was small, with a pencil-thin mustache and a personality so sniveling he almost needed to be twins. He stared into space, his lips moving silently, though he did not answer. "Dr. Fitch?"

"Well, obviously the parents of the children are lepers."

"We know their parents are lepers. How do you vote?"

"It's hard for me to say. I'm just saying the children can't stay on Molokai. They might contract leprosy." The committee chairman spoke to Fitch as one bureaucrat to another. "Dr. Fitch, do you agree that staying on Molokai presents a dangerous situation to the children?"

"I agree, in principle, that the danger may or may not exist."

"As such, would you then agree that a 'Yes' vote would be in the children's best interest?"

"I wouldn't say no to the point that a 'yes' vote may or may not be in the best interest of the children."

The chairman sighed and marked a "Yes" for Fitch. "Superintendent Anderson, your opinion?"

A corpulent balding man replied in a thick State-of-Maine accent. "I think the children are better off working in the clean environment of a private hospital in Honolulu. There is no hope for them on that outer island. Their future is brighter working for me. I vote 'Yes' for removal."

"Thank you. For the final vote, Reverend Paisley?"

"Not sure. Not sure I trust these damn Asiatics. Had a whole household staff of them quit just yesterday. More damn lies about my wife beating them, fondling them. Liars all!" He reached for a glass and drank deeply the clear liquid—his "water" as he called it.

"Reverend, the issue here isn't uh... one of trust or... where they'd work." He looked briefly at Anderson. "It's one of protecting their welfare."

The reverend thought for a moment of what life would be like on the estate if there were no servants to do his wife's cooking, her cleaning, her... "Reverend?"

"Yes, yes, right. Vote 'Yes' to remove the dirty little buggers."

"So be it. Let it be known that a resolution has been passed by this body whereby uninfected children of infected lepers residing on the island of Molokai shall be removed from said parents. Children will be disbursed to Oahu and other islands for their own safety and benefit. A physician will conduct an in situ exam to determine the extent of leprosy in the parents determinate for the children's removal. They will be moved calmly and with great care."

There would be no physician "in situ". There wasn't a physician from San Francisco to Fukushima that could be begged, bought, or held at knifepoint to set foot on Molokai. The only ones "in situ" to remove the children "calmly and with great care" would be out-of-work mercenaries, out-of-jail convicts, beached sailors, corrupt cops, the lot.

The fabric of Hawaiian society—the family—would be torn asunder. Children would be wrestled and ripped from their parents. Mothers and fathers, aunts and uncles, would be clubbed into unconsciousness, their children dragged away and tossed wailing in terror into the hold of a filthy schooner. It was a thirty-year-old desecration that descended upon Molokai time and time again.

The name of the terrible schooner was *Gemini*. She was a former blackbirder that still sported barbed wire for handrails. It would take a full day for her to reach Molokai, departing Honolulu at night to take advantage of favorable winds. About noon, her mast, as seen from the island, would pop over the horizon. As the vessel gained the wind and came into full sight, the islanders would know her identity and intent. Panic would ensue.

There is no foolproof way on earth to fully protect a child, less so on Molokai in advance of a raid. Common sense and instinct sent the children to the valleys or the jungle. But that, too, was fraught with danger. In the past, when the terrible schooner was first sighted, the Colonel, smiling in delight, would send his minions off to "Collect strays" the invading brigands might have missed.

There were wild boar, keen and voracious hunters that a healthy adult could scarcely protect themselves against, much less a terrified child. Also scattered amongst the hills and some of the caves were the human chancres present in every society, twisted individuals who looked upon the children not as children but as prey. To the parents of Molokai, the schooner was a gangway to the gates of hell with a first-class ticket to its lowest levels.

*

Dear Son,

It is with no great reserve and no small understatement to write that your mother and I miss you very much. More grievously so, and more than your mother will admit, for the reason we may never see you again.

When we first heard from Congressman Gibson that you were lost in the Pacific, we did not grieve or give up hope. When we later were informed you were alive, joy! Until...

It has been a sine curve of happiness and horrors for your mother and I. We are breathless that you are alive, and breathless that you have been diagnosed a leper. My son...

You and I have excelled at dispute. You know I never approved of your lifestyle and career. Your brothers are now the lead legal counsel for a rapidly growing company named General Motors. It is an up-and-coming corporation which produces automobiles. The future of both your brothers seems very bright indeed. You could have been right there beside them, yet you chose to philander in the tropics, you god-damned insolent – Forgive me; my grief overwhelms and anger takes hold. I must force myself to come to terms with what is, rather than what was not.

My son, what I can glean from your letters is that through and because of your crash, your "ordeal", and the contracting of

*this horrible disease, you have become a
man and then something more. When we
wrote to enquire of your needs, you replied
you only need a few pair of khaki pants, half
boots, some cotton shirts, but mostly,
"Mostly," you said, "dozens of blankets for
the poor souls with which I cohabitate."
When we asked of books to help you pass the
time, you requested titles on gardening,
philosophy, and caregiving. We were
surprised and proud. We love you.*

*I beseech and beg you on your mother's
behalf to write often, daily if you can. We've
heard of a Doctor in Scandinavia who has
been making great inroads in the treatment
of leprosy. I have recently been named
chairman of the United States Chamber of
Commerce and, as such, my influence and
reach is significant. If what we are hearing
about this doctor is true, I will have him on
the first steamer to Molokai. There is always
hope.*

*In closing, I pass on the regards of your
nieces and nephews. Young Molly is asking
for a letter on island life, and she and her
sister, Grace, are sending you a collection
of autumn leaves to remind you of
Cincinnati.*

Your loving father

*

The thugs, thirty in all, waded ashore, and like foul
moths, were drawn to the flame of two torches on the
beach. The leader held up his hand for the mob to stop as
he alone drew close to the torches. He stopped and stood
still, sensing, searching. The wind gave a minor howl
and backed a few points, changing the direction of the

209

fluttering torch flames. Sean emerged from the shadows and the direction of the wind. "Ah, Augustus John, I see you graduated from union busting to kidnapping. Fitting promotion for one such as yourself."

"Corcoran, you bog-trotting bastard, I heard you was on this island. Typical of you mick fucks—you finally make it big, and you catch the king hell clap of leprosy. I'm gonna laugh over the years hearing about your guts rotting away."

"Laddie, what makes you think you'll be alive to enjoy the show?" His tone melodious, even in this tense passage, but this thug was not impressed by his voice or his threat, and advanced. "Tell me, Augustus John, was it once or twice I broke your jaw in New Zealand?" Augustus John smiled furiously and Sean lashed out. A loud crack echoed across the beach. "No need to answer, lad. I'm sure now it was twice."

His opponent stood rock still. With great care, he reached into his mouth and withdrew a piece of bloody bone and tossed in the sand at Sean's feet. With slightly gurgled speech, he said, "That'll cost you, Corcoran."

"Aye, maybe, but not tonight."

The thug bristled. "Oh, no? And whose gonna stop us from picking up as many maggoty brats as we choose? Some broke-down cripples, or this midget priest we been hearin' about?"

"Aye, that's who it be." And from the ink of the night, a murmur arose, movement unseen but sensed, a danger moving in. The first to be seen stepping in from the darkness and behind Sean was the village leader from "The Village of the Deceased," the man who had first taken in Jack Tanveer. By the light of day, his appearance would fold one's imagination, but by the flickering light of the torches… his hands were enlarged, his fingers elongated, his grisly, white-boned knuckles protruding like knots on a wooden club. The skin on his face was all but gone. Only an apache crescent of hair remained atop his skull. Because he had no skin, he could neither sneer, nor grimace, nor spit in hatred. When he spoke, his death's head barely moved—only the dusty white jaw and teeth move vertically, clicking with each word, the Grim Reaper's journeymen. He raised a skeletal hand in the air and the rest of his band, the lepers of lepers from his village moved into the torchlight. He spoke directly to Augustus John. "It is time, haole."

And the heat began.

CHAPTER THIRTEEN

The sun came up unnoticed. A dry offshore breeze touched the sands of the cove, and the small surf came upon the beach uncaring as it intertwined and lapped around the limbs of the dead. As Damien gazed down upon them, he said, "We must entomb our enemy as though they were our friends."

"No, Father," said Sean somewhat sternly, "not even the cold earth would take such as these, nor will the dogs or the pigs chew their foul flesh. Besides," he added, wiping the blood from a gash on his forehead, "we have our own dead to bury."

All of the thugs who came to the beach either fled in horror, swimming blindly into the sea, or died in the fight on the beach. Most of the lepers who came to battle were dead, though not all. Each, however, had been very far along in the disease and had become, themselves, a walking weapon, both against their enemies and to themselves so that even minor wounds were fatal.

Damien attended their comfort and their last rites first, though he would find a way to honor their fallen enemies, even against Sean's wishes.

The chief who led this struggle now lay gasping where the waves thinned upon the land. He was, despite his impending death, pleased. He had long imagined the disease would fell him as it ravaged his body and left him weakened and pitiful. To die as a warrior was an unexpected honor.

Damien knelt alongside and anointed him, offering the sign of the cross. Between labored breaths, the leper raised an unsteady hand. It was mostly devoid of flesh and crawling with unseen maggots, but Damien grasped it, fearing his last words were coming. "Did we get them, Father? Did we save the children?"

"Yes, we won." The leper, who had no eyelids, could only stare. While the light in his eyes dimmed, his jaw moved, attempting a smile. He felt his flesh becoming whole again, and as he passed into the next life, he did so with pride, as a man intact.

Without malice aforethought, Damien had lied to the man.

Sean then hears a scream on the wind. A lone kokua raced across the sands. She was battered and bruised, shrilling in a mix of Japanese, Hawaiian, and English. Sean, recognizing her, rushed over. "Maksuno, what's the matter? What happened?" She stood wide-eyed and babbling. Sean shook her, attempting to focus her so he could understand and act. "Maksuno, please!"

As it dawned on her that she was among friends, her panic receded and she spoke, her words rushed but intelligible. "Sore wa hidoi monodeshita…"

Sean's shoulders sagged and he wavered slightly in the wind. To no one and everyone he said, "All that bloodshed, all that goddamn bloodshed." He closed his eyes.

By now, Damien had reached them. "What is it, my son?"

With eyes still closed, Sean went off in monotone. "They killed Mr. and Mrs. Fukino. They beat them to death and stole their daughter and son. They went next to the Epileas, burned down the shanty, and stole two toddlers."

"But how? All the blackbirders are dead."

"Some must have slipped away during the fight."

"We'll scour the island. They can't hide here." In an instant, a thought dawned on them both. Simultaneously the heads of the two men swept to the west. On the ocean's horizon, the terrible schooner sailed uncaring toward Honolulu, its once empty holds now laden with a cargo of four.

In the valley, the Colonel and Terry were locked in a game of chess on a sleek board of ebony and whalebone, the pieces carved from the digits of various mammals. "I'd say that's checkmate, old man."

"Huh," was all Terry would concede. He sat back and drank deeply from his glass, the contents of which could be mistaken for red wine. The Colonel, satisfied with the outcome, also sat back in his chair and drank deeply. He pondered the joy of existence. Did the disenfranchised and near-dead humans really think they could pull it off? His gaze shifted to the peninsula. He laughed a cold laugh.

The carnage on the beach had barely ceased when Jack began to dig the graves. He was stripped to the waist, as even a cotton shirt brushing against his skin caused his burns to sing painfully. His legs and buttocks also pained him, but modesty did not allow him to strip further.

The digging was soothing to him, giving him a purpose on an island where, even among the grotesquely distorted, he stood out. The pilot took time to catch his breath after finishing the third grave and leaned on the shovel. Jack stretched out his right arm and marveled at the burns. *Perfect little pictures*, he thought. The story on the arm showed the migration of seabirds and dolphins throughout Oceania.

He understood it all; could see the great depths and the towering islands; could feel the blue of the sky and the wisp of the clouds. He could understand a great many things now. While his body strove to heal his skin, casting away dead cells and replacing them with new, his soul endeavored to enlighten his heart and unfold his mind. Old memories, old desires, old conceptions died away. Replacing them were different premises on life and an outlook almost infinite. The comfort and joy were almost unbearable.

He inhaled the sea air and thought there was so much to give here. He happily resumed the digging.

Behind the post office, three men sat at a table. Jeemo stood leaning against the trunk of a small palm tree. There was much discussion, both heated and calm. For the calm, it was decided that the lepers who had perished on the beach would be buried in state. For the heated, there was no resolution. Sean screeched with a passion no one on this island, and few on this earth, had ever heard. Judge Lae slammed his fist many times on the table in violent demand, but Damien was adamant. "No, we cannot…"

Between the seventeen open graves, nine to the left, eight to the right, were the coffins of those Damien would later declare "the martyred." Atop and draped about each coffin were the flowers of Molokai—night blooming jasmine, blue, red and purple hibiscus, and the beautiful white moonflower, which opens and glows after evening twilight. At the head of the two rows, someone stood a large piece of monkeypod wood and had painted

These people our friends
Rest in peace

No one knew their names. They were among the first to be unceremoniously and ruthlessly dumped on the shore. The Honolulu Board of Health had them declared legally dead before they even arrived. To the law, to their families on *the other* islands, and to the world, they did not exist, but to the lepers of Settlement Molokai they were heroes, and the lepers came to pay their respects.

Word was passed that the gates to the cemetery, of late being referred to as the Garden of the Dead, would open at sunrise, and services held just before sunset. This would allow plenty of time for the ambulatory and less-than-so to arrive, view the departed, and pray.

And they came. As the sun's upper limb cracked the eastern horizon, there were already a dozen or so ready to enter the cemetery. Jack Tanveer opened the rusty gates to let Damien and the mourners pass through. Damien stood at the head of the row, next to the sign, rosary in hand. He would remain there silently throughout the day.

The lepers passed the coffins in a silent, unending flow. They came from the village. From the scattered shanties. From the caves and lean-tos. Upon crutches. Unable to see or hear or speak. They came in rags, and they came naked. They came and they stayed all day. Les Horribles.

Damien stayed, too, stood, silently saying his rosary over and over again. He noticed only the sun, its ascent to the meridian searing his face. At sunset, he turned and walked to his charges, who stood behind the departed.

He wanted a eulogy to praise these dead. He wanted to say, "Though we may now shiver in darkness, the morning will bring God's light." He wanted to speak of the divine; he wanted to say that these dead would live in the heart of Hawaii for eternity. But when he opened his mouth, no words came. Panic and breathlessness enveloped him. Outside the cemetery fence, he saw Jack Tanveer walking calmly in the distance. Damien's breathing resumed and he calmed. He noticed among the lepers the presence of the Kahuna Ana woman. He smiled to himself and looked again toward Jack, but the pilot was gone. All Damien could see was the island— split rock crags and foreboding thunderhead clouds to the east, calm crimson light to the west. The surf swirled and smashed upon the shore as the waves lulled behind, ancient and subtle. At The Wall of Pali, a creep of green met the rainbow cascades of waterfalls.

Molokai.

The words came, though he was not conscious of them as he spoke. "We have had our souls spit upon and our hearts lashed." The murmuring of the group ceased. "We lepers have been mutilated and tortured by unseen enemies from within our bodies and even enemies from without. But we are still people, men and women, young and old, and we deserve to live as God's people under the sun." The lepers fixed their gaze upon Father Damien., pure silence on the promontory. "We have been created in His image, and they that trample upon us trample upon God, and as He cries out, we must ACT out." Damien spoke to them from his heart, and the bodies of the whole began slowly to reach for each other's hands. He pointed to the flower-draped coffins.

"These people died as settlers, as lepers, as friends. They offered their lives as individuals in common for you. They died so that the children, the children of our flesh and the children of God, may continue life, such that our existence may reverse from horror to joy." The speaker and the spoken became one. "And though they now lay here above the earth and soon below it, know their spirits will soar the skies and sail the seas at one with God." Then, as a slash on his conscience, Damien saw in his mind the terrible schooner sailing across the horizon. He screamed out, "Lawa! Enough!" The priest lowered his head, then raised it in slow deliberation. He said to them in a soft voice, "If this is allowed, we share the sin."

The lepers stared, frozen. He nodded imperceptibly to Sean, who did the same to Jeemo. The boy sprinted into the gathering darkness.

Two days later, the mail steamer arrived. The sailors who picked up the outgoing mail were both surprised and ecstatic to find only three letters: two headed to the Tanveer family of Cincinnati and one to an Uncle Jon Boey, care of the Sanford Plantation.

Jon Boey was a leper. When he noticed his left hand beginning to turn grey, he held it over a burning hurricane lamp. He felt no pain. He was far more worried that someone would betray him, then the sheriff would beat him unconscious, shackle him, and dump him aboard the cowboat. Upon arrival, he'd be cast into the surf and washed upon the idyllic crypt that was Molokai.

Jon Boey had an uncle who had been denounced as leper and had run for the jungle. Jon knew where he was and sought him out.

The uncle told him he would be killed or banished to Molokai if the white man found out. He also told him there were hundreds of lepers throughout the islands hiding in plain sight, working with and for the haoles.

There was money to help them escape to the less-populated areas, money to provide opium to ease the pain, even pallbearers to surreptitiously bury the dead so their families would not be identified as "afflicted". It was a secret society of the doomed. The old man told Jon that he must disguise himself by hiding the disease, no matter how difficult.

Come the dawn, Jon reported to the Sanford Plantation pineapple fields where he worked at the coring machine. Pineapples were picked and placed on a moving boom crane with a conveyor belt. The belt would hoist the fruit up a slight incline, which then tumbled down to Jon's station. Each pineapple would land horizontally and be punctured, stem to leaf, by a two-inch hollow pipe. The pipe would retain the fruit for canning, ejecting it later down the line when full. Jon's job was to whisk the empty husk of the fruit away in preparation for the next arrival. It was fast and simple work. It was also dangerous. He thought he'd best get on with it.

The scream when it was heard was responded to quickly and with urgency, but with little surprise. Mutilation on the plantation was a common occurrence, especially at harvest time. Jon's spurting stump was wrapped in denim and his hand, its telltale tinge of gray now covered in blood, tossed casually into the firebox of the boiler that powered the boom crane and coring machine.

Jon bribed the Chinese comprador and secured himself a job as plantation runner, entrusted with messages to the banks in Honolulu, the machine shops at Pearl, and the outlying plantations. The pain of his amputation had, over time, been reduced to a dull throb, though his resentment increased. *Why would the white man hunt me down and either kill or banish me because of a disease they brought here?*

As he drank deeply from the bowl that contained his fourth draught of kava, he felt a tugging on his sarong. He looked down to see a smiling young girl. She had a note in her hand. "Dis for you," she said and handed it to him. He was in a mild daze from the kava, so he experienced no surprise—only a comfortable curiosity. He read the note, a jumbled scrawl of the backwards "S's" and "E's" of a child's handwriting.

Dear Uncle,

Life here on Molokai is hard but I think someday maybe getting better. Mommy and Daddie teaching me about power of sun and ocean and ancestors and gods. Tell me Hawaii islands come from Pele who create from fire. Dis scary to me but I think also important. Please write soon.

Love,

Ukupanipo

Below the name, in the center of the page, sat a striking image both hypnotic and powerful. The sophistication of the drawing was unearthly. It was the visage of a hammerhead shark, its silhouette poised to strike from below. The shark was covered with Maori moku, each symbol indicating an epoch in the lives of Pacific Islanders, though there was a space across the forehead and between the ancient eyes that seemed unnaturally blank.

The lightness of the kava instantly vanished. *The rage of haoles will be infinite.* Dropping his head in resignation, his next thought was that it must be done. Jon Boey vanished into the jungle. He would return to the Sanford Plantation once more, but it would be the last time in his life.

It took Jeemo almost eleven days. Twice a day without fear or exhaustion, he hiked the west spine of The Wall of Pali. The trail, scarcely a foot wide and pummeled to hardness by generations of mountain goat, felt warm beneath his feet. He paused for a moment, shifted the load on his back, and moved on. He climbed steadily for hours, the smile never leaving his face. As he ascended, the scent of the sea left him, but the power he felt from it did not.

He could see the mass of the surf, aquamarine and white foam flecks silently smashing the coast below. The trail twisted and turned, ever rising. He enjoyed the shadow play of the cumulus clouds as they blocked out the sun, turning The Wall to gray then back to green and gold. Jeemo loved existence on The Wall; it was where he felt his people lived. At a turn in the trail, a rock the size of a person's head blocked his path. He judged it little more than an inconvenience, but the trail was only as wide as his feet and the wind was increasing. He thought it best not to step over it. He balanced the bladder bags as he kneeled, but still spilled some of the palm oil within. He smiled; no worries.

With his right hand on the trail, he lightly pressed the rock with the back of his left. The rock teetered, and without resignation fell into the sky. Jeemo watched as it touched The Wall with a click, then again another click, half the rock disintegrating. Then came the spiraling silence as the rock, which spent eons upon the face of the earth, plunged to infinity.

The trail ended near the summit, but it was not his trail's end. Jeemo stopped and faced the sea. He smiled again and backed himself against the face of The Wall.

The dense liana vines gave way, and he stepped calmly into the cave. There was little darkness—an overhead hole in the rock ceiling gave way to sky. To the left and right, Jeemo gave notice to the ancient petroglyphs, proud that he understood their meaning. He reached his hands up easily, grasped the edges, and hoisted himself once again into daylight.

On the first day, he cut the clearing in the brush. It was a specific shape, very large. He took great care in its precision. On successive days, he hauled the bladders of palm oil to the site and saturated the ground within the perimeter. Today was the final time. From this Olympian height, he scanned the points of the horizon.

He could see the peak of Mauna Kea on the big island of Hawaii, Red Hill Peak on Maui, The Garden of the Gods on Lanai, and the Sacred Falls on the Koolau Range on Oahu. It was at these places people would be waiting. With a great swing arc, Jeemo cast the empty bladders over The Wall and into the deep. His task almost complete, he settled himself into the changing breeze of sunset and napped.

Momentarily eclipsing the star Arcturus which hung overhead, the flash of a shooting star awakened Jeemo. He arose with great lightness and approached the shape he cut over a week ago, the strong scent of palm oil welcoming him. It was time. Removing a flint and nap that he had tied to his arm, he scraped for sparks. Scrape and nothing. A second scrape and nothing.

He used a bit more care and a bit more force. A lone blue sparked fell with impossible slowness to the oil-soaked ground. Jeemo thought it died, but it did not. The oil and air and the minutest of flames intertwined, then coalesced and exploded. Jeemo was knocked to the ground, unconscious but alive. The perimeter was a solid mass of fire. From a gods'-eye view, it was the visage of a hammerhead shark poised to strike from below.

Ukupanipo.

The fire could be seen on Maui, Lanai, the Big Island, and Oahu. Men and women who saw the flame knew what to do. The immolation of Hawaii had begun.

Chapter Fourteen

And though it had been over a year ago, the Colonel could still see the burning of Hawaii.

He had awoken with a start and rushed to stand atop the ghost stones outside the bachelor lepers' club inside the Colonel's compound in the Wailau Valley. Standing atop them gave him no advantage in height or distance sighted, but it had become his habit since it scared the natives. He saw what was happening on the other islands as though it were happening right before him. Played in the vapors as though on stage, he saw the translucent shape of Jon Boey holding a burning torch and whispering to three other lepers armed with flame. A moment of silence, a nod, and they scattered swift and fleet to the four quadrants of the Sanford Plantation, where they touched torches to pineapples, nearly ripened and soon to be picked. Within three hours, nearly 400,000 acres of pineapple were ablaze.

The Colonel burned within as the fires burned without. He turned atop the ghost stone to the coffee plantations on the big island of Hawaii. One by one, from Kealakekua to Holualoa, row upon row, field upon field, the coffee bushes burned, saturating the tropical air with the deceptive scent of a calm morning in the kitchen. On Oahu, the flames from the arsonists' sparks raged like a demented child. One by one, the great plantations were incinerated, the Hawe, the Waianae, and the Koolau, the sugar blackened and turned to cinders, indiscernible from the volcanic ash in which it grew. On Kauai, copra, the currency of the South Seas was conflagrated, a million acres in all, and on Lanai, the tea and orchid plantations were reduced to ashes. On all the islands, only two plantations were spared.

The Colonel stood atop the ghost stones for days watching the destruction. He turned his concentration to the Sanford Plantation where his plan to destroy American influence in the Pacific had been only days away from execution.

It had taken him two years to infect all the pickers and workers with a venereal disease. Shortly after the harvest, and when the pineapples were aboard ship outbound for the States, an announcement was to be made about the "health" of the Sanford employees. It would cause fear and panic in the stateside market, the pineapples kept in the harbor away from the docks. The confidence in the Hawaiian fruit and vegetable markets, as well as coffee, tea, and copra would be shattered. The Americans would be driven out, their experiment with "Democracy" and the "Rights of Man" deemed a failure. It would be a stunning victory to the Colonel and his master. But not now. As the Colonel watched the last wall of the last drying barn on the Sanford Plantation burn to the ground, he knew the coolies he infected were now unemployed. The pineapples were turned to ash and now sympathy, rather than accusation and condemnation, would be turned toward the islands.

Upon the swirling vaporous stage, the Colonel saw Dolan Sanford, along with other planters, sitting around a large table negotiating a contract to sell his unemployed coolies to an English concern that would transfer them to a British plantation on New Caledonia to pick tea leaves. *Bastard humans.* The Colonel raged and howled like a terrible beast, one not heard on earth for millennia.

After a week, he stepped down from the stones, and utterly unexhausted, strolled with a spring in his step. *It was,* he thought, *the lepers who were ultimately behind this. Them and that diminutive priest.* Well, that couldn't be allowed to stand. It would take months of demonstrative devotion, as well as serious work and prayers to his Master to accomplish what he had in mind. One of the Colonel's followers ran up behind him to ask a question, but before the man could speak, he received a backhand to the neck, severing his head from his shoulders. It rolled into the surf and was immediately set upon by crabs. The Colonel felt a touch better. As he walked, he whistled an old regimental tune.

*

It was Jeemo who first saw the mast of a schooner break the horizon. As though a brother to the wind, he swooped to Judge Lae's home, then to Sean's. Word quickly spread.

The islanders gathered at Kalawao cove. The elderly and infirm stood side by side with the able and stout. As the schooner approached, a whisper was heard, "Never again." It was passed from mouth to mouth and became a murmuring chant.

In their hearts, every leper vowed that their children would never be stolen from them again; that the white man would never harm them again. Never. They would fight bone and nail to their own demise and that of their foe before they'd allow the haole to tread in malice upon Molokai.

As the schooner neared the cove and dropped its mainsail, the chant of "Never again" grew louder. The schooner slowed, and those who could read, read its name. The name struck fear into their hearts, but girded them for combat. A lone figure on deck unlaid a slipknot on the capstan, releasing the anchor to hold the vessel fast. *Curious. If the white man were here for plunder, he'd not drop anchor. He'd want to turn and run at a moment's notice.* The man on deck, satisfied the anchor was holding, cupped his hands and shouted, "Ahoy the island."

Sean tersely replied, "What is it you want?"

"Permission to land."

"Land who, or what?"

"Myself."

"No landings are allowed on this island. Go home."

"I've come all the way from San Francisco."

"Then it's a testament to your seafaring skills that you haven't wound up as shark bait. But if you took the time to read one of your charts, you would have read the most noticeable words "NO LANDINGS PERMITTED ON MOLOKAI. EPIDEMIC LEPROSY PRESENT"."

Over the wind the man shouted, "I was invited."

"Invited by whom?"

"Jack Tanveer. I'm an old friend of his."

"I'm sure many men know Jack Tanveer. Go home."

The man on deck pulled something from his shirt. "I have a letter from him. It says I'm supposed to tell you Jack goes by the name Brother Joseph now."

Sean softened a notch. "Aye, that's true enough, but not enough for you to come ashore. By what name do you call your own self?" The man shouted his name to the cove. Sean replied, "Stand hard on your anchor. We'll let you know."

The tall man and the judge had a quiet conversation. Sean whistled to one of the teenage boys as the judge approached the elders. After a likewise quiet conversation, the elders departed the beach, taking the infirm with them. The teenage boy who had been speaking to the planter nodded, then ran at full pace inland. Only the fit and the strong remained on the shore.

It took a few hours. Some of the lepers sat in the sand, but none averted their eyes from the schooner. Sean began to light a cigar, but tossed the match when he saw the boy break the brush and trot toward him. The boy relayed the message. Sean turned toward the sea, "Ahoy the schooner! Brother Joseph informs that you're supposed to tell me something."

The man on deck smiled. "Yep, that's true."

"Well?"

"Semper fi."

Sean turned his head inland, nodded a smile, and everyone on the beach exhaled. He turned his head back to the schooner. "Permission to land. Welcome to Molokai."

Introductions were made, and the man from the schooner shook hands with everyone on the beach. To all but him, shaking hands was strange, though a welcome act. Sean told the man that his friend was in the valley helping Damien on his rounds, and that he'd be back in a day or two. He was welcome to stay ashore or head back to his boat, but an insistence was made that he stay for supper. "I'd be glad to."

"I think it would be a greater delight if we were to know your name."

"Richard Zachary."

"And besides friendship, what brings you to our island, Mr. Zachary?"

"I'm a writer looking for a story."

Judge Lae, ever wary, asked, "Mr. Zachary, I noticed you no bat an eye when see the lepers here. You mebbe got dis disease?"

"No, but I have been to a leper colony before." Sean and the judge looked at each other in disbelief. "It's true. I was once starving and frozen and some lepers took me in, gave me food."

"Where dis?"

"The Northwest Territories in Canada. The Athabasca Indians have a valley where they banish other tribes' people who have leprosy. It is a village on a stream. The people there are very content, but live too short a time."

There was silence between the three, then Sean boomed, "You're *that* Richard Zachary! The famous writer!?"

"Yes."

"I knew your name sounded familiar."

The man smiled, and the judge chimed in, "Seems Brother Joseph knows some important peoples."

"When I knew him, he went by the name Jack, and yes, a great many people knew him—bookies, bartenders, women's husbands..."

"He not same man. Good man, yes, but not same as in your time."

"I could tell from his letter. It's part of the reason I came here. Can't wait to see him again."

"It'll be a few days, so why don't you stay after supper? We built a cabin by the beach for guests we thought we'd never see. You'll be the first to grace its presence." The man smiled, patted the judge on the back, and shook Sean's hand once again.

It was predawn, that time of day when shapes are discernable but their details hidden by the receding darkness. The form approached the cabin in an easy, almost flowing pace. The man sitting on the porch, up early to enjoy the sunrise, rocked his chair slightly. The softness of the form gained some angles, but it was still only a silhouette in front of the emerging sun. It tacked smoothly, its course clearly laid for the front porch. As the sun lugged up a further few degrees, the man on the porch saw the details of the form: white hair and beard, twinkling eyes, slight smile, "Tanveer..."

"Richie!"

"You always were a fuck-up."

They hugged with a thunderclap, the embrace felt down to the ground.

The writer stayed on Molokai for two months. He would daily swim out to his schooner to check the lay of the deck and the anchor, but spent the rest of his time roaming the peninsula with his friend, breaking bread with the inhabitants, and helping construct a new pier. An hour before sundown, he could be found behind the post office sitting at Mr. Mah's patio, scribbling in his journal. When done his musings, he'd enjoy a pint of kava or bootleg rum and do some more visiting.

Richie and Brother Joseph could often be found in deep conversation. They enjoyed hour after hour walking the beach and hiking the low reaches of The Wall of Pali, Brother Joseph always pointing to this or that. The two men seemed as one man, very happy.

Finally introduced to Father Damien, the writer and the priest became fast friends. Richard Zachary taught Damien shorthand to help him keep track of building supplies and maintain a journal for future reference. Damien confessed to Richard some of the pitfalls and frustrations in his mission, but Richards noted with great pride in humanity that the little priest's devotion was unflagged. *Happy in his work,* he thought. The writer told Damien the world would soon be hearing of his mission.

A quiet midmorning found the author on his knees in the sand. Beside him, clutching a rosary, sat Damien on a simple wooden chair. "Your confession is complete, my son. Your sins are few; your penance is your own. Go with God,"

"You go with God, as well, Father."

The two shook hands warmly, and Damien departed the beach to serve morning mass. Richards turned to the sea. The schooner was riding nicely on her anchor, and Sean, Brother Joseph, and the Kahuna woman stood in the surf. Upon approaching them, Sean spoke first, "And where you bound first, laddie?"

"Honolulu to wire a story to San Francisco, then the Fanning for water, Micronesia, the Solomons, Borneo, then I don't know where."

"Fanning Island has good water. Load as much as you can." The Kahuna woman looked at Sean, who then added, "She says head south one day from Fanning, and keep your eyes open for a kelp bed. Follow it west for nine days. You should have a favorable current. As soon as you see pelicans flying east in the morning, head north and that should put you abeam of the Ponape." The writer nodded his thanks to her. Tanveer told him there was an American Coast Guard station on Guam and a cutter on permanent patrol off Howland Island. They were always good for charts, smokes, and local knowledge. The two shook hands, encapsulating a certain sadness that his friend Richard was on his way.

The writer then spoke to his longtime friend. "Everyone back home is real proud of you: your family, the old-timers, and me most of all." Tanveer smiled in appreciation.

The Kahuna woman approached and produced a lei, a garland of hibiscus Molokai and plumeria, a traditional Hawaiian gift to those arriving and departing. The writer, a man who earned his living using words, found himself speechless. The islanders, to his relief, said in unison, "Aloha!" Still without words, he smiled, put his hand on his heart, and turned to the surf. The three on the beach remained till the schooner dipped below the horizon.

The pier and jetty had been completed on the Kalaupapa side, snaking its way into the surf. The settlers added a simple hoist so that cargo could be offloaded directly from the steamer instead of being dumped from the vessel's stern to float at leisure, and sometimes its demise, to the shore.

The arriving settler/inmates, however, did not rise to the status of cargo, and the poor unfortunates were still forced to jump into the sea. But at least now the new lepers needed only jump in and swim a few feet to a ladder affixed to the pier. They climbed soaking wet and not a little frightened, but at the top of the ladder their fears would subside as Father Damien greeted them with warm blankets and cups of steaming soup.

The night before this Steamer Day, Judge Lae shot a wild boar, a terrifyingly feral beast with red eyes and tusks as long as a man's forearm. The judge removed the tusks, the largest he had ever seen, and hung them blades down over his front door. The pig was far too large for the elderly judge to move and skin himself, so he saddled one of his mares and rode to Sean's to invite him to butcher duty. Aid acquired, the two rode back, meeting Jeemo on the way. The boy was quick to volunteer. Even skinned, bled out, and eviscerated, the boar was of such weight that it took all three men to load it into Sean's wagon. They transported the swine down to the beach on the Kalaupapa side so some of the Hawaiians skilled in luau could roast it for tomorrow's event.

Steamer Day was always full of anticipation. The people of Molokai would receive letters from families, and sometimes family members would arrive as kokuas. There would be occasional scant foodstuffs and clothing from the Honolulu Board of Health, and lately, an increasing amount of building supplies—paint, wood, shingles, home furnishings, chairs, mattresses, curtains, and an occasional carpet.

It had become custom that all islanders in all clutches of life would show up to the beach to watch the steamer tie up to the jetty. Damien would, very early in the morning, borrow a wagon from Sean and make his usual rounds to hear confessions, give last rites, and bandage wounds. He also helped the very young, the very old, and the infirm board the wagon so they could be brought to shore. He made many happy trips throughout the day, and though the trips were rugged and dusty, everyone arrived at the beach with broad smiles.

Today, the intoxicating scent of pig roasting for over twelve hours in sage, cumin, and pineapple greeted the arrivees. A girls' choir, though limited in repertoire, sang the hymns *Shenandoah* and *Amazing Grace*. Hawaiian ditties were sung by the men while strumming ukuleles. The beach, the pier, and the post office eclipsed the bathhouses as the center points of gossip and gatherings. Laughter and conversation peppered the air. It may as well have been Independence Day on Coney Island.

No great hush overtook the peninsula when the mast of the steamer cracked the horizon. All knew at this point she was still sixteen miles distant, and as she was bucking a strong headwind, it would be hours yet.

As the little ship halved the distance, Damien took note of its color. It wasn't the gray and rust hulk of the converted cattle transport. Its hull was gleaming white, and that could mean one thing. The priest rushed to the post office and asked to borrow one of the mules hitched to a post. "Dat's okay, Father. Sure thing, take Anni. She da one with the straw hat. She friendly." And true enough, Damien found her to be a comfortable and agreeable old Jane.

The two clomped out to the Puhala tree. Damien had been tempted to move into a more comfortable shed on the island, but as building supplies poured in, he was able to fix up his surroundings to his satisfaction. The rest of the extra supplies were used to build a home not for himself, but for another. He named the new church Saint Mary's after his mother.

He dismounted the friendly old mule to let her chop the grass unhitched. The foundation of the church was composed of solid native stone and mortar laid out in the classic cruciform style of the time—the knave facing east; entrance to the west. Within the foundation and still in the open air, Damien constructed a wall-less shed with a palm-thatch roof.

Beneath were a small desk, chair, and the steamer trunk that had accompanied him from Belgium. From within, he retrieved a gunny sack and withdrew his long-barreled Navy colt revolver, fully loaded. Damien tucked the pistol behind his belt and let his linen jacket disguise its bulk. He mounted Anni and rode leisurely back to the beach.

As the Board of Health steamer approached the newly built pier, the inmates of Molokai flocked to the beach to view the vessel's maneuverings. The small white ship sailed surprisingly fast and parallel to the dock. Just as it seemed it would pass the pier, it came full about, pointing its bow to the high seas. For a moment, all conversation on the beach stopped. Was she leaving? Relief swept over them as a bell rang out from inside the wheelhouse and the muted words, "Stop engine, aye!" followed. The wind, blowing a Force Two from the west, gently nudged the vessel to the dock. The islanders, realizing a job well done, applauded.

Damien, his appreciation complete, shouted a polite, "Ahoy the bridge!"

A grizzled old man chomping a cigar stepped out to the bridge wing. With a small amount of gruff and no small amount of tobacco juice in his beard, he called down, "Bridge, aye."

"Nice bit of seamanship, Captain."

The old salt beamed. "If it bain't be me old friend, Father Damien . Glad to see ye ain't dead."

Damien blushed and said, "Glad not to be dead," then added, "I have something for you."

The ancient mariner paused, inhaled his cigar, then exhaled a draft the size of a small cumulus cloud. "Aye, I bet ye do. I'll be down in two ticks to be receivin' it."

The captain stomped down the crude gangplank in grand, boisterous fashion and eyed the priest. Damien reached to his back and slowly withdrew the Navy colt. The sailors on deck and the lepers on dock froze. The priest eyed the man before him. "Do you recall?"

"Aye." The wind had ceased and the sea no longer lapped the hull and the dock. "I recall tellin' you to take that there Navy colt. That you'd be needin' it, and that someday you wouldn't, and on that day, I'd come ashore to collect it."

"And Captain, I am most pleased to inform you that the first part was as true as the second, and I'm as thankful for one as the other." Damien handed the pistol butt first to his friend.

"Them be some words well-spoken and..." He waved his hand to the peninsula "...some seas well

234

sailed." The seamen on deck and the lepers on deck
exhaled, each proud of the men before them. "Now,
Father, why don't ye come thee aboard? We've a new
cook from a French clipper. He's uglier than a bulldog's
grommet, but sure knows his way around a galley. We
also shipped some whiskey from a place called Ken-
tuck-ee. Right tasty bilge water it be, known to pare well
with meat, fish, poultry, grains, nuts, breakfast, legumes,
octopus, and the odd seagull or two. Come thee and
welcome aboard!"

*

Deep in the Wailau Valley, in the Colonel's domain,
the last of the insurgent lepers was dead. After
completing the task requested of them, the Colonel
executed Terry and Willy. It was a fine murder. The
Colonel broke both their massive backs and staked them
on the beach. He was disappointed, however, when the
crabs, the gannets, and the gulls feasted on them that the
two Maori failed to cry out. *Ah, well.* The Colonel turned
his gaze toward Kalaupapa, and though the vision of his
one eye was blocked by flora, fauna, and terraform, he
could see the scene unfolding at the pier and later at the
post office as clearly as if he were there. He smiled a
very satisfied smile.

*

The ship's boom swung the last of three crates to
the dock. Brother Joseph and one of the islanders helped
it land, unshackled the lading, and sent the boom
shipside. A hand from on deck shouted, "Got the invoice
for them crates addressed to one Jack Tanveer."

"I'm he. I'll sign for them."

"Nah, it's okay. I ain't touching anything what's
been touched from someone on this island." He tossed
the envelope on the dock. It landed on one of the crates.
All three of the wooden boxes were of a shape similar to

235

billiard tables but much larger in length and width. Brother Joseph opened the envelope.

My beloved Son,

I hope this letter finds you well. As your mother I drown in tears every night at the thought of the malady you have contracted, but smile every morning as I read your letters and recently the fine article of the good works you are doing.

All the neighbors say hello; your nieces and nephews, too. A great many of your classmates from Annapolis have written asking for your address. I have written back to each and everyone and have honored their requests.

Your father has retired from his law firm and has left it in the capable hands of your brothers. He has taken an interest in defeating your disease and is approaching the battle with a zeal that exceeds his previous zeal toward the law and business. As of this writing, he has embarked aboard a liner, The President Lincoln, for Copenhagen, to visit the doctor he wrote you of earlier. He will send everything he learns to our own Doctor Parker, who will send them out to you and the Honolulu Board of Health.

After Denmark, your father will board the Tsuna Maru for Japan. Dr. Parker has corresponded with a physician in Yokohama who is claiming one hundred percent success in alieving the sores and erosions of leprosy using topical oils and unguents. I pray this to be true, and I pray your father's voyages to be safe. He loves you very much.

*I was more than delighted when I heard
your friend was constructing a chapel for
his flock. Bravo! No doubt you have seen the
crates we shipped your way. Within are gifts
to Damien and yourself for the construction
of this house of God.*

Brother Joseph's curiosity bested him, and he called
over to the steamer, "Any chance us borrowing a pry bar
from you fellas for a minute?"

One of the sailors stepped inside, came out, and
tossed a pry bar to the pier. "Keep it."

Joseph pried open one of the crates and marveled at
its contents. *They are the works of a Mister John
LaForce, a Master in the painting and assemblage of
stained-glass windows. He crafts in the style of Lois
Tiffany, creating tiny mosaics and infinite shades of
color. What do you think?*

Joseph was breathless. When he regained the ability
to speak, he called out to the vessel, "Ahoy the bridge."

Captain Ross appeared on the wing, wiping his face
with a kerchief. "What be it now?"

"Begging your pardon, Captain. When you and
Father Damien finish lunch, could you come on down?
There is something here I think he'd like to see.
Something I think everyone would like to see."

By the time Damien and the captain emerged,
Joseph and the Kanaka had uncrated the windows and
leaned them vertically on the seawall. The tropical sun
and rippling sea painted beautifully upon the panes.

When Damien spotted the magnificent work, he was
breathless. As a boy, he had viewed the Façade
Windows upon the Cathedral of Chartres and
remembered thinking, *They cannot be made by the
hands of men.* But these... these lifted his soul to lofty
heights. He spoke quietly to no one and everyone.
"Behold this" he said, pointing to the first pane. "This

work depicts Saint Christopher, patron saint of travelers and sailors. What we're seeing is Christopher fording a great river with a boy on his back."

Some of the people on the beach, sensing something special, gravitated to the pier. "The boy asked to be carried across the expanse of the river, and Christopher did so without hesitation. Notice the golden halo about the boy's head as he rides upon Christopher's back?" And those on the dock stood captivated by the circle shimmering in the dappled light. "Once they were across, the boy revealed to Christopher that he had just carried the resurrection of Christ across troubled waters and that now, safely ashore, he would spread the word of God his father."

Damien pointed to the next window. "Ah," he sighed, "Saint Xavier, second only to Christ himself in spreading the word." The priest was almost giddy, reveling in his lecture and recollection. "We see Xavier kneeling in petition before Pope John the X of Portugal. The scene takes place in a palace garden outside Lisbon. Look at the glass to the east and behold how it is alight." And it was true, but it was not pigment or tone that beguiled the eye—there was something almost alive gaining in hue and albedo reflecting all points of the compass.

"Saint Xavier traveled to India, Ceylon, Java, and Japan to preach the Word. He was received as a teacher and friend throughout Asia, and even the emperor of China declared that, 'He has brought light to the world.'"

Not a sound could be heard on the dock save the soft cotton caress of the breeze and the sea gently lapping the pier. Damien continued, the happy professor. "See how the artist creates individual murals, individual scenes to bring the whole to life? Amazing be the shadows, the highlights made irregular in the changing

238

sunlight, opalescent in their own right and captured between the frames."

The lepers on the dock no longer felt their own wounded and damaged bodies. They were more alive than they'd ever been, alive amongst the scenes of great devotion and enlightenment. There was an increasing silence, a growing feeling of the divine, most especially as their gazes fell upon the last window. Damien took a few steps toward the third window. The sun brought out gold and silver strains, full of power and glory. The priest inhaled, brought his hands together, and raised them to his face, thumbs lightly upon his chin. To himself and others he said, "For this one, I have no words."

*

As he watched the vaporous scene unfolding before him, the Colonel said, "No priest, no words, and soon no place to speak them. No life..."

The murder and mutilation on his side of the valley were but mere offerings. What was soon to transpire would prove to his Master the Colonel's worth. He was a serious supplicant worthy of honoring his dark lord and synthesizing all his efforts on earth. *A bit more fun than my sack of Carthage,* he thought.

*

The windows were lovingly re-packed and horse-carted to the foundation of the future church. One of the lepers, blinded from the ravage, a man who originally hailed from Terlingua, Texas, helped Damien store the crates beneath the pole shed. The Texan said, "Damn, Father, if'n you'll excuse my language, thems were some beautiful words y'all spoke back there. I've been as blind as a Carlsbad bat since this goddamn disease, if'n you'll pardon my language, took my damn eyes away. But I'm tellin' ya right now with what you said, I could see them windows just like I had eyeballs. I thank ya."

Damien, more than a little moved, said, "Your welcome, son. Why don't we get back to the post office and retrieve our mail? If you have any that you'd like read, I'd be proud to do it."

When Damien and the Texan arrived at the post office, there were more than a few settlers about. Some were lounging on the steps finishing off the last of the monster pig, while others enjoyed rum or kava in the nearby shade.

Before Damien could climb the three steps to the post office, Brother Joseph called to him. "Father, come out to the patio. There's news."

As the two men sat, Mr. Mah brought out fresh tea and mangoes. "Good news, huh? Okay, I go back inside. Much mail to hand out."

Joseph held up a copy of the *Seattle Post-Star,* but before he could reveal the news, Damien spoke. "Has anyone seen Sean or His Honor today?"

"Sean's with Jeemo out at the judge's. Well ran dry. They're digging out a new one."

"What about their mail? I could drop it off before I turn in."

"No worries there, Father. Jeemo said he'd be along to pick it up for all of them."

"Grand. Now tell me what's in that newspaper?"

"There is an article on page four and five about us."

"About you and I?"

"About you and I and everyone on the island. It's about the new buildings, the new gardens, everything."

"Who would write such a thing?"

"Our good friend, Richard Zachary."

"Of course. I should have known."

"Well, Father, he's a very important writer; very popular, too. Not just in the States, but the world over. He never told you?"

"No, he never much spoke 'bout himself." Damien gestured to the newspaper. "May I?"

IMPRESSIONS OF THE SOUTH SEAS
Richard Zachary

To the reader: This is the first article in a planned series in which the *Seattle Post-Star* has commissioned the author to write a firsthand account of island life in the South Pacific. I will be sailing my own vessel, departing San Francisco for the Sandwich Islands, the Line Islands, the Micronesian Crescent, the Solomons, Borneo, and finally Batavia. My account begins on Molokai, a small island in the Hawaiian chain, and one I hope is of great interest to the reader...

(Molokai, Hawaii) I sailed the *White Fog* once around the entire island of Molokai before landing. I did this not in search of a suitable pier, for there were none at the time, but to get a feel for a place the outside world holds with great derision and infamy. Indeed, stamped on my nautical chart were big black letters impossible to miss: WARNING! ATTEMPT NO LANDINGS! MOLOKAI ISLAND EPIDEMIC! LEPROSY PRESENT! The reader may well ask why I chose so foreboding a place to commence the travelogue. The answer is really quite simple: I was intrigued by a place South Sea islanders refer to as "A living mausoleum."

And also upon that island I had a friend.

White Fog dropped anchor in Kalawao Cove. My friend was not there to meet me. However, a band of the islands "settlers" were. The reception I received was neither friendly nor warm. These people are viewed as "Living corpses" by the outside world, and they know it.

They live in a world not of their own choosing, banished by a people who neither care about nor understand them.

I remained aboard the vessel for several hours while members from the band attempted to locate my friend. Finally, I was hailed from the beach and informed that my friend was unavailable but had confirmed my bona fides. I was thus permitted to come ashore.

A band of male lepers greeted me as I emerged from the surf. I was received with great caring and concern, as though I were a shipwrecked sailor washing ashore or a friend returning from a long journey. They escorted me to a guesthouse meant for non-lepers, where, not surprisingly, I learned I was its first resident. I later found that such compassion and friendliness are traits shared by all the islanders, as embodied in a concept known as *Aloha*.

Make no mistake: leprosy is a horror, but lepers, contrary to popular opinion, are not horrible. Leprosy has been called "The Separating Sickness." This moniker is terrible, but terribly accurate. Settlers lose limbs and digits at a catastrophic rate, though the islander takes this for granted, almost to the point of nonchalance. Blindness is epidemic and preys on every age and either gender.

Antiseptic surgery is standard in the contiguous United States, or the "Mainland" as the Hawaiians call it, but not so on Molokai. The practice of cleansing wounds or a surgeon's hands and instruments are looked at as a joyous miracle by these lepers. Before these practices were introduced by a missionary, the death rate was quadruple what it is today.

So quickly has the concept of sanitation caught on that all the settlers whitewash their homes on a regular basis, and immaculate quarters are set aside for pneumonia patients and hospice. Should I ever fall gravely ill, I would prefer treatment on Molokai than in similar facilities in the Five Points section of New York City or Boston's Southside.

So that I may be welcome upon my return home, I would like to inform the reader and the authorities that the contagion of leprosy is not as voracious as perceived. The disease cannot be contracted from "Breathing the same air as a leper," or from simple skin contact. Thoroughly washing oneself with hygienic soap after simple contact, as well as daily baths (which I enjoyed in the blue Pacific), are sufficient for self-immunization.

The scenery here is staggeringly beautiful and epitomizes one's perception of a South Seas paradise. The settlement was built upon a peninsula. On the east bank is Kalawao Cove, the first point of immigration in the early days of the colony. It is crescent-shaped and fringed by a white sandy beach. The sea shimmers when viewed from the beach, but when swimming is crystal clear, limitless to vision, with fish and coral the colors of which would embarrass a rainbow. It is so quiet, one can hear one's heartbeat, and at Kalawao Cove the heart beats slowly.

Not so, though, on the western side of the island. Here, Pacific currents from the west meet the northeast trade winds in a mighty collision of elements. The angry blue seas heap high and crash upon the shore with the excitement of a Broadway opening and the suddenness of an artillery barrage. When the sea meets the land, the water shatters into spray and vaults itself one hundred feet into the air with an elegant violence.

The entire low-lying jut is surrounded by The Wall of Pali, the world's tallest sea cliff. This writer has sailed the inside passage to Alaska, where the fjords are numerous and spectacular, but compared to The Wall of Pali, the fjords are a children's playground. Its massive buttes, blue from the reflection of sea and sky, are verdant with infinite vegetation. Thousand-foot waterfalls plunge from its heights, some a needle of white, some a roaring road of foaming froth. Above The Wall, the island is uninhabited, but legend has it that a lost tribe of Polynesians live there, though no one has ever seen them. The valleys that bisect The Wall are lush with all manner of tropic fruit, including olive trees said to have been planted by Spanish navigators. Even the names of these valleys carry a melody both tropic and mystic: Papalau, the Pelekuna, and the Wailau.

At the base of The Wall, at the draw of the valleys and penetrating into the sea, is the Kalaupapa Peninsula. This triangle of earth is composed of sand dunes, rolling hills, large streams, and an extinct volcano, and is home to over one thousand lepers, kokua (their helpers), and one missionary. Some of the settlers live native style in the deep valleys, while others live in caves. At one time in the not-too-distant past, everyone lived outdoors, prey to wind, weather, and wildlife. At present, and contrary to the rumors I hear stateside, the majority of lepers domicile in neat, whitewashed bungalows, some with roofs of tin, others of shingle, most with thatch. Walkways of crushed white oyster shell act as sidewalks to the homes, and a hard-packed dirt traverses the entire promontory. Many yards contain small plot gardens and livestock. At each cottage, a friendly word is given and refreshment offered. There is a small whitewashed building for orphaned boys and a similar building being constructed for orphaned girls. Planted throughout the island, serving as wind breaks, are Norfolk pines and Royal palm trees. When the wind blows, they sway as a person entranced, towering sentinels of peace.

Seven days after my arrival, I met the agent provocateur of all this industry and charity, Father Damien deVuester, a native of Belgium and a Catholic missionary. This diminutive and devout man *volunteered* for this posting on Molokai. A magnanimous and deeply caring individual, he is the sole inhabitant on Molokai not afflicted with the most reverentially feared disease in the history of the world. It seems in his good deeds comes good fortune and God's favor.

Over the course of my stay, I enjoyed many fine conversations with this man of God. I told him that less-informed people believe Molokai to be an "Island of Horrors". Damien took this information graciously and indicated that in the past things were "difficult," but of late, were much improved.

"You may have heard," he explained, "that a natural disaster struck the other Hawaiian Islands." And indeed, months before my departure, the Governor General of the Hawaiian Territory reported to the world that the Islands' industry and agriculture had been devastated by fire. The Hawaiian Growers Association indicated these fires, originating from lighting strikes, had run rampant and laid waste to entire plantations. Father Damien told me only Molokai was spared the ravage. He said "Only by the grace of God were we untouched."

Not only were they untouched, but the only plantations not to suffer damage on the other islands are owned by lepers currently residing on Molokai: Judge Lae, a native of Hawaii, and Mister Sean Corcoran, late of County Donegal, Ireland. The former was a strong advocate for the rights of Hawaiian peoples and opposed banishment under leper laws.

When he himself was diagnosed with leprosy, he willingly presented himself for exile. Judge Lae owns the second (now first) largest pineapple plantation in the islands. Owing to the fires, Mr. Corcoran is now the owner of the largest coffee plantation in Hawaii. Both men have very generously donated a large portion of their profits to improving the quality of life on Molokai. Now, the monthly supply steamer from Honolulu brings building and infrastructure materials so that the settlers may enjoy our common comforts.

Much has been said about the charitable work of Father Damien. There have been many glowing accolades as people in the world take notice of his efforts, but, as in any grand endeavor, there are detractors. Such miscreants have categorized the good father as "No different than any other settler." This is a less-than-subtle lie. The priest works, prays, builds, and doctors daily, the scourge and specter of leprosy looming over him like a diseased sword of Damocles. To minister as he does under such a threat is nothing short of miraculous. From the moment he came ashore at Kalawao Cove, he embraced the people. He spews no fire and brimstone, nor does he proselytize. He embraces all interpretations of the Almighty. Everyone in his flock is a child of God.

Damien cannot purge the island of rotting limbs as St. Patrick did Ireland of snakes, nor has he cured infant mortality or blindness, but his good works have purged this place of despair and brought his "Children" into the light of the world.

Throughout the South Seas, there is a code that describes a way of life. It is known as Aloha. Aloha is as uncomplicated as it is beautiful. Children learn that they have a responsibility not to themselves, but to the poor or oppressed. Molokai is isolated, but its residents do not live in isolation. People here live as an extended family, enduring the disappointments and sharing the joys of family life. This is Aloha. There is a concept within Aloha known as "Hili", which means to string flowers together as a lei. It symbolizes bringing diverse peoples of every age and color, in all manner of despair and happiness, into the beautiful fragrance of life. And it is here, two degrees east of the International Date Line, on the Island of Molokai, in the Hawaiian Trust Territory, that the spirit of Aloha is most alive and most richly felt.

It is hoped the reader has enjoyed this first installment of *Impressions of the South Seas*. Fair winds prevailing, the next missive will come to you from the island of Saipan via undersea cable to San Francisco. Till then—ALOHA!

*

Damien exhaled as though all his cares had sailed over the horizon. "It is the second time today words have failed me." Across the table, Brother Joseph took a long draught of his tea and gave an understated smile. "Yep, my boy Richie's still got it. Do you know what this means, Father?"

"I do. Now the Church and the world will know we are not monsters here."

"More than that. From now on, your requests to the Board of Health for food and clothes will no longer go unanswered. When we beg the Navy for a doctor, they won't be able to ignore us. There will be volunteers and donations arriving from around the world. All your projects, all your dreams for the people of this island, will come true."

"I suppose… you could be right." No one, living or dead on the island of Molokai, had ever seen Father Damien relaxed. Calm yes, happy at times, but never was he known to release himself from his self-induced pressure to accomplish. He slouched slightly, put his arm over the back of his chair, and tipped his teacup to Brother Joseph as if in a New Year's toast. As he did, a man appeared on the patio. It was the ex-sailor, the one who first used the baths Damien, Jeemo, and Sean had built.

"Father Damien, you need to come out to the baths." Delivered in monotone, the words were numb and foreboding.

The three men left the patio in a hurry.

But only Brother Joseph noticed that no one milled about the post office, or the beach, or the pier. The fire that cooked the pig was extinguished, the steamer gone, the music silenced. He urged his companions to double their pace.

CHAPTER FIFTEEN

Cresting the top of a sand dune, Father Damien saw Mrs. Leander frozen, pity deep in her eyes. His fear rose with each settler he passed, a gauntlet of mourning glances.

Damien no longer felt his footsteps or the animation of his body. He only heard his breath, himself a mere vessel. When he rounded the turn to the bathhouses, he saw something he thought was only in his mind.

But as he looked to Joseph and the old sailor, he knew the vision to be true.

He noticed, absurdly, that the wood used was from a monkeypod tree, and that the vertical and crossbeams were stout. The nails were the same as those used to construct the baths. In the seminary, Damien read how the Roman army constructed such devices, and his carpenter's eye told him the height and spacing (in cubit units) was correct. The directions had been followed to the letter. A thought sailed so quickly through his mind that he momentarily forgot it—who but a religious scholar or demon would know such a thing? But as his denial diminished, the truth took root. Damien sank to his knees. The ankles of all three were correctly crossed and properly nailed, as were the outstretched hands. There was even a liturgical lance wound inflicted post-mortem between the right third and fourth ribs.

The priest was not as disturbed by the naked bodies upon the wood as he was the hair of the men slowly blowing in the wind like dead ryegrass. What did transcend his reality was the final and obscene mockery; The letters "I" painted atop each crucifix and above the lifeless heads of Sean, Jeemo and Judge Lae.

The islanders continued to arrive in clumps, silent and muted, to witness a scene previously played out two thousand years before. In the last version, soldiers played dice games, merchants sold wares, and onlookers chatted. Here, there was only silence and profound grief. The empathy of deep and poignant distress penetrated everyone in attendance en solamente, en masse.

Damien, upon one knee, forced himself to look upon the crucifixion, and as he did, his soul hollowed out like a violent wind blasting through a rotten palm tree. Closing his eyes and nodding his head, he regained himself. *The island,* he thought, *this* island.

Brother Joseph recalled how he had once been a hard man, a man of war. He even recalled witnessing crucifixions in the Philippines, a favorite pastime of Spanish mercenaries when engaging prisoners of war. He recalled acting with violence and frothing vengeance. Now, upon this beach, upon this island, he carried no thoughts of vengeance or human destruction. His only meditations were of sympathy for his friends upon the cross and commiseration with his friend upon one knee— a friend who might be wrecked, whose soul might have taken flight. Brother Joseph shimmied up the back of the first cross and pulled the nail from Sean's feet, then one nail each from his palm. Two lepers caught the body and lowered it to the ground. Jeemo and the judge were respectfully brought to earth in the same manner.

Upon The Wall of Pali, upon a ledge that could not be reached, stood the Kahuna ʻana woman. She watched the scene in silence much the same way another woman witnessed it two thousand years before. The woman of antiquity grieved calmly and in silence the rest of her life. The reaction of the Kahuna ʻana woman would be altogether different.

The sun rose and set three times upon the beach where Damien knelt. His head remained bowed, his whispers, his prayers, never stopping. After a fourth day, a woman brought out a calabash of water. It went untouched. Mr. Mah brought him a blue fish steamed in lime juice. It, too, lay untouched. And so it went day after day, the islanders bringing meals, blankets, and tobacco, all untouched. There had even been torches lit about the little man to ward off wild boar and cobras, but the boar and cobra were unafraid of torches. They chose not to come for their own reasons.

Brother Joseph brought an urn of fresh water to his friend every day, though it remained as untouched as the food. On the seventh day, while drawing water from a pool at the base of The Wall of Pali, Joseph noticed a small steamer on this side of the horizon closing fast. He wondered why he had not seen it sooner, and after delivering water to Damien, hurried to the pier.

When it arrived the mate on deck said to Joseph, "Is you the guy that can sign for all this?" Joseph absently nodded. The *offloading* commenced.

Damien not only prayed on the beach, but reflected on his life in its totality, and it was so clear…

…Apprehension when first arriving on Molokai, then backwards to joy upon learning his request to be a missionary in Hawaii had been granted. Then back

again to his voyage out... His wonder at the high seas...
The immensity of America... The thrill of Ellis Island...
The Atlantic... Becoming a priest... and backwards
still...

The sublime grind of the seminary
Marseille and Lyon and his father teaching him
about on bridge-building and construction
Carefree summers in Wilgenhof
Chasing butterflies as a boy
Morning mass with his mother
Lunches of cold rabbit in mustard sauce
Sparkling water
Starched blue skies
A brief lull as infinity paused to gaze upon its son,
then...

A toddler rolling unsteady to his first steps
An infant's laughter
A lullaby in his mother's arms
Baptism after birth...

...And now birth. A muted alluring flow of warm
waters both within and without. Decreasing hues of a
falling sunset enveloped him, the temptation to yield to
the eclipsing comfort was powerful...

On the beach, twin girls in white summer frocks and
blue trim walked hand in hand. They were precocious
and determined. "Do you think he will like the food?"

"Of course he will, silly. Mommy cooked it." They
trudged through the sand to where Damien knelt.

The twins holding hands and Damien's supper
rushed to the unmoving and kneeling priest. The smaller
of the two, holding cooked pig and poi wrapped in
banana leaves, said, "Father, we sure hope you like..."
but before she could finish, she stumbled headlong into
the priest.

As he reached a hand out to the comforting
darkness, a gust of light entered his soul. He ceased his

252

whisperings, opened his eyes for the first time in seven days, and looked up. Between the sun, the sky, and himself the faces of two little girls looked down. One fought back tears as if she had done something wrong; the other beamed, holding sand-encrusted pieces of pork and poi. "Father Damien," she bubbled, "you should try this. Mommy made it."

His hand, outstretched toward eternal comfort, withdrew to cover his heart. Damien yielded to the light.

Word spread quickly that he had risen. As he walked the beach with the little ones, lepers came to greet him. He was offered flowers, picked hastily along the way, and cups of cool fresh water. He drank deeply the liquid and deeply the spirit. Settlers with only stumps for hands patted his back; those without speech came to wish him well, and the blind staggered in, greeting him back to life.

He had endured a crisis of the spirit divine, but had prevailed. He had received the gift of misery in all its largesse, and had now become one with the spirit. Now his people were one with him. When he finally caught sight of Brother Joseph, Damien said simply, "All is well my son."

The two men sat on the stone foundation that one day would support the church. A few gulls whirled overhead and a light breeze swayed the grass around them. "Joseph, were they buried properly?"

"Yes, Father. I buried Sean myself in the cemetery and planted clover and hibiscus atop the grave. I wrote his family and requested a headstone. I spared them the details."

Damien nodded. "And of Jeemo and the judge?"

"Both were buried in the Hawaiian fashion, though in different form. Some of the old seamen hollowed the trunk of an Acacia Koa tree and carved a small outrigger canoe. Jeemo's body was placed within and pushed to the surf. A dozen or so of the strongest paddled on wave boards alongside. They escorted the canoe to the edge of the Thunder Road current and said their prayers to the sea. The current took hold, and Jeemo was carried off toward the setting sun."

Damien gave a wistful smile. "Beautiful. And Judge Lae?"

"It was different for him. I helped sew the shroud in which he was encased. There was a ceremony and viewing period outside the cave."

"Cave?"

"Over toward the west side of the peninsula. The islanders claim it was once a place for the burial of Hawaiian kings."

"I didn't know there was a cave over that way."

"Nor did I. Do you recall telling that place where you found some artifacts—bone fishhooks, ladies' earrings?"

"Yes, of course."

"The cave is close by."

Damien tilted his head down, shaking it slightly. "Go on."

"His Honor will be placed within and a sentinel will remain in perpetuity outside the entrance."

Damien's astonished look asked the obvious question. "It is true, Father. The sentinel will remain beneath a lean-to. The lepers will bring him food and water. When he passes, another will replace him. It is a custom they take quite seriously."

Damien recalled something his mother once told him: *Mourning is to honor the dead; bereavement is to console the living.*

So be it, he thought. Then to Brother Joseph, he said, "I will visit the cemetery, the seashore, and the cave tomorrow."

"Yes, Father. I realize it is a difficult time, but there are some other matters that require your attention. They are matters of some import."

Damien smiled, ready for any challenge. "Of course."

Death and suffering were the métier of the Colonel, though this last bit was not for enjoyment alone. It was meant as an offering to his Master in preparation for the favor he was about to request. He walked into the surf, and as he did so, the sharks within distance ceased swimming, dead from electrification. So did the other fish of the sea, and even coral lost its brilliance, turning ash gray. The Colonel raised his arms to the sky, then lowered them to the sea. Palms facing outward, he said, *Oh, quaeso tenebris dominus...*

It was conceived where the ocean was deep, eighteen thousand feet below the gentle swell. In an area known as the Ring of Fire did it gestate incomprehensible power at incomprehensible depths. At the bottom lay *two* masses of the geologic known to later scientists as "plates". The world over these plates struggle against each other, two massive walls grinding, yearning throughout deep time for even the smallest horizontal give-way. Throughout the course of human events, the plates have been denied movement, except when acted upon by some event or entity.

Standing in the surf off Molokai Island, the Colonel's body began to tremble. *Pariet irarum munditiam...*

One of the plates relinquished both its advance and its opposition and sank beneath the other. The second plate, almost two thousand miles long and running north to south, rose an astonishing ninety feet. It displaced a column of water that same height to the very surface of the ocean. A seawall briskly raced across the Pacific.

The monster was alive.

Damien gazed in wonder at the beach and the pier. "You mean to tell me the steamer is arriving every day?" Brother Joseph nodded. "Or at least every other day. I reserved a piece of beach for building and medical supplies and miscellaneous items."

"Miscellaneous?" In response, Joseph handed Damien a stack of letters.

> *Dear Father Damien,*
> *Please accept this four hundred feet of piping to help you build Molokai.*
> *Fraternally,*
> *Brotherhood of Pipefitters Local 256 Carbondale, Pa.*

> *Dear Father Damien,*
> *We do so hope you enjoy the enclosed painting Madonna at the Shore by Elio Sobrero. Perhaps when your church is built, you may find somewhere nice to display it.*
> *Sincerely,*
> *The Ladies Mission and Garden Club of Turnbridge Wells, United Kingdom*

> *To the Mission Father, Molokai Island, Hawaiian Trust Territory,*
> *These one thousand blankets each have a weaved history of our people. We are in sympathy of your endeavors.*
> *Council of Elders, Navaho Nations*

> *Dear Father Damien,*
> *Please accept this donation of six dollars to help you help the lepers.*

Your Friends,
Miss Lannon's fourth grade class,
Baldwin, NY

And on and on by the stack.

Father Damien was so moved that he vowed to re-double his efforts. He gave up his sunrise meditations to move building supplies to the sites before anyone on the island stirred. He reckoned himself physically fit and therefore denied himself lunch, preferring instead to whitewash the boys' orphanage and plan the girls' orphanage in this newfound hour per day. The one thing he would not deny himself was visiting the resting place of his three friends.

Damien knew roughly the location of the cave in which the judge was interred, but could not for the life of him find it. As his first stop would be The Garden of The Dead, the cemetery in which his Irish friend (as he had taken to calling Sean because he could not bear to think his name without crushing anguish) was buried, he would stop by Mrs. Kepihe's house, the mother of the twins who brought Damien back to the world. She was also one of the storytellers of the peninsula and a keeper of Hawaiian myths. Damien was sure she could provide directions.

"Father, you need only go where The Wall of Pali meets the peninsula and the sea on
    the west side. Boulder there mostly flat on top.
Climb on boulder, reach hands in brush, find
    small steps. Steps be many, long time climbing.
They take you up to cave."

Thank you, Mrs. Kepihe."

"Dat's okay, Father. Know you love Judge. We all love Judge. Father?"

"Yes, my dear?"

257

"I no feel good today." She passed a hand over her lower abdomen. "Stomach tight." He nodded. "Okay, you take girls today; watch. I take rest."

"Of course, ma'am, I'd be delighted." And with the tiny lepers in tow, Damien began his first visit to say his final goodbyes to his three friends.

Damien looked over the oceans horizon in memory of Jeemo. It was hard. The visit to the grave of Sean was hard, too, but the twins made it easier. They gamboled, held each other's hands, and gathered flowers. Before leaving, they sang a Hawaiian hymn, two angels with a single beautiful voice.

"What are you doing, Father?" She caught him in a reverie

"Oh, Mili, saying goodbye to a dear friend."

"You mean Jeemo?' said her sister.

"Yes, Lili."

The little girl reached to the sand and picked up a small seashell. She offered it to Damien. "Here, this for him."

"Why don't you place it in the sea? Jeemo would like that." As she did, her sister, not to be outdone, placed a starfish next to the shell. The calm surf left both undisturbed.

"Father Damien?"

"Yes, Mili?"

"Mommy said you want to know where the big boulder with the flat top is."

Lili said, "It's right here." She pointed to a boulder green and shiny with seaweed. "There's a hole halfway. Just put your foot in, climb to top, find stairs."

Out of the mouths of babes, he thought. He lifted first Lili, then Mili to the top, then knelt to remove his sandals. In doing so, he noticed something curious. In the sand was a small polished shape, white in color, the size of an index finger. He picked it up, curious—it was a small carving of a shark. He looked down and saw other bone carvings: buttons, fishhooks, shells... a fish flopping in the sand gasping for oxygen, then another and another. Damien was confused. *Was the sea receding?*

And the monster roared. A wall of water mighty and tall, thousands of miles long, charged unchallenged across the Pacific. In deep water, the monster is *fearsome*; in shallow, ferocious. As it approached the sloping shoals, the shallow water was drawn into its maw, the taste angering it and causing it to rise, to roar, to bare its teeth...

The Colonel walked farther into the sea. He ceased his ancient prayer and remained still. No human could hear the ugly and distant roar, but he exalted as the symphony built. The Colonel soon stepped smoothly from the surf and calmly shook himself off just as the incomprehensible wall of water smashed into Kalaupapa.

Damien's eyes followed the receding sea to the horizon. At first, it appeared a thin black line north to south, but it grew in height as it approached. He watched, mystified. It was the absence of reality that stunned Damien into movement. "Little ones," he said to the twins, "climb the steps as fast as you can. Do not look down, do not look back. I shall follow!" He placed his right foot into the hole in the boulder and grabbed for a handhold, but the rock was slick with seaweed. He fell back upon the beach.

The wall of water turned from sky blue to deep purple to black as it began to shoal. Although Damien did not know what a tsunami was, he was certain what he was witnessing was not an act of God.

The mind records the past as permanent. Its images are indelible and perceived to be reality. Richard Zachary exhaled an audible gasp when the schooner rounded Okala Rock and entered Kalawao Cove. The cove, fixed in his mind as the perfect example of a Pacific paradise, lay before him devastated and unrecognizable, a coastal ruin. The white sand beach formerly shaped in an easy crescent was all but gone, now a narrow horizontal strip littered with debris. The sea no longer lapped the shore, now a bloated swell sloshing, haphazard, pushing oceanic garbage inland and sucking sand to sea. The blue-green jungle wall of lanta and bamboo had been scoured away, leaving only a rude slag of pummeled volcanic scree.

He was so jarred, he decided not to land till the next day, perhaps hoping he would awake once again in paradise. He spent the night aboard ship, writing in his journal with a less steady hand than he was used to.

Before first light, Richard filled a canteen, packed some hard tack and tinned sardines, sharpened his Gerber knife, and made a final check of the lay of his anchor. Satisfied, he dove into the sea and swam for shore, fearfully willing to embrace the landfall torn asunder.

The trail he frequently used on Molokai was blocked, heaped upon with thousands of tons of decomposing seaweed. He could either scale the muck, scale The Wall of Pali, then move horizontally across its face, or swim half a mile to regain the trail east of the seaweed and rocks. He chose the swim, though he noticed no fish or colorful coral reefs, and that the water was no longer clean and embracing, but tepid and slimy.

Emerging, from the repellant water, Richards saw no signs of life—no birds in the sky, nothing scurrying in the bush. He looked east to Kalaupapa for signs of humans, but saw nothing. He walked on with great trepidation, forcing himself to hold on to a glimmer of hope, but he only saw more and more signs of destruction: broken furniture, wagon wheels, uprooted ebony trees. He came across the corpse of a mule wide-eyed and bloated, then another and another, carcasses torn, entrails askew. There were beached and dead whales, dolphins, countless seagulls rotted and gray. But among all this viscera there were no carrion, no flies. *Where were the flies,* he wondered?

Richard Zachary began the hike up the extinct Kaunako crater, one of the highest vantage points upon the promontory, to search for signs of life from its rim.

The last time the writer scaled this crater had been with his friend, Jack Tanveer. Jack told him the crater was the domain of the Night Marchers, long dead Hawaiian warriors who nightly emerged from the bottomless lake to roam the precipices. Back then, Richard remembered feeling "something" odd. Last time, the wind blew with hurricane force; now the sky was void, dead silent, as though he had been cast back into a time before wind, before weather.

"Hello, Richard."

The writer simultaneously drew his knife, choked back a scream, and spun so fast he almost lost his balance. "Jack!?"

"Well, it's Brother Joseph these days, but I'll let that one slide."

Brother Joseph and his friend sat at ease watching a crackling campfire. "How many do you reckon, Joseph?"

"Over a thousand."

"That's damn near the whole settlement."

"We estimate less than fifty left." The writer shook his head in disbelief. "Any bodies?"

"Yes and no. Most were carried out to sea when the wave receded. Even some of the survivors were carried out, but clung to debris, then washed in with the corpses."

"You, too?"

"No, I was in the judge's tower scouting for boar when I saw it roll in. Didn't believe it at first, but when I saw the ebony and monkeypod trees snapping like match sticks, I knew I was on hell's front porch."

"Whadja do?"

"I jumped from the tower to The Wall of Pali, holding onto vines and shimmying like a squirrel. I didn't even see the thing, Rich. It rolled underneath me. After it receded, I climbed down and walked out over the valley."

"How about the judge?"

Brother Joseph relayed to his friend all the details of the deaths of Sean, Jeemo, and Judge Lae, including the impact on Damien.

"What of him? Did he make it?"

Joseph eyed his friend calmly.

"Fire's dying, Rich. Let's get some shuteye."

*

For two months, the Colonel remained inert under a ton of muck and detritus. One random morning when the first ray of light split night into day, he exploded from the mass and rose. He stood in the valley, naked and burnt. No patch upon his eye, the socket black and limitless. He walked not propelled by ligament or limbs, but by hatred and revenge.

The Colonel took little notice of his surroundings as he went from walk to trot to full run. In fact, he noticed nothing, his mind set on a pure bloodletting, ugly and brutish, starting with the priest. He'd slaughter all but one, so the survivor could live to tell the world. The

Colonel allowed himself a smile, confident no human could stop him. He was right.

*

Rich said, "What are those large circles of ashes?"

"The tsunami carried some of our livestock to sea, but most drowned on land. We were worried about a cholera outbreak like at Pearl."

"Pearl has cholera?"

"Yes. I'm glad you didn't land there. Cholera is epidemic, and martial law has been declared. You probably would have been shot. Anyway, we decided to burn all the deceased livestock. The piles you're seeing are the result."

"The piles are everywhere. I don't recall that many animals."

His friend hesitated, then said, "It wasn't all animals."

"Eh?"

"A great many of our people were swept into the sea, including the dead." Richards gave him a look of incomprehension. "So powerful was the wave when it first made landfall, it unearthed and exhumed those buried in The Garden of the Dead. That's ten years of internment. Days after the monster struck, most of the bodies washed back to shore."

"So you..."

"The Coast Guard sailed to the Kalaupapa side and rolled tents, barrels of lime juice, and kerosene to shore. We cremated all that washed on shore. The health hazard to the living was just too great. Damien was loathe to do so, but..."

"So Damien is alive?"

Brother Joseph nodded. "Yes, he was visiting the grave of Judge Lae. His Honor's tomb is a third of the way up The Wall of Pali. He and two little girls, and the docent of the tomb, were spared."

263

"A miracle."

"More of a fulfillment, I should say."

"Jack..."

"Please call me Joseph."

"I'm sorry. Brother, when I left 'Frisco, I wanted to write a story about the Pacific, but this..." He waved his hand in a sweeping motion across the promontory "...this is the story of the Pacific."

*

"You're telling me he doesn't sleep?"

"Not since the crucifixions. When he came in from the wilderness, we expected him to be shattered and destroyed."

"And?"

"Just the opposite. It was as though he were reborn. There was a light about him, and he drew remarkable strength from every difficulty. When bandaging the ulcers of survivors, he was buoyantly chatty. When we butchered a beached Orca, he spent twenty-four hours in the guts sawing and passing out slabs of meat, all while singing."

The writer exhaled. "He's has turned misery into a life force."

On the Kalaupapa side, some beach grass tried to push up from the soil. Richard took a long pull from his canteen and handed it to Brother Joseph. A wind arrived, a gust from the east. "Strange," said Jack. "I haven't felt the wind since I landed."

"No, nor has there been one since the wave hit."

They crossed over a dry streambed and crested a slight rise where the church came into view. The writer commented, "I have great difficulty believing it survived."

"It didn't survive intact. Two of the four walls were washed away, as were the stairs and two of the stained-

264

glass windows my mother sent. The stone masonry of the foundation is what saved it."

"Brother, this promontory has been decimated, pounded like the devil's own anvil. How is it a clapboard church survives?"

"First off, it's hard for the eye to notice because the rise is gradual, but its location is the highest point on the peninsula."

"What made you build there?"

"It wasn't my choice. Damien chose the spot."

"How did he know?"

Brother Joseph ignored the question. "The wave came from the west. The Wailau Valley took the brunt of it, filling up like a trough. As it mauled its way across, the land wounded it. It lost energy, transforming from a monstrous tidal wave to vicious flood. When it reached St. Mary's, it was sick and dying, a bloated, arrogant swell. Its last act in life was to punch out the walls of the church, a childish reminder it had been there."

Only nine of the twenty tents encircling the remains of the church remained occupied. The residents of the other eleven perished in the days after the tsunami. Brother Joseph and Richard Zachary sat down at a community table just outside the ring of tents. The table was a crude affair cobbled together with driftwood and old rags. "I thought we'd have breakfast. Before mass, there's something I want to show you."

There weren't any utensils left on the island, nor pots to cook from. One of the kerosene barrels the Coast Guard floated ashore that split in the surf served as cauldron for the survivors' repast. Breakfast today was mollusk and shark entrails served on a bed of seaweed. Richard Zachary enquired if he was to serve himself, but Brother Joseph told him someone would be around. He reminded his friend not to start eating till everyone was served. A woman used a sea shell as a ladle to spoon the meal onto flaps of seaweed held by Mili and Lili. The little ones stomped purposely about the table, then so served, sat down themselves.

A young lady spoke in Hawaiian, and breakfast was served. There was animated conversation and even some backslapping. No one took notice they were eating half-cooked fish guts, or that they were living in sodden tents. If the lepers of Molokai realized they were an endangered species, they did so with brave faces and hearts filled with joy.

*

The Colonel rounded the south rim of the crater and spit in memory of the Night Marchers. He then stopped for a moment, not to take a breather, as he didn't respirate, but to plan. How would he kill the priest? Something soviet? Not too modern… medieval perhaps? Too boring. Then a thought. *Ah, yes, the Inquisition. How apropos.*

*

After breakfast, the lepers splashed into the sea for ablutions, then to their tents to freshen for mass.

All that was left standing were the east and south walls. The north and west were carried out to sea, and the roof collapsed on the remaining walls before caving in altogether a few days later. The pew benches and flooring were dismantled for the tents. Joseph led his friend up the rebuilt stairs laid from sea smooth rocks. Once in the roofless church, the writer stopped. "That stained-glass window behind the altar is breathtaking."

"The best is yet to come."

Between the communion railing and the front of the pew benches was a large gap running the width of the church. Richard looked at the floor and once again stopped. "How?"

Brother Joseph said nothing, allowing his friend to revel in the moment. The writer's eyes beheld something that couldn't be: dolphins swimming on the floor, blue and white creatures purposeful and happy. They undulated naturally in a light blue hue, sunfish and minnows flickering around them. "Is it a vision? A miracle?"

"We thought so at first. In fact, settlers stayed here for days watching it."

"Well, if not a miracle, how the h…"

"Look at the glass behind the altar." And indeed beneath the visage of the Virgin were subtle glass cuts of dolphins and fish. Richard held his hands out in a gesture of confusion. "C'mon" his friend said, "I'll show you." They went behind the altar, and Brother Joseph pointed. "We believe there's not just one pane, but hundreds of panes joined together. The dolphins and the fish don't exactly overlap, and their positions are ever so slightly different. Don't forget, the sun never stops moving. As it rises in the east, it casts its rays into a slightly different picture each time, the glass reflecting the illusion of movement every single moment of the day."

"How could the artist have known the vision would lay upon the floor and be in such perfect consonance with its surroundings?"

"I think that's the miracle here. Or at least one of them."

"I see you two are admiring our dolphins," said Father Damien. "Welcome back, Mr. Zachary." The writer was taken aback. Contrary to his expectations, the priest was not haggard or beaten. Quite the contrary. He looked ten years younger. He wasn't even wearing his spectacles. The two men embraced. "Nice to see you again, my son. Will you be staying a bit longer?"

"True enough, sir. Fact is, I'm never leaving."

Damien offered an indulging smile. "Never is a long time, my friend."

"Father, it is my int…" His words stopped abruptly. The three men snapped their attention to the back of the church.

The Colonel stood at the top of the stairs where the back door once was. His naked body was burnt black, hairless, ash emanating slightly from his mouth. His one eye gleamed with the satisfaction of obtaining a long-awaited goal. A smug smile formed on his lips, then suddenly rescinded into neutrality.

Just a step below, and behind him, stood the Kahuna 'ana woman. The Colonel turned and advanced, vitriolic hatred and fury in his eyes, then froze.

His paralysis was unintended; he tried putting one foot before the other but could not. The woman whispered and the arms of the Colonel froze, though he was able to turn his torso. As he did, he saw the lepers gathering in a circle around him. With practiced arrogance he procured a snide smile. Mili and Lili approached, both holding a single object between them—a small squirming squid which they dropped at the Colonel's feet.

A silver-haired Hawaiian, ancient and powerfully built, likewise stood before the paralyzed entity and squashed the squid beneath his feet, grinding it into the sand as he turned his back and left. The Colonel lost movement of his torso, his smug smile fading as the Kahuna whispered, the arrogant smile on his mouth frozen into a frightened half smirk. Damien knelt upon the chapel floor alongside the light play of the reflecting dolphins and began to pray in Latin.

At Kalawao Cove, the Pacific lapped gently upon the shore; on the other side of the peninsula at Kalaupapa the surf pounded the coast exploding blue sea into the air…

... and at the half built St. Mary Church, the circle of lepers closed. Brother Joseph stood in front of the Colonel and said, "There is a star directly above your head. Even if you could move, you wouldn't be able to see it in the daylight, but it's always there. It's called Hokule 'a, and it never sets. It remains above the heads of these people ever watching, ever watchful."

The Kahuna woman spoke in full voice, though in a Hawaiian dialect not heard in centuries. The Colonel felt the bones and membranes in his cheek soften. One of his cheekbones collapsed, and the socket with no eye stretched and ripped, his body still frozen while his remaining eye circled and darted in terror. His digits elongated and separated. It was within him; the bacillus leprae. Blindness ensued, the single eye becoming opaque; then heat, suffocation...

The Kahuna 'ana, once again whispered the words, "Wa hei moe." The being that was the Colonel folded into ash, wisping wildly away in the northeast trade wind.

After a moment Damien rose and said, "E nominae padre, espiritu sanctu," offering the sign of the cross. He smiled calmly and called the lepers to mass, looking forward to the celebration of life.

The End

EPILOGUE

This story is historical fiction based in part on the life and works of Father Damien DeVeuster, a Catholic priest and missionary who served at great cost to his health, the lepers of Molokai. The following is some information on his life.

Excerpts from a letter by Robert Louis Stevenson to the Reverend William Hyde of Honolulu:

Sir—It may probably occur to you that we have met, and visited and conversed; on my side, with interest. You may remember that you have done me several courtesies, for which I was prepared to be grateful. But there are duties which come before gratitude, and offences which justly divide friends, far more acquaintances. Your letter to the Reverend H.B. Gauge is a document which, in my sight, if you had filled me with bread when I was starving, if you had sat up to nurse my father when he lay a-dying, would yet absolve me from the bonds of gratitude. You know enough, doubtless, of the process of canonization to be aware that, a hundred years after the death of Damien, there will appear a man charged with the painful office of the Devil's Advocate. After that noble brother of mine, and all frail clay, shall have lain a century at rest, one shall accuse, one defend him. The circumstance is unusual that the devil's advocate should be a volunteer, should be a member of a sect immediately rival, and should make haste upon himself his ugly office ere the bones are cold; unusual, and of a taste which I shall leave my readers free to qualify; unusual, and to me inspiring. If I have at all learned the trade of using words to convey truth and to arouse emotion, you have at last furnished me with a subject. For it is in the interest of all mankind, and the cause of public decency in every quarter of the world, not only that Damien [DeVeuster] should be righted, but that you and your letter should be displayed at length, in their true colours, to the public eye.

To do this properly, I must begin by quoting you at large: I shall then proceed to criticize your utterance from several points of view, divine and human, in the course of which I shall attempt to draw again, and with more specification, the character of the dead saint whom it has pleased you to vilify: So much being done, I shall say farewell to you forever.

[To] "Rev. H.B. Gauge.

Dear Brother—In answer to your inquiries about Father Damien, I can only reply that we who knew the man are surprised at the extravagant newspaper laudations, as if he was a most saintly philanthropist. The simple truth is, he was a coarse, dirty man, head strong and bigoted. He was not sent to Molokai but went without orders; did not stay at the leper settlement (before he became one himself) but circulated freely over the whole island (less than half the island is devoted to lepers), and he came often to Honolulu. He had no hand in the reforms and improvements inaugurated, which were the work of our Board of Health, as occasion required and means were provided. He was not a pure man in his relations with women, and the leprosy of which he died should be attributed to his vices and carelessness. Others have done much for the lepers, our own ministers, the government physicians, and so forth, but never with the Catholic idea of meriting eternal life.—Yours, etc.,

C.M. Hyde"

I know I am touching here upon a nerve acutely sensitive.

You having failed, and Damien succeeded, I marvel it should not have occurred to you that you were doomed to silence; that when you had been outstripped in that high rivalry, and sat inglorious in the midst of your wellbeing, in your pleasant room- and Damien, crowned with glories and horrors, toiled and rotted in that pigsty under the cliffs of Kalawao—you, the elect who would not, were the last man on earth to collect and propagate gossip on the volunteer who would and did.

...we will (if you please) go hand-in-hand through the different phrases of your letter, and candidly examine each from the point of view of its truth, its appositeness, and its charity.

"Damien was coarse."

It is very possible. You make us sorry for the lepers, who had only a coarse old peasant for their friend and father. But you, who were so refined, why you were not there, to cheer them with the lights of culture?

"Damien was dirty."

...Think of the poor lepers annoyed with this dirty comrade! But the clean Dr. Hyde was at his food in a fine house.

"Damien was headstrong."

I believe you are right again; and I thank God for his strong head and heart.

"Damien was bigoted."

...But the point of interest in Damien, which has caused him to be so much talked about and made him at last the subject of your pen and mine, was that, in him, his bigotry, his intense and narrow faith, wrought potently for good, and strengthened him to be one of the world's heroes and exemplars.

Is it growing at all clear to you what a picture you have drawn of your own heart? I will try yet once again to make it clearer. You had a father: suppose this tale were about him, and some informant brought it to you, proof in hand: I am not making too high an estimate of your emotional nature when I suppose you would regret

272

the circumstance? That you feel the tale of frailty the more keenly since it shamed the author of your days and that the last thing you would want to do would be to publish it in the religious press? Well, the man who tried to do what Damien did, is my father...and the father of all who love goodness; and he was your father, too, if God had given you the grace to see it.

On October 11, 2009 Father Damien DeVeuster was canonized, making him a saint of the Catholic Church.

Pope Benedict XVI proclaimed: "The figure of Father Damien teaches us to choose the good fight—not those that lead to division, but those that gather us in unity."

The laws requiring lepers to be banished to Molokai were rescinded in 1969.

Leprosy, now known as Hansen's Disease, is completely curable through antibiotic multidrug therapy.

It is believed 5% of the world's population is susceptible to leprosy.

Dedicated

To

Alison

In Whose Arms I Have

Been Reborn

273

Disclaimer

God Made Us Monsters is a book of historical fiction and largely based on the life of Father Damien deVuester.a Catholic Missionary who, although uninfected until the later years of his life, chose to devote himself to caring for the lepers on Molokai Island.

To view other books by Ari Publishing go to:
http://aripublishing.com